Saga of the Myth Reaver

Joshua Unruh

Published by Pulp Diction Press, 2012.

SAGA OF THE MYTH REAVER

First edition. September 5, 2012.

ISBN: 978-1497750838

Written by Joshua Unruh.

Also by Joshua Unruh

Arcanoir
Hob Lesatz for Hire

Gripping Tales of the Impossible
Werewolves of Mass Destruction

Six-Gun Supernatural
Hell Bent for Leather

Standalone
Saga of the Myth Reaver

Watch for more at www.JoshuaUnruh.com.

1. Brotherly Love

Five winters is too young to start breaking bones. But two of my older brothers were foolish enough to let me get my pudgy child's hands on them, so I broke their bones anyway.

The twins wore identical wicked grins as they approached me. At first I thought little of it. Though rarely cruel, my numerous siblings were nevertheless a scourge upon me, as all older brothers are to the younger. So it was that the twins came to me where I played and called me names. I knew better than to react, so they decided to throw rocks along with their taunts.

I weathered the storm of stones, already wily enough to know that any retaliation would result in a beating, until one particularly well-thrown rock hit me just below my left eye. I had recently seen a warrior return from a-viking with an empty socket. The sight had terrified me. In my child's mind, my brother Skulli had nearly put my own eye out. I lost my temper.

I roared my tiny battle yell and leapt at Skulli. His face grew slack with shock as I hurtled toward him, his arm pulled back with another stone to throw. One tiny hand found his throat while the other grabbed his poised wrist. He fell to the ground beneath me, and I forced his wrist farther and farther back until the arm gave a moist snap. I'd never heard such a noise before but found it irresistibly satisfying. Skulli's screams climbed high and shrill. I turned on Snorri, his twin, and watched Snorri's eyes widen with shock and terror.

A red haze descended over my vision as I looked into the pained, terrified faces of my brothers. I remembered nothing for a while except for rage, though when the red receded, my second-eldest brother Hallbjorn pinned my spindly arms to my sides and lifted me off one of the twins. My throat was raw, but still I screamed defiance. Hallbjorn shook me like one of our sisters' dolls and bellowed in my ear.

"Look around you, lad; the battle's over! And 'tis a battle you've won, you tiny bear shirt!"

I stopped yelling long enough to turn my attention toward the beaten, bloody, broken messes that had been my twin brothers. Indeed, they looked as though they'd been mauled by a bear cub, not attacked by a boy four winters their junior. I went limp in Hallbjorn's grip, suddenly very tired. He slung me over his shoulder like a full grain sack and said, "Now you must visit our father and see if you survive the war."

That was how I came to stand under the full force of Styrr's mighty scowl.

Among the mightiest of all the Northmen kings who ever ruled, Styrr Warborn governed with courage and greatness. Styrr was a well known wrecker of mead-benches, shatterer of foes, scourge of tribes, and taker of many tributes. This rampager and terror to raven-feeders grew into kingship and became a generous giver of rings, prudently purchasing loyalty in peace that had been hard bought with his sword arm in battle. That was one good king.

Odin and Tyr looked fondly on Styrr in matters of war, but the mighty Warborn was most blessed by Freyja during the long years of his rule. Or perhaps what seemed to be Freyja's gifts were truly curses from those gods of war. Most kings were fortunate to claim two or three sons, and luckier still if even one managed to survive long enough to continue his rule. My father sired prince after prince until they numbered seven in all. Then came a healthy smattering of daughters, each one more comely than the last, able to fetch a high price in either dowry or treaty.

But all was not well with so many Styrrssons. A first son was crown prince. A second was a strong right arm to his elder brother. A third felt almost from birth the push of gentle hands on his back, thrusting him into the wide world to make his own fortune. After that, a king's sons had only a handful of options: pious poverty, honorless banditry, the assassin's dagger, or the poisoner's draught. Lastly, and only if they boasted great strength in arms and could inspire true loyalty, a lesser son might have chosen civil war. Brother pitted against brother. Two sons could tear a nation apart, but seven could lay waste to the whole world. And there were always sons-in-law who might look with greedy hearts and itchy palms upon the Warborn's kingdom.

With each new birth, war loomed in the future of my father's kingdom, as cold, life-stealing, and inevitable as winter.

My father hoped to stave this off by instilling a strident sense of duty in each of us. And by not creating any additional potential contenders. Once again, the gods or Norns had the last laugh...in the form of a shockingly powerful and charismatic youngest son. Me.

I was last of Styrr's twelve children. The long years and royal jealousies between me and my brothers stacked up like sharpened spears. This was especially true with Grímarr, the eldest and most sure heir to father's throne.

Grímarr disliked me from the cradle. He distrusted me, saw evil and fault even in a mewling babe. Once I toddled about enough to be out from under mother's skirts for any length of time, Grímarr decided I, as the coddled baby, needed a lesson in humility. This was why he convinced Snorri and Skulli that I needed a thrashing. Fiery haired and fiery tempered, quick to fight even as children, and nearest my own age, they were just the brothers to give my well "earned" beating.

But it was they who had been bloodied. And now Styrr demanded that I make an accounting of myself. It had not started out well.

"Styrrssons will *not* fight amongst themselves. Not now, not ever. And certainly not with help from outside the family!" Styrr bellowed at me.

Outrage filled me, but I could only squeak out "I fought alone," before his baleful scowl silenced me again.

"Boy, don't you lie to me," he said coldly. "How did you alone do all *that* to your brothers?"

I did my best to meet his heavy glare, but my knees knocked in terror. I curled my fingers into tiny fists to keep my hands from joining them. Styrr's hall was empty as he sat upon his kingly seat, but he would have looked down on me regardless. I was but a child while Styrr was...well, he was Styrr.

"Father," I began, but my thin voice cracked. I snapped my jaw shut and took control of my jangling nerves. I began again, and this time my voice held strong. "Father, my brothers came to me, challenging me to a fight. I gave them what I thought they wanted. Is this not the Northman's way?"

At my words, Father's mouth fell open in surprise, and his bristling beard relaxed. He sat back in his high seat and considered me for a long moment. Just as I felt sure the harangue was to begin again, he burst into hearty laughter. He stood from his throne and thumped down the steps to stand beside me. He slapped me on the back.

"That it is, lad, that it is. You've the fine beginnings of a man's mind. Someday you'll have a man's strong body to match." He waggled a finger at me. "When that day comes, you must be a mighty right-hand to Grímarr while he's in my place. Styrrsson will not turn upon Styrrsson; I won't have it. Duty, loyalty, honor. These, more than any strong arm or stout shield, will preserve my kingdom past my final breath."

Styrr stared at me in sternness, but when he realized I'd taken the lesson to heart, a grin cut across his sharp features. He shook his shaggy head at me. "Imagine, a true berserker! And before you've seen even six winters. I'm mean, lad, but that has to come from your mother's side of the family."

He winked at me. It made me smile. He smiled back, and we laughed and laughed together. But from the corner of my eye, I saw my brother Grímarr tucked around the door that led to the family rooms behind the hall. His calm face was like the mask for which he was named. But his eyes weighed me. With my father's lesson still in my ears, I had an insight beyond mere child's wisdom. I understood what my eldest brother must wonder.

Would I obey Father's law and become Grímarr's greatest thane? Would I take the throne by force and leave him as only rotting meat? Or would our people support me in revolution no matter what Father, Grímarr, or I commanded?

I vowed to myself at that moment that neither he nor any of my other brothers would have to wonder about my loyalty. I inscribed my father's admonition upon my child's heart. I would be the greatest thane my father, my brothers, or any king could ever hope for. Neither life nor glory would come before this vow, even if keeping it meant something I could never have expected. Even if it meant leaving my father's house forever.

After a tryout such as that, my training began immediately. As I grew, so did my strength and skill at arms. When I finally reached the winter of my manhood, I had become high-born and powerful, the mightiest of men, a binder of a dozen beasts on my first cattle-raid, and holding the strength of thirty men in each grip. Beardless and untested in any combat save one-to-one, I rowed forth with my brothers to weather my first storm of weapons in the name of Styrr Warborn. My destiny held larger battles and foes both more numerous and more dangerous. Yet this battle, even with what came after, always held a special place in my heart. For a young man, a first war was as unforgettable as his first maiden. With a song in my heart and on my lips, I went out to sate the hunger of an eagle's flock with my father's enemies. Or, should I fail, with my own body.

The eight of us warred side by side, as comfortable together in the tides of battle as pike in a school. Yet alongside seven mighty princes, I was the mightiest. I fought on the eastern front with the twins, I battled on the western front with Magnus, I protected the rear while Jorund the archer rained down death, and I clashed with the vanguard alongside Hallbjorn and Grímarr. I was everywhere.

I stood with Grímarr when we broke the enemy's front line and first laid eyes on the head of the opposing tribe, Seaxwulf the Axe-Toothed. Ever one to take advantage of even the smallest opportunity in war, Seaxwulf drew back his javelin and let fly at my eldest brother. I plucked the missile from the air a scant inch from Grímarr's impassive eye.

I beamed at him, the battle-joy fully upon me. It was a strange moment to feel my heart swell with brotherly love, surrounded as we were by the din of strife and the groans and gasps of the dying. I had shared similar though lesser feelings with my other brothers this very day, but I had not saved any of their lives so directly. I felt ready to burst, such was the affection for Grímarr at that moment. He and I had been far from bosom companions, but I thought perhaps there was a chance his glacial face might melt and grace me with a smile of appreciation and nod of recognition.

Yet without a word or even a brow's flicker, he turned his back upon me and made for the enemy king.

Still I leapt ahead of him and tore into the huscarls and personal guard of Seaxwulf. I beat back a dozen men with sword and shield, hacking them to pieces so as to clear a path for my brother that he might save the strength of his sword arm for the rival king.

None could stand before my charge; none went unblooded when they entered my death-circle. Finally I burst through the last of his most trusted guardians, and Seaxwulf stood before me. His eyes rolled like a frightened horse's, all white and mad. He swung a sword at me, its tip broken off in the fighting. I carelessly caught his wrist and jerked him past me. He slipped and fell to his knees at Grímarr's feet. He looked up into the cold stare of my future king, his gaze meeting eyes as bereft of warmth and hope as Hel itself. Grímarr placed the tip of his blade beneath the fallen hall-chief's chin. To his credit, Seaxwulf still spat defiance.

"You will not face me yourself, Grímarr? You will only sic your father's brute wolfhound upon me?" Seaxwulf spoke through teeth long since shattered in battle, the source of his honored name. Flecks of blood and foam fell from his lips, caught in the bed of his beard.

My brother removed his sword and allowed the enemy king to stand. Seaxwulf recovered his sword and shield from the muck and grime into which combat had churned his land. The two men squared off in a trial of battle. I loomed over this fight, the shadow of my presence warning all other warriors from either side to stay away.

Grímarr was magnificent. His blade darted in and around Seaxwulf's guard. Grímarr stabbed into the rival chief's shield shoulder, forcing him to drop his blocking board. Seaxwulf's return attack was powerful but clumsy compared to Grímarr's studied precision. He swung wildly at my brother, but wherever his blade's edge passed, Grímarr was an inch to the left or right. When finally the Axe-Tooth dropped to one knee, panting in exhaustion, Grímarr kicked the broken sword from his lazy grip.

"Do you yield? Will you and yours pay tribute to the Warborn? And to all kings that follow him?" Grímarr's voice could have taught icicles how to freeze. Chest heaving, eyes downcast, the exhausted Seaxwulf nodded his head.

Grímarr turned his back on the rival king in disdain, but I still looked upon the tableau proudly, trying to etch every detail into my memory. That was how I saw the furtive movement of Seaxwulf. The sun glinted along the edge of the small knife he'd held hidden on his person. He moved toward my brother, ready to drive the short blade between ribs and into Grímarr's heart. Seaxwulf was deadly fast as a viper, but I was faster.

An angry, guttural sound escaped my lips, and I swung my sword with all my incredible strength. I landed a ringing blow on the crown of Seaxwulf's helm, but the metal did not stop my stroke. Neither did bone, muscle, sinew, or chain. I split our rival king from pate to groin like a side of beef, and he fell on the battlefield in halves.

Seaxwulf's men who were close enough to witness my mighty stroke threw down their weapons immediately. Grímarr spun at the racket of steel clattering to the ground, and saw what I had done. I held my arms as wide as the broad smile I had for him.

"Seaxwulf's treachery dies here, brother! We are victorious!"

He stared at me for a long moment, his face unreadable as ever. But his eyes, they betrayed something of what went on in his thought-hoard, something too complex for me to measure. If Grímarr had stood on the opposite side of a chasm and whispered the secrets of the world to me, I would have been more likely to hear and understand them than delve to the bottom of those eyes. Finally, turning on his heel, my eldest brother left my embrace unanswered. It chilled me, and I spun on my heel only to find myself face to face with Hallbjorn.

"Let it bother you only a sliver, littlest brother," Hallbjorn said. "After all, Grímarr has never been one for showy displays."

"Aye," I growled, a sullen self pity falling over me. "But that is no reason to disdain a brother who saved his life. Twice."

Hallbjorn's eyes grew tight. "Simple Finn, do you truly not understand?" I shook my head. Hallbjorn sighed. "He fears you, and you alone. You above all our brethren are a threat to Grímarr. He fears that whomever father chooses for the throne, the people will choose *you*. Finn the mighty, Finn the reaver of hundreds, Finn his father's beloved."

Hot rage washed through me. "I would never break father's law! I love and honor my father by loving and honoring all my brothers. Especially Grímarr, who will be king one day."

The tightness of Hallbjorn's features washed away like clean water, and pride shone in his clear eyes. "Know, Finn, that I have never doubted you. Grímarr doubts enough for all." He looked away toward our eldest brother in the distance. "You must not hate him, littlest brother. But you should fear him."

I scoffed. "Fear Grímarr? Even you, Hallbjorn the true, would raise a hand to me before he would."

Hallbjorn's stare was far away as he said, "It isn't Grímarr's hand you ought to be wary of."

I had no time to ponder Hallbjorn's cryptic words. Tidings of Seaxwulf's spectacular end spread across the battlefield like fire in dry grass. Everywhere, his men threw down their weapons to pledge their lives and tribute to Styrr Warborn. My brothers and I were vanquishing heroes, triumphant and soon to be glorified once we returned to our father's hall.

We sailed back as soon as the tribute and treaties were secured with whatever conniving regent replaced Seaxwulf, our victory burning in our hearts and on our lips. Upon making port, we left the boat and headed straight for the hall. When we entered, I was still unsuspecting, bolstered in blood from crown to heel, and proud of the victory my brothers and I brought home. Alongside my kin, not merely surviving the battle but returning as victors, I would never again feel such camaraderie with anyone as I did in that moment. How might my Norn-thread have woven differently if all my brothers had felt the same way?

Grímarr stepped ahead of us, saluted proud Styrr and said, "We, your sons, return from the field of spear's din with glad tidings of victory, great king. Each of us acquitted ourselves valiantly, but one of your mighty princes rose head and shoulders above the rest."

My satisfied smile froze harder than Jotunheimr cliffs as Grímarr turned to me, his face as unsearchable as always. My eldest brother typically spoke tersely, protecting his word-hoard more fiercely than a miser dragon watching its gold. He rarely lied, but he also never said more than need be spoken. One thing I knew, this uncharacteristic praise, true though it may be, was not meant for my good. I'd thought the heat of battle had burned away any worry about my loyalty as noonday sun does to morning mist. I'd thought it had left us brother to brother, future king to future thane.

I had been a fool.

It isn't Grímarr's hand you ought to be wary of.

Grímarr, continuing the charade of friendship, clapped his hand on my shoulder. "For every man slain by one of your other sons, Finn slew ten men. For every strike of our blades, Finn hewed three times as often. He split the lie-smith of a king, Seaxwulf, like a lamb for roasting. I am no skald, my lord, no teller of tales, but I need not a silver tongue to tell you your sons did the work of heroes. Only a poet, however, could spin a tale of how your youngest son did the work of mighty Thor himself."

Styrr beamed down at me, and his voice rang through his hall. "Finn...my greatest son."

The other people in my father's hall, man, woman, child, warrior, smith, or farmer, raised a cheer loud enough to shift the roof's timbers. Thatch and dust sifted down and obscured the now stony faces of my brothers. I peered at them in turn. Tall Hallbjorn, bristling Magnus, bouncing Osvald, dark-eyed Jorund, and tussling Skulli and Snorri; each suddenly only had eyes for my father. All of them shifted half a step away from me and toward Grímarr. I looked from the betrayers up into Styrr's noble face and saw a total lack of understanding at Grímarr's maneuvering. I looked at my mother, a beatific smile barely concealing the tears welling in her eyes.

The crush of my father's celebrating subjects propelled me onto the dais until I was pressed between my parents. My father clapped my back, and I did my best to return his proud smile. Knowing it might be the last time I'd embrace her, I lifted my mother and spun her, much to the whooping delight of the crowd. My father laughed from his belly, deep and loud in my ears even over the triumphal din. It stabbed me to my heart because I knew I would soon replace mirth with bitter shame.

Finally, I looked at Grímarr. That look was in his eyes once again, the same one that had filled me with such dread on the battlefield. His motives flashed like a leaping salmon, still too fast and far too slippery for me to catch. Perhaps it was merely satisfaction at knowing once and for all if my father would elevate me past him.

I knew now that my other brothers would forever follow Grímarr's lead in the name of father's peace if nothing else. And bright Grímarr, shining Grímarr, first in birth, first in kingly wisdom, and, save for me, first in battle prowess, would never, ever trust a thane as powerful and beloved by his people as I.

But Grímarr didn't know, none of my brothers *could* know, about my childhood vow of loyalty. He couldn't understand how deeply our father's law had etched itself into my heart in the years since. Now my brother's conniving gambit left me only one way to fulfill that law.

I turned to my father's people and lifted my hands to signal them to silence. It took some time, but eventually the tumult died down to rumbles and, finally, to hissed whispers.

"Grímarr's words do me too much honor," I said to the throng. Then, though it cut me to do so, I spoke not as myself, but instead as a preening, puffed up fool. "But not by much."

The laughter that erupted from both my father and his people cut deeper than could any axe strike. With a heavy heart, I had to cut them back, even deeper, and sever myself from them forever.

"In fact, I believe what Grímarr is suggesting, and I agree wholeheartedly, is that the lands of Styrr stretch across my wide shoulders like a child's garment pulled thin across a warrior's back. I must either exchange that garment for one larger, perhaps as large as Midgard itself, or—" I faltered as I looked into Grímarr's impassive face. "Or tear it asunder."

The hall fell silent. Many faces looked to me in confusion.

"Son, what are you saying?" Styrr asked, hurt and bewilderment making his voice hollow in my ears. I turned to him.

"I'm saying it's time for me to leave these tiny lands and find a destiny greater than mere thane to Northmen kings." I looked away before I could see my father's face fall. "And there's no time to strike but when the iron is glowing. Enjoy the victory festivities, father, mother, brothers. I'll see to my own departure."

I stepped down from the dais, my father's silence, his sadness, his sense of betrayal, like a wall behind me. My mother let one quiet sob escape, and the wretched noise caused me to hesitate on the final step. But the outburst lasted only a moment before she clamped down on her emotions, setting me free to continue without a backward look. I stalked past my brothers, staring straight ahead so as to make no eye contact with any of them. Nor did I look into the face of any of my father's subjects. My grim visage focused only on the door at the far end of the hall. If I had looked away from it for even a moment, my resolve would have vanished like breath.

As I neared the door, a hulking, cloaked figure detached itself from the crowd of horrified onlookers. Despite my resolve to see nothing until I had shaken the dust of that hall from my boots, my eyes flickered toward the hooded face of this man. Much to my shock, I saw the piercing eyes of my brother Hallbjorn looking back at me. How he had made it from the front of the hall to the rear and found time to disguise himself, I'll never know. However he had managed it, Hallbjorn had decided it important enough to give me a farewell even though any sign of his support could undo what I had wrought. I wanted to be angry that he would chance a civil war, but I could not slap away this final gift.

Somewhat against my will, I looked into his eyes. A world's worth of words passed between us without a sound. He nodded once, making plain his understanding of Grímarr's plan and his approval for my own in one curt motion. I never slowed, never missed a step, never gave anyone cause to pass a second glance over this cloaked man. I moved by Hallbjorn and continued out into the harsh, cold sunlight. I swore to myself the flicker of my eyelids came from the sudden brightness and not from tears no Northman reaver should ever shed.

2. A Warrior's Shame

I went down to the docks alone, all others too stunned to follow me. I found the booty-laden longship my brothers and I had ridden home at rest in its dock. We had been so anxious to bring news of our victory to our father that no one had taken the time to unload any of the battle tackle, swords, shields, or axes, let alone the gold torques and rings we had taken as tribute. The ship carried a fortune fit for eight princes...or just for one whose home had been stolen from him. Alone, with no home or people to call upon, I would need such things to make my way. If my brothers missed what I took, then they would be missing me. I suspected there would be no outrage at my presumption. No, they would simply breathe sighs of relief that I was gone.

But our snekkja ship had benches for twenty rowers, and none had volunteered to accompany me. Not that I would have allowed them to if they had. I looked down at my broad fists. For years, my father had bragged that I had the strength of thirty men in each grip. I had never had occasion to question the boast. Today, I would put it to the ultimate test.

I found lengths of stout, thick rope, several loose oar rings, and a blacksmith's hammer. I pounded the rings into the ends of the oars and threaded the rope through each one before affixing it with giant knots to the oars at one end of the boat. It was no challenge to push the longship into the water alone, hop the side, and settle myself at the master set of oars. I spat on each of my palms, rubbed them together vigorously, then grasped the oars.

I hauled against them, my muscles bulging from the effort, and the oars creaked like old trees in a storm. I thought for a moment that I'd asked too much of them, but they held fast until my trembling arms overcame the drag of the entire boat. The master oars moved under my grip, the other nineteen sets following their motion like puppets pulled by strings, and my ship shot through the waves as though carried on Sleipnir's eight legs.

It was surprisingly easy to keep going after I got it moving. Once I lost sight of my homeland shore, I spent some time practicing the changes of direction that made my people's ships so maneuverable amongst the ice floes and so devastating in battle. What I lacked in skill I made up for in brute strength.

I tore through the waves, only a small part of my mind paying any attention to the stars for navigation. Bitterness and anger are powerful fuel for Northman thews, but they don't lend themselves to forethought or planning. I had no destination in mind, only that I should put as many leagues between me and my homeland as I could manage before my limbs gave out.

I had taken gold, mail, and weapons, but in my sorrow, I had not thought to pack provisions. Thank the Norns someone had left a few waterskins behind in the boat. They sustained me for two days, and I refilled them from a passing ice floe once. But some time after that, my vision began to swim and even my strapping arms began to weaken. Bitterness and rage are a strong spur but make for poor meals.

On the fifth morning after leaving my people, blackest night gave way to a gray and woolen morning. I took it as an omen since it mirrored my own disposition. The black pit of despair lightened to a realization that I desired not an ignominious death of starvation. No son of Styrr would be a cracked and undead skeleton rowing an infernal ship in attack against his kinsmen. Besides, was I not the mightiest prince, born from the loins of a mighty king? Was my destiny not greater than choking to death on my own bile?

Hopelessly lost but considering it a new dawn of both this day and my own life, I turned my ship in the direction of the morning sun and pulled against the waves with leaden limbs. The morning whiled away, my eyes growing heavier and my oars moving with ever more difficulty. I began to think I'd snapped from my melancholy too late and I'd die of privation despite my newfound desire to live. To live and thrive in spite of my brother's machinations.

Thoughts of my brother and my own doom turned my mood dark again, but only for a moment before my hawkish eyes spied the telltale wisps of smoke and tumbling outline of a settlement atop a high cliff. My heart soared in my chest. A village, and with it salvation. I angled my boat toward a beach that looked as though it had a path that led off into the cliff face and, eventually I hoped, the village.

I ran my ship aground at the beach nearest the high cliff. I leapt over the side with as much enthusiasm as I could muster, though much less than I wished. As my booted feet hit the soft sand, my knees buckled slightly. I overcame my weakness and straightened, though the pause helped me hear the sound of hoofbeats over the muted bell-chimes of my mail shirt. I realized at that moment I was still rigged for battle, complete with boar-helm and sword at my hip, though I had left all the shields behind on the boat. I had worn my gear as a victor in my father's hall, and my black mood had not given me leave to change it. I looked up to see through dim eyes a similarly armed and armored man bearing down on me on horseback.

Doubtless the coast guard's confusion was the only thing that brought him up short. He reigned in his charging horse, wheeling the beast around to keep it from trampling me. The horse looked at me sideways, the whites of its eyes showing it to be a beast with its own battle fervor and none pleased at being kept from a fight.

"What manner of man are you to arrive rigged out for combat in a coat of mail, sailing the whale's way alone in a steep-hulled boat made for a score of men?" he demanded. His voice was clear and keen, accustomed to yelling a warning to his people when raiders accosted his sandy fortress. He leveled a pike at me. "I have been the coast guard here for a long time. Never before has a single man disembarked so openly, not bothering to ask for safe passage. State your business on this sandy shoal or be skewered for impertinence."

The coals of anger at my brother, burned low in my belly over the last few days at sea, briefly fanned into a mighty flame. Despite my weakness and hunger, I reached up and grasped the end of his pike in my fist. I squeezed until the haft splintered in my hand. The guard's eyes went wide, and his horse screamed at the sharp crack. The guard reined in the side-stepping horse, and his shocked eyes narrowed as he looked me over a second time.

"Sooth, I have ne'er seen a mightier man-at-arms 'neath Ymir's massive skull. Unless I'm mistaken, you are truly noble, no mere hanger-on in a pillaged hero's armor. I greet you, honorable warrior, in the name of Klibo, village on the cliffs. But before you proceed, you must tell me who you are and where you hail from."

I grunted in my anger but then sighed in resignation. This man only sought to do his honorable job in the name of his lord, no less than I'd meant to do for my father. Besides, under usual circumstances, even astride that beast, this man would be no match for me. But mounted and with me weakened by days of battling the swan's road with no meat or mead, he'd likely have the best of me. Politeness, and shame at the foolishness of leaving myself so weak and open to attack, won out. I unlocked my word-hoard rather than the wound-hoe that rode at my side.

"I, too, belong by birth to a Danish people, and, until mere days ago, owed allegiance to Styrr Warborn, my father and king. My father continues to outlast winters, and men who faced him in battle continue to say his name with dread even as men wise in counsel recall his name fondly. I have recently left the protection of his hall and have run low on provision. I saw your fair village, the shining walls of Klibo, afar off and came in good faith hoping it might afford me a place of rest and a hearty meal. No great errand brings me, though the right advice and direction toward the friendship of your village would be of true help."

The guard's eyes weighed me for a long moment, his splintered halberd dangling loosely in his hand. Finally he spoke.

"I believe you are a man of war who comes in peace. I will bid my comrades on their word of honor to watch over your craft and possessions on the strand, to keep her safe in fresh tar until her curved prow preens the waves again. So follow me with your arms and gear and I will guide you into Klibo, for I see that you are somewhat desperate in your privation and will not be dissuaded." He shook his head, a dark cloud coming over his face. "Though you may wish you had sailed us by ere long."

~

I heard the wailing while still several leagues away from the village. Mayhap the canyon's shape magnified the noise, causing it to carry farther than it normally would. Or perhaps the lamentation was just that deep and heartfelt. Whatever the cause, as I walked on shaky legs next to the mounted coast guard, I heard the high keening of women, the low sobbing of men, and the pathetic sniffling of younglings. It sounded like half the village wept. I looked toward my guide, but he refused to meet my gaze.

When we arrived, I realized my estimate of who in the village wept had missed the mark by half. Only the fighting men didn't have tear-tracked cheeks. Yet they looked drawn and resolute, like men on the losing side of a siege. What in Hel was going on in this town?

The guard gestured to a small, one-story inn. "There, traveler, you'll find what hospitality Klibo still has to give."

A fat man, one of nature's innsmen, sat on a rocking chair in front of the inn staring blankly at the ground. Next to him stood an equally round woman, her rosy cheeks matched by a running red nose. She sniffled lightly and dabbed at her eyes with her apron. Every few dabs she'd punctuate her misery with a loud emptying of her nose into the same apron. Everywhere I looked, the townspeople were in the same morose state.

"I thank you for your courtesy and helpfulness, guard. But what evil befalls this town? Are you *all* bewitched?"

The guard looked at me sadly then shook his head. "Aye, that we are. But you'd do better to hear the tale from Rafarta and Valgerd." He gestured towards the innkeepers. "I must return to my post and to the protection of your ship."

Before I could speak again, he wheeled his horse about and galloped back the direction we'd come from. No one in the town came to meet or greet me. None gave me questioning looks. None reacted to me at all. I may have been a wandering spirit, invisible and dead to the world of the living, for all the reaction my presence made in accursed Klibo. Poor, damned Klibo.

I walked a few steps toward the innkeeper and his wife. Even standing on their doorstep, obviously haggard with hunger and need for rest, with nine rings of gold wrapping each arm with which to pay, the two failed to notice me. They remained wrapped in their great, thick blankets of sadness.

"Hail, innkeeper," I rumbled. "I have need of hearty fare and quickly. Tell me this place isn't simply for show and that you have stews and ales aplenty for hungry warriors."

Nothing. They didn't even blink in my direction. A flash of anger washed over me.

I leaned down toward the seated man and bellowed, "Who do I have to put on a spit to get my belly filled?"

That got their attention. Rafarta stood up straight as a rod, mustered a pathetic smile for me, then said, "No spitting necessary, master. There's bread in the oven, ain't there Valgerd?" Valgerd squeaked and curtsied to me before vanishing into the inn. The warmth of fires and ovens wafted through the door and breathed life back into my cold bones. The smell of fresh bread reached through my nose, into my empty stomach, and grabbed a fistful to twist.

"Right this way," Rafarta said and gestured inward. I hardly needed the invitation.

He held the door for me, but I still had to duck and turn sideways to enter the place. They apparently built them small in Klibo. I sat down at a bench as near the fire as I could stand.

"I'll have a stew with that bread, or whatever else you have to eat, along with a flagon of warm mead. Keep plates, bowls, and cups full until this runs out." I reached up and snapped a ring from my arm and tossed it to the fat man. Sausage-like fingers snatched it out of the air with a deftness belied by their thickness.

He made to dart off into the kitchens. "Stay," I ordered. "Leave it to your woman. From you, I'll have the tale of what's befallen this village."

He still stood with his back to me, but I saw his shoulders sag. He turned slowly, his slumped, ashen cheeks drawn down around his frowning mouth. "I'd rather not dwell on it, master."

"I'll have a story along with my meal, innsman. Open up your word-hoard and pour out your tale until this," I snapped another ring off my arm, "runs out."

I tossed the ring to him, and he caught it with decidedly less enthusiasm this time. But he was still an innkeeper, so the gold was never in any danger of hitting the ground. He shuffled across the floor, bumping tables and chairs with his wide hips, until he sat across from me.

"Gather your thoughts, man," I said. "I won't be able to listen to a word of it until I've some of that bread in front of me. The smell is driving me near to madness."

Rafarta fiddled with the golden rings, refusing to look up at me. A handful of minutes crawled by before Valgerd came in and placed before me a bowl of thick stew, a plate of warm, buttered bread, and a large cup of steaming mead. Though it scalded me, I shoveled the stew into my mouth and emptied the bowl in minutes. I threw back the mug in one large gulp, then began sopping up the stew with the bread. A thunderous belch escaped me.

"Another of everything, woman," I said to the hovering Valgerd. She scurried off, and I turned to Rafarta. "And you can begin your tale now."

Rafarta took a deep breath before finally looking up into my eyes. Valgerd unobtrusively dropped another meal in front of me, and I dug in while Rafarta took a second deep, shuddering breath.

"There isn't much to tell, master. Klibo is beset by a wolf."

I barked a laugh, bits of stew flying across the table. "The town drowns in a flood of its own tears over a pack of *wolves*. I saw your coast guard, he seems able enough. If you have just five more like him, then even starving wolves shouldn't be a problem to root out. Or have you no torches, either, to frighten the beasts away?"

I chuckled to myself and went back to eating. Wolves, of all things.

But Rafarta only looked grimmer as he awaited the end of my outburst. "I didn't say wolves, master. I said *wolf*. A great, black beast, larger than a warhorse. It attacks the town nightly, having no fear of man's weapons, be they steel or flame. Worst of all..." He choked on a sob, and tears streaked the man's face anew. His shoulders shook as he wept quietly. I still had stew to eat, so I could afford patience.

Rafarta regained brief control of himself. "Worst of all, the monster steals our—"

But that was as far as the man got before burying his face in his apron and degenerating into blubbering sobs. I finished my bowl of stew, mopped it out, and I had drunk the rest of my mead.

I smacked the table with my open palm. "Steals your what, man?" The wracking sobs continued. I rolled my eyes. "In Thor's name, *pretend* to be a proper Northman long enough to tell me what this monstrous brute steals that's so terrible. Guardsmen? Sheep? Cattle?"

Valgerd appeared at my elbow, and quietly said, "Our children." She served the third round of food with which she was laden. Then she sat down across from me, next to her husband. She patted his back and said again, "It steals and eats the village children."

I stared at her blotchy face and thought back to what I'd witnessed outside. There had been no rush of young boys out to see the fighting man just into town. There had been no girls picking wildflowers. There had been no delighted yells of children at play, no stepping around racing moppets. I thought back and stared into her tear-filled, bloodshot eyes, and I felt shame.

I had been betrayed by my brother, forced to leave all I knew behind. But though I left 'neath a cloud of my own creation, should I ever decide to go back, people who loved me would welcome me. Even if I never returned, my name would still be remembered with some fondness. Leaving that place felt like losing everything. Now I understood that I had lost much, but there are those who lose far more precious things than I'd ever had. Shame now burned alongside the coals of hot anger Grímarr had stoked. Together, they became a blazing bonfire. I owed this small village a penance for my selfishness, a penance to be paid in blood. Wolf's blood.

"Worry not, woman. I swear by Odin's missing eye, your wolf has had its last feast of youngling flesh. It will either eat me, or it will eat my steel, then nothing ever again." I grinned, mirthless and grim. "And if it bests me, then I vow it will choke to death on my bones."

3. The Fame Wolf

I slept the day away to rest my weary muscles and recuperate from my foolish, self-destructive journey by boat. Valgerd had been so happy at my declaration that she insisted I take her and Rafarta's personal room. I didn't argue since it was likely the only bed in the place that could reasonably guarantee sleep without bedbugs. A handful of nosy villagers crept up the hall, but I heard Valgerd shoo them all away, insisting I needed my rest. Thanks to her mothering, I slept well enough.

As evening approached, I roused myself and went into the common room. Valgerd had prepared for me a feast of meats and warm bread. I ate plenty but did not stuff myself full and drank only water.

I stood from the table, strode out the door, and loudly asked, "From whence comes this wolf?"

The villagers had gathered to see me off, and many pointed farther inland to the east. But only one spoke. An old man who hissed and murmured through gums that held no teeth.

"He comes from the forest, raven feeder. It was ever a fell and evil wood, but this beast has mastered it and made it his den. Surely none less than a grandpup of Fenrir himself could have managed the quelling of that dark and ancient wood."

I looked at the old man. "Grandpup? You think a wolf as big as a warhorse is a grandwhelp of cruel and humongous Fenrir?"

The old man chuckled at me. "Fenrir's pups will eat the sun and the moon come the Aesir's Twilight. They must be a sight larger than a warhorse to manage that feat. No, I suspect the Lokison's blood roars through this monster's veins, but it is thinned by lesser beasts. Fear not, hero, there's still plenty of monster for ye to battle."

I laughed along with the old man at that. He was likely right, if the legends of Ragnarök, the Twilight of the Aesir, held true. I hadn't considered it much since I only expected to see it from the warrior's paradise of Valhalla's golden fields.

I had requested someone fetch a shield from my ship, and a villager delivered it to me now. He also handed me a set of throwing javelins, and I strapped these on my back. My mail shirt and boar's helm gleamed in the guttering torchlight the villagers used to stave off the quickly falling dusk. I took the largest of the torches for myself and struck off silently eastward, toward the so-called haunted woods.

I covered the distance to the forest's edge quickly. It was a heather, mostly clear save for some large boulders and what might have been a true standing stone, though I could not see well in the purplish gloom. Even with such speed, by the time I reached the forest's edge, full night had bloomed. Clouds obscured the moon and most of the stars, leaving my torch the only source of real light.

I had thought about leaving the torch behind. After all, in this darkness, it shone a beacon, pointing toward just where enemies should attack. Leaving it behind would have given me an edge in stealth against men, but I didn't think it would help against the wolf. Wolves had better night vision than a man and "saw" the world through their noses anyway. With the torch, the wolf could see me a mile away, but without it, I wouldn't see it coming at all.

I followed a path into the woods. Once Klibo had used it for hunting and building lumber, so some trails still criss-crossed the forest. I was sure the wolf had made itself aware of its new stronghold, including trails used by men. It would expect a man to stay on the trails. But, just like the torch, to leave them would offer the wolf the advantage without gaining any for myself. Better to remain predictable in a stronger position than unexpected yet foolish, old Styrr used to tell me.

Right away I noticed oddities about this forest. No animal noises echoed. Nothing chittered, scrabbled, squawked, or sang in this wood. As I moved, I looked to the ground for pawprints. I found none, but what I did find explained the lack of noise from the usual woodland creatures. Gnawed bones littered the forest floor. They ranged in size from the smallest bird or mouse up to what must have been a large wild boar in life.

I inspected the ground even more carefully and noticed something else. Even the usual creeping things I'd expect to see in the forest were absent. No maggots clung to any of the scoured bones, no beetles crept, no centipedes ran on many legs, and no snakes slithered. The wolf had hunted and eaten the life from this forest.

Distantly I heard a great, warbling howl that chilled my blood and turned my bowels to water. Even though I had been blooded on the battlefield, this was not the battle cries of men, nor any normal wolf call. This was a yowl meant to announce the end of the world. Hearing it, I could nearly believe I heard Fenrir himself stalking these woods.

Leaves rustled small and hushed from just outside my circle of torchlight. It had to be the wolf, but his howl had sounded miles away. Could the massive beast move so quickly and so quietly?

"I smell your fear, little hero," a voice said from the darkness. The voice spoke deep and throaty, with the purr of a wolf's growl a constant undertone for every word. It nearly unmanned me. I had expected tooth and claw, not a beast clever enough to use the speech of men. But then I thought of terrified children torn from their mothers' breasts and dragged into the dark of night to meet some unspeakable fate. The thought put anger in my belly and a spine once again down my back.

I slowly turned in a circle, squinting into the darkness as I spoke. "I think it's your own fear you smell, pup. You've had your way of things with sparrows and squirrels. Now you take mere children. But it isn't the tiny and weak you face now. It's a Northman warrior born."

A husky laugh that escalated into another bone-chilling howl rang around me. "Manling, what you take for weakness I take for sport. Just as I did here in my new home, I started small so as to give the more powerful, the guardians, a chance to come to me in strength, to face me in combat. These stupid animals ran and hid, just as your village has." The laughing howl came again. "Your countrymen are no better than field mice and rutting boars."

"You face no cowering villager now, whelp," I said and threw my torch high into the trees above. It caught in branches and threw a wider net of illumination around me. I thought I saw a darting shadow to my left that might have been a wolf flank trying to remain outside the light. I pulled free my sword and turned that direction, ready for a fight. "I'm Finn Styrrsson, heir to the Warborn, noble and stalwart. Combat, and your doom, has come to you, monster."

A throaty chuckle answered me. "None who have faced Hróðvitnir Sköllsson have yet been my doom—" I interrupted him with my own laughter. "What do you find amusing, manling?"

"You claim a great heritage there, pup. Who named you one of Fenrir's own many names? Surely the sun-chasing cur you claim as your father didn't have the audacity."

My only answer was a growl, much lower and more menacing than the one that had accompanied the wolf's playful words before now. I laughed again and threw my sword lightly up, letting it spin edge over handle before catching the grip again. The spinning blade flashed in the torchlight.

"Never mind who named you 'fame wolf.' If fame you will bring, then I shall wear your hide as a winter cloak and your guts about my neck."

Stealthy and swift, the shadow-stalker flashed to my sword side, just on the edge of my vision. For all the world it appeared that a shadow with green, glowing eyes and yard-long fangs had decided to rip me limb from limb.

The wolf snapped at my face, but I swiped my sword in a darting arc and hit the charging beast full strength. The power of my parry brought its bite up short, but its hot breath blasted my skin and stung my nose with the fetid stink of dead things. Saliva dripped from the tips of vicious teeth, speckling my face and revolting me. But I broke the initial rush, at least.

The fight might have finished in victory right there, save that the movement had been so swift I failed in bringing the blade's edge to bear. The flat of my sword had slapped against the wolf's hide with a noise like two shields crashing together. A yelp escaped its maw, and, just as quickly as it had pounced, it retreated. It circled me again.

Large as a warhorse, the villagers had said! Lies and shite! Big as a small cottage, more like! Each green eye glared large as my helmed head, and the four most pronounced canine teeth stretched as long as my own broadsword. Hair bristled across its hackles as stiff as a boar's and so black it looked purple in the torchlight. Its pink tongue lolled out the side of its gargantuan muzzle as it panted. I saw an impression in the fur left from the impact of my sword, but there I found no evidence of an injury. For all I knew, I hadn't hurt the beast as much as startled it.

The beast circled me, staying just inside the line of light cast by my torch, and I circled with it, keeping my shield between its slavering jaws and myself. I heard a loud crackling above us and chanced a look upward. The torch had caught the dry tree branches and fire overtook the small copse above me.

"All the better to see you with," I said.

The wolf snarled. "You men and your fire, bringing your light and heat to the world as if you need no other weapons to defend yourself against the wilds."

I hefted my sword and swung it casually. "Light and heat aren't the only weapons *I* bring. I'll put my steel tooth against your mouth of fangs any day."

The wolf stopped pacing and looked at me straight on, head cocked to the side in the questioning way that dogs do. I saw a considering, measuring intelligence behind those eyes.

"True, manling, a tooth for a tooth. Yet you still have an advantage over me." The wolf's muscles coiled and it sprang directly toward me. Going from a rest to battering ram in a flicker, the wolf's bulk was so large and its movement so swift my mind reeled. I had no time for my sword, could only throw my shield between us.

Which was exactly what the wolf had wanted.

Too late I realized it hadn't been an attack of tooth or claw. It barrelled its shoulder into my ash shield. I heard the wood crack with a sound like thunder. The tremor of impact rode up my arm and into my shoulder, worse than any berserker's axe strike. I felt a knife of hot ice stab into my shoulder, then something went loose inside the joint. I fell backward, rolled, and came back to my feet. I dropped the shield's boss with its clinging slivers of wood. That motion made my shoulder flare with painful heat, igniting my temper into a conflagration that loosed itself from my chest in a roar. My arm fell uselessly to my side.

The wolf pounced to the edge of light. Which, thanks to the growing bonfire above us, burned three times larger now. Small bits of ash and smoldering sparks fell around us like snow on the riverbanks of Hel. The monster's tongue lolled out again, and this time the muzzle fell open wider. I had the impression it smiled at me.

"Nothing to hide behind now, manling," it growled. "Bright light to see one another by, tooth versus tooth. We appear to be on even footing."

So I threw a javelin in its eye.

I snatched one of the short, throwing spears off my back in a smooth motion and threw it directly into its bright green left eye. I did so with my injured left arm, and the effort, the pain, nearly caused me to black out. But as bad as that was for me, the wolf had it worse.

The iron spike on the end of the shaft sank into the soft, green orb and popped it like a soap bubble full of gristle. The wolf yowled in pain and tried to gingerly paw the bobbing shaft out of its ruined socket. The beast could not shake the javelin loose. The tip had not penetrated to the brain or this fight would have been ended once and for all, but it must have lodged in the skull. The wolf shook itself like it had just come in from the rain, but the short spear only bobbed harder, bringing louder, higher pitched screams from the monster.

I ran forward, grabbed the still vibrating shaft, and yanked it free. Blood and other juices sprayed across the bed of leaves and needles that carpeted the forest. I swung my sword around. I moved too slowly, though, or the wolf too quickly. It snapped its gaping maw around my forearm. Pain flared bright sparks in my eyes and I screamed something horrible at the wolf. My sword fell from suddenly numb fingers. I tugged the arm, testing if I could get it free. My flesh tore against the monster's teeth, but the wolf bit down harder, holding me fast.

I screamed again. The pain in my left shoulder had faded into the background of the agony in my right forearm, like a screaming child in the face of an earthquake. So I swung the javelin back down, this time using the butt as a club. I slammed it into the leaking socket once, twice, and a third time. On the fourth collision, the fire-hardened shaft shattered against the wolf's thick skull. The beast's jaw went slack and it stumbled away from me in a daze. I leapt back, cradling my gashed forearm.

Blood pumped from the arc of puncture wounds, the holes created by the four largest fangs in front squirting my life water in time with my heart. The wound was ragged, but I wouldn't soon bleed out, and the bone was unbroken. I flexed my fingers and my grip still worked, thank Odin. I glanced at where my sword lay glinting in the firelight. It lay more or less between giant paws where the wolf shook its head, trying to regain its senses. I grimaced and cursed. No way I could get that back easily.

I reached over my shoulder for another javelin, but the low growl from the wolf made me stop with it half drawn. It had its head cocked to the side again, trying to see me with its one good eye.

"What, don't care for—" I started, but it pounced again. I cursed myself for a fool, getting caught the same way I'd caught it. At least I was swift enough to fall backward with the pounce, lessening the crushing power. But raw force hadn't been the point of the beast's attack, not this time.

A heavy paw pinned me to the ground, and neck muscles as thick as the ropes on my ship propelled the gaping, slavering jaws toward my face. I brought my two injured arms up quickly, gripping the underside of the beast's neck as hard as I could. I heaved upward against its lunge, and, once again, scant inches were all that separated my face from being torn free. Had I been a normal man and not had the strength of thirty warriors in each grip, I'd never have turned the bite aside.

We stayed there for the span of ten heartbeats, wolf sinew straining against human thews. My arms trembled and somehow, even though its mouth opened wide, the wolf chuckled.

"Do you weaken, manling?" it purred.

"I do not." I dug my fingers deeper into the flesh of the wolf's neck. Even through its thick hackles I knew I had a hold of tender flesh. I saw its remaining eye go slightly wider in surprise. I squeezed again and heard the beast wheeze, splattering my face with more of the hot breath and rancid saliva. I felt something else dripping. I looked down at my chest to see blood, my blood, leaking from the fang holes in my arm. That reminded me of my shoulder, and suddenly I couldn't think of anything else.

"I will eat you, manling. I will crack your bones and slurp the sweet, meaty marrow from them. I will sate this night's hunger on you and allow those foolish villagers to think their hero has succeeded in killing me. Then, when they lay snugly in their beds, thinking themselves safe, I will come again to them. And I will not leave one child behind. How much will they curse the name of Finn Styrrsson then, do you think?"

My anger came, just like the day my brothers had taunted me. I would not allow that village to be ravaged. I would not allow more children to be dragged into these woods. I would not allow myself to be remembered this way. I would not allow Grímarr to lean into my father's ear when the news reached his hall and whisper, "Just as well he left, eh, Father?"

My vision went redder than the warm glow of the bonfire above us, and I *squeezed.* I throttled. I strangled. As if from a long way off and through the pounding surf of blood in my own ears, I heard the great wolf gurgle. I saw its sides heave, trying to suck in air. Finally, it had to slacken its neck in hopes of drawing even a thin breath. The ropy muscles loosened barely a fraction, but it was more than I needed. I yanked hard to the right.

I snapped the wolf's neck like dry kindling.

The wolf did not immediately die, but all the tension in its body drained away like water. It slumped forward on me with a pup's whimper that seemed terribly at odds coming from the throat of this great beast. The noise stole the bulk of my rage, and I barely shifted the wolf aside against the protestations of my wounded arms. I lay there staring up at the smoldering treetops above me, trying to catch my breath. I listened to the labored breathing of the paralyzed animal beside me filling my ears like a blacksmith's bellows.

At length I heaved myself to a standing position. The wolf's single, remaining eye had gone a cloudy green. It watched me but didn't speak. Perhaps whatever damage I'd done to it had rendered it incapable of communication. It didn't matter. Nothing it could have said would have filled me with more disgust than the sight of its powerful form now broken and languid. I made a sound in my throat and turned to retrieve my sword. I grasped its hilt and came back to stand beside the wolf.

"You were a great and worthy adversary. It would be my honor if your death at my hands brought me fame. I don't know if Valkyries come for wolf-spirits, my foe. If they do, you will see one soon. You are one of the worthy dead."

The green eye closed. I struck.

4. My Triumphant Return

I stood panting over my vanquished foe. My nerves were drawn taut as a bow-string, and my skin tingled as though I stood in a storm with lightning about to strike. I felt larger. Not physically, but in spirit. As though, should that lightning strike, I would simply absorb its power and add it to my own. If my pulsing thews glowed from within with a hero's light, I would not have been surprised.

"You look proud as a brat taking its first steps. Have Northmen around here not killed wolves before?"

The voice held a teasing tone that desecrated the moment and polluted my limbs with fatigue. But the derisive lilt also rekindled the fire of my temper, and I spun upon the speaker with a snarl. I lunged toward my antagonist, sword humming in the air.

My mocker snorted and brought up his own blade to bat my strike away. The movement was as careless as if I were smoke drifting too closely to his eyes. No blow of Finn Styrrsson had ever been so easily rebuffed, and my own shock brought me up short. I looked at the man before me and horrified realization crept across me.

"Lord Tyr! I did not expect to find a shining Aesir in this misbegotten weald. I beg your pardon for my ignorant, arrogant insolence." I bobbed my head in respect, but no more. I expected to die, but I would not die on my knees.

The Aesir, the god, standing before me sneered at my words, but the disdain did little to mar his beautiful features. A gleaming helm of polished gold sat high atop his fair forehead, pushed back so he could consider me with his piercing, hazel eyes. The two honey green orbs were twin stars gazing down at me from on high. Hair the color of polished chestnut wood dangled in complicated braids from beneath his helmet. His lustrous, tightly woven mail hugged a tall, rangy frame.

What I could see of his skin was pale, lighter than my own, yet bore the blemishes and scars of a lifelong warrior. Somehow, the wound tracks were so at home upon this lord of heroic glory that they only enhanced his beauty. The shining figure was perfect save for one glaring flaw. Where his right hand should have been, there was instead only a hideously scarred and disfigured stump. The missing hand of Tyr, the greatest testament to his courage and strength, long ago vanished down the gullet of Fenrir—the Fame Wolf my dead quarry had claimed as ancestor.

"My pardon is the least of the things you'll beg for, Northman. If you don't explain to my satisfaction what became of this wolfling, you'll also beg for an end to pain and the sweet release of Hel's embrace."

"I did battle with the beast then killed it, Lord Tyr."

He gave me an appraising look from my head to my feet and back again. "Did you now?" I nodded. "That's the work of a hero, boy. And I would know."

I stammered my thanks, but he waved his stump at me to stop my faltering words.

"What is your name, boy?"

"Finn Styrrsson, milord."

Again, he pondered me, his scarred wrist tapping against his chin. "I have not heard of you before."

"I would not expect you to, milord. Not yet. I am mighty and deadly, but young and barely tested."

Tyr scoffed. "Barely tested? So says the manling who killed a grandwhelp of the hated Fame Wolf." He spat in the general direction of the massive wolf corpse. "What brought you on this quest?"

"The wolf accosted a village, milord. Yon Klibo. The beast preyed upon their children. When I heard, I couldn't abide it."

"So came you into this wildwood in search of glory, then, Finn Styrrsson?"

The question caught me off guard. I thought for a long time before answering. "Glory is ever on the mind of every Northman warrior, Lord Tyr. But I did not set out against this monster primarily for renown."

Tyr stared at me the way an old farmer stared at the sky, trying to discern the coming weather. He sheathed his sword and squatted, the movement compact, graceful, and deadly. His eyes stared, smoldering green coals that burned into me...and through me.

"Then what? Honor? Duty?"

I shook my head. "Honor, also, is dear to any son of the Warborn, but it was not my foremost ambition. Neither have I any particular duty to the village of Klibo."

The gleaming warrior sighed impatiently. "You're an oddity that has caught my interest, but I grow weary of guessing, boy. Spit it out."

I straightened my back and met his frightening gaze. "I stood for Klibo because none other would or could. I fought for Klibo because I am recently lost to my home and have no lands and no people to protect. I have no place to call my own. I didn't know if Klibo would have me even after this, I could but hope my valor might carve me out a place in the world. A place where I could be welcomed and appreciated, where my power could be a shield to my loved ones and a sword to their enemies."

Still that flashing gold-green focus affixed me in place. Then Tyr shook his head and sighed. "You will be disappointed. This Klibo, if it is like so many of Midgard's villages, small and afraid, will not have you. Not if you can do such as this." He gestured toward the dead wolf. "They will only fear you."

I shrugged. "Then I will find my way in the wider world of men. Or one of the other eight if necessary. Somewhere will welcome me. The gleaming halls of Valhalla will bring me home if nothing else."

Tyr snorted. "So you trust Odin's wisdom and justice then?" He shook his head and spat again. "I forgive you this folly; you are young, even for men. But I tell you, any man capable of feats such as these will have a hard time entering Valhalla, and Odin is not a forgiving soul. Someday you will face his narrow minded injustice. I will be most interested to see how you do."

These words dumbfounded me and surely my confusion showed on my face. I opened my mouth to ask for explanation, but Tyr merely waved me quiet.

"Worry not, Styrrsson. Tomorrow will answer your questions soon enough. Tonight, celebrate your triumph."

My shoulders slumped with fatigue. "I cannot yet, Mighty Tyr. I have more work to do this night. Unpleasant work to soothe the troubled brow of Klibo."

Tyr chuckled, the burbling like a clear stream on a spring day. "You are an odd one, Finn Styrrsson. It is good that I find you so amusing since you stole from me my entertainment."

I looked questioningly at him, and he gestured toward the wolf.

"I do not well abide Fenrir's descendants." He thumped his stump with the left hand's knuckles. "I find them whenever I can and make good sport of them. I'm often able to torture them for the better part of a year before they surrender to my ministrations."

I didn't know what to say to that, but a contrite heart went far with Aesir. "Again, my apologies, Lord Tyr."

"Worry not over this trifle. I suspect you will be at least as entertaining and for at least as long." He looked hard into my eyes, and though I wanted to look away, I stood transfixed. "I have my eyes on you, Finn Styrrsson. We will meet again." He turned to leave but stopped after only a step and spoke to me over his shoulder. "Yours is a good name, but it is not the name of a hero. When next we meet, I expect better. Inspire stories, Finn. Let men name you something worthy of your greatness."

Then shining Tyr, Aesir and god of glorious heroes, was gone as though he'd never been. After a moment of standing rooted and bewitched, I shook myself. Had I just spoken with a god? Or had it been an apparition borne of battle fatigue?

It mattered little. I had a lot of disgusting, repugnant work to do to. I'd likely spend all night in this forest, and sooner started was sooner finished. I spent hours stumbling around that accursed forest looking for the wolf's lair. In the end, it wasn't as hard to find as I had initially feared. I simply followed my nose to the strongest source of rot and decay. At the end of the odorous trail, I discovered a cave hollowed out by the great beast's claws so its gargantuan bulk could rest comfortably atop a collection of bones. I dug through the refuse to collect my spoils of war. It would have been difficult enough even without my wounds. But I felt I owed the people of Klibo this last penance for my petty self-pity.

I made a trophy of the wolf's hide. It would prove to the villagers that their nightmare had ended and would serve as a bag to bring back the only battle plunder that could give them a ray of hope. The ray would be tiny, the barest sliver, but I had no other to give.

Around midday, I stalked back into town, dragging my burden behind me. At first, only hushed whispers and sharp, frightened intakes of breath met me. The village had clearly given up on my return. Perhaps they mistook me for a vengeful spirit, back to take more redress on them for my own death. Who could blame them, since I surely looked a spectre? Covered in dried, sticky gore and forest detritus, one arm's wounds inexpertly wrapped, the other arm hanging loosely, and the look of grim determination only a night of truly grisly work can give a man. And over it all rang the racket made by a multitude of dry bones clacking together with every step I took.

I shambled into the town center and, with one last heave on the tail, threw a humongous, still-seeping wolfskin, complete with head and single, glowing green eye, upon the front steps leading to Rafarta and Valgerd's inn.

"Inside my trophy you will find the bones of your children." I shrugged, my manner bleak. "Or at least all of them I could find. Forgive me for any I may have missed. They can share a barrow even as they shared a doom."

I sat down awkwardly on the steps next to my grisly prize, exhaustion finally overcoming my willpower.

Some bystander muttered, "What manner of man would do *this*?" but he was quickly shushed by the rest of the crowd. Valgerd's voice rang out over all the hushed noise.

"A hero, that's what manner of man. And you're not fit to trim his beard, so you can just shut your hole, Olaf."

Someone, probably Valgerd, placed a mug in my hand, and I brought the mead to my lips. It tasted good and was made all the sweeter by defying death to drink it. I heard yells and many running feet moving away from me. Shortly an old woman with a bag that smelled of spices, herbs, and other less pleasant things knelt beside me. She roughly unwrapped my wounded forearm, made the usual *tsk tsk* noises of healers everywhere when they see work that isn't their own. She then went to stringing catgut through a bone needle. A young woman next to her mixed things into a bowl until a sharp smell permeated the air and threatened to make me sneeze. For my shoulder's sake, I hoped I didn't.

They poked and prodded me in painful ways. I yelled, but the old woman simply ignored me and dragged my wounded shoulder around in a truly uncomfortable position until it made a popping noise that made the previous pain a mooncast shadow. Someone handed me breads and cheeses, and my mug never remained empty. Somewhere along the line, the children's bones must have been collected because, when the crowd tending to my wounds and physical needs briefly parted, I saw a few men looking at the wolfskin distastefully as though deciding what to do with it.

"Tan it!" I bellowed. "That's my trophy, and I plan on wearing it this winter. Just the thought of killing that beast will be enough to keep me warm." They started to wander off together, I assumed in the direction of the tanner, but I hadn't finished. "Wait! Stuff that head with salt and cure it. I'll have it ride the prow of my ship ere I leave Klibo."

Eventually every scrape, scratch, and puncture I'd received from the wolf had been scrubbed and daubed by the evil-smelling unguent. The old woman wrapped the worst of my wounds in clean linens. She then strapped my left arm to my body to, according to her, "stop me doing anything else stupid until it's healed." I wondered for a moment if she knew my mother.

I had eaten enough during these less than tender ministrations that I'd filled my belly and I retired, once again, to the innkeepers' bed. I slept for so long I lost count of the hours, but daylight invaded the room when I eventually emerged from sleep. Getting my stiffened muscles out of bed with one arm entirely unusable and the other one throbbing like Loki's own fire felt like more of a challenge than killing the wolf. I gave up on dressing myself and left the room skyclad. Valgerd, to her credit, reacted with little but a glance downward and a smirk before fetching me a breakfast. Thank Freyja for that woman, for I was famished.

I ate for a long time, plate after plate, bowl after bowl, mug after mug. When I finally finished, I belched mightily. I yelled for Valgerd and asked, "Which way to the hot springs?"

She looked at me pointedly. "How do you know there's a hot springs?"

"Don't play with me, woman. Every village has a hot springs. Even if it's a hundred miles away and shared with three other remote villages, it still has a hot springs. My sinews and bones ache, and I would have a soak."

"I'm not surprised after you spent four days abed."

This took me back a bit. "Four days?" I frowned. "Did I meet an Aesir?"

She blinked at me. "I'd been in to make sure you'd fog a knife blade a few times. I'm surprised you could even stand on your own."

She helped me out of the wrappings that held my left arm immobile. The joint, like much of my body, had stiffened, but it no longer held a core of molten lead. I unwrapped crusted linens from around my forearm and other parts of my body, cast them into the fire, and then strode, still naked as the day my mother bore me, along the directions Valgerd had given me. Many in the village greeted me, and I greeted them back as though it were perfectly normal for a naked Viking to stride through their town.

The long walk did my aching joints good even if the brisk air didn't. A joy to be alive and to have a monster dead overtook me, and a hymn to Thor and Odin escaped my lips as I approached the hot springs. Once ensconced in their steamy environs, I finally eased my weary and aching body into the blazing hot water.

I stayed at the springs over much of the day, easing myself into hotter and hotter areas until it felt like my skin would blister. When the sun sank and the sky purpled, I reluctantly hauled myself from the springs. It was more than time to head back to the village. Even I didn't want to walk in the dark with nothing but the stars to guide me and naught to keep me warm but pleasant thoughts.

I returned to the inn to find the healing woman waiting for me. She re-dressed my wounds, then I re-dressed myself before Valgerd and Rafarta served me dinner. They sat with me, anxious to bring me up to date on what had happened while I slept. I was anxious to eat and, if at all possible, to get blind, stinking drunk.

"The whole town's been beside itself since you came back with that wolf-skin," Valgerd told me. "We have so many children to bury. But even so, it's hard not to be a little happy that the ordeal is finished."

"Until you arrived, we thought for sure the village would be slowly devoured by that wolf," Rafarta said, nodding hard enough his jowls bounced.

Through a full mouth, I said, "That seems a bit dour even for our people, doesn't it? I mean, how long had the wolf been here? A month?" I thought about how long it would take to clear every living thing out of a large forest. "Two?"

"Six," Rafarta said flatly. A bite stopped halfway to my mouth. After a moment, I let it continue on its journey, then chewed it thoughtfully.

"How long before it came for your children?"

"That had only been going on a few weeks," Rafarta said. He sniffled lightly and blew his nose. "Right after the last of our livestock was taken."

"Surely you petitioned your king. Why has he not answered? You aren't *that* out of the way. And that slip of beach is good land should he find himself in a fight and need to move men."

Valgerd snorted. "King Hrapp. The worthless prince of a middling father. He hasn't won a fight against anything but a mead horn in his entire life. Frankly, even the mead horns tend to get the best of him."

I laughed at that, hard enough it made my shoulder ache. "But your coast guard seemed a good man, strong of arm and true of word."

"Aye," Rafarta agreed, "our guards here are good men. But they're also lightly garrisoned. And, as you say, that strip of beach is a good place to sail men from. Or to land them."

I saw the problem. Throw their lives away and maybe save the village from the wolf, or keep doing their job and possibly vouchsafe the entire fiefdom. I sighed at the dilemma. "Well, it's done now. You can try and replenish your livestock and your happiness. More younglings would be a step in the right direction for the latter, I wager."

The couple glanced at one another nervously, a gesture I couldn't miss. I sighed again and put down my mug. "It's not done, is it?"

They shook their heads.

"What's the problem?"

Rafarta answered first. "Koll, the guard who met you on the beach, he felt it his duty to report what had happened to King Hrapp. He left three days ago, riding like a Valkyrie chased close on his heels." He looked at his wife. "We're not sure what to expect from Hrapp. He's lazy, and you solved a huge problem for him, so he may arrive with many thanks. But he's also jealous and petty, seeing slights where there are none. So he may see what you did as an affront to his honor and may arrive with many fighting men meant to bring you back for an audience."

I cracked my knuckles. "Wounded or not, they'll have their hands full with Finn Styrrsson."

"Finn the Wolfslayer," Rafarta corrected.

"Finn of the Fame Wolf," Valgerd agreed.

Before I could reply, a hue and cry arose from outside. I heard voices I recognized, like the old woman who had tended my wounds and one of the men who had wondered what to do with my wolf pelt. Just at the edge of my hearing, I heard the pounding tattoo of hoofbeats and the clinking music of men in mail. I took one final swig to empty my mug, then silently stood and went to the innkeepers' room.

My clothing awaited me, cleaned and mended. My boots had been shined and the steel toes polished. My mail shirt had been draped across the bedding. Someone had cleaned the gore and bits of sticks and leaves from it, leaving it shining and whole. The holes where the great wolf's fangs had penetrated had been mended so expertly I could only find the imperfections by matching them to my still-healing wounds. My boar-helm had been similarly cleaned until it shone brassy and bright. I belted my sword around my middle and pulled a couple inches from the scabbard to check. Just as I expected, it too had been well cared for and sharpened to a razor's edge. Another shield had been taken from my boat and waited for me.

I stepped from the room, prepared to battle men that I, by all rights, ought to quaff ale with. Valgerd met me, a smile on her lips but tears in her eyes. She held in her arms a cloak of fur that bristled like a boar's hide but was thick enough to be wolf's hackles. It was so dark a black that it shone almost purple in the candlelight. I looked from it to her, a question in my eyes.

"We saw to it while you rested," she answered. "You brought back a lot more hide than this, so we made a few for you."

"And don't worry for the head," Rafarta interjected. "It already adorns your boat." He shivered. "Odin help the man you're bearing down on with that thing watching the waves for you."

I smiled at them both. Then I knelt so Valgerd could throw the cloak over my shoulders. She fastened it at my left shoulder with a large, onyx brooch in the shape of a broad wolf's head. Two emeralds the size of my smallest finger's nail sat in for its eyes and its teeth and whiskers shone in gold and silver. I looked at Valgerd, another question unspoken.

"We owe you all this and more, son," she said and patted my shoulder.

Emotion for these people overcame me. These strangers whom I had come to while wallowing in my own sty of self pity and anger, these folk I helped only because I felt I owed them something for my own selfishness. They had adopted me and made me their hero. I hugged Valgerd fiercely and, when that long embrace broke, I slapped Rafarta on the shoulder as though he were a fellow man-at-arms. I stepped past them and out the door to face the soldiers whose voices I heard beyond.

Full night had fallen at this point, the only light coming from torches held by the warriors and, it appeared, most of the villagers who had turned out to welcome their king's men. Or to watch their king's men get slaughtered. Right now, one was as like as the other.

Twenty warriors stared down at me, all of them fit, with my friend, the coast guard, at their head. They didn't appear as rough and ready as the men who followed my father, but they nevertheless wore their mail well and looked comfortable with swords at hip and halberds at hand. Based on what I'd heard of King Hrapp, I wasn't sure how they got their practice. Not that it mattered. I reckoned I could beat them, but sheer numbers and my still stiff body meant I'd have to move first and move hard. My muscles tensed and the wolf's cloak I wore bristled as though the hackles still connected to a battle-ready mind.

The obvious leader of the men, a royal huscarl by the look of him, turned to the coast guard and asked, "Is this him?"

The coast guard nodded once. "Aye."

The huscarl turned his eyes upon me, gray as the stormy sea, and said, "We've heard a tale of who you are and what you've done from this man, as well as the nattering of the Klibo-folk. I'd have it told by you."

I bridled under his rudeness. Then again, if he failed to introduce himself, then he probably didn't expect to have to kill me shortly. If I was to die, he'd want me to know who had slain me. It seemed I had a few peaceful moments left to me, so I answered.

"I am Finn Styrrsson, come across the whale's way from my the hall of my father, Styrr Warborn. Being his youngest son and weighed down with the sidelong glances of too many older brothers, I left his hall to make my fortune however the Norns would weave my thread. I came to this village, found it under siege by a wolf, a grandpup of Fenrir Tyrbiter himself. The beast stalked huge and fell, but still I bested it on behalf of a people who could not protect themselves." I paused a moment with a sharp retort on my tongue, had better judgment of it, then ignored that prudence. "They deserved protection from their liege. I know not what waylaid those safeguards."

I watched those gray eyes go hard as slate. Though I refused to break his gaze, I heard the creak of leather that told me his men shifted in their saddles, probably readying to attack. The huscarl's right hand convulsed on the reins as though it wished it held a sword. No great surprise. I had insulted his king's wisdom as well as his own military prowess. But I didn't care. Any people as besieged as these would not have had to wait six months for ol' Styrr to send men to their rescue. In fact, the Warborn would like as not have led the charge himself. Some kings do not deserve the title of ring-breaker. I feared this Hrapp was one such.

The huscarl considered me for several long minutes. The silence grew thick between us and I feared only a wound-hoe's cut would split it. He took a deep breath, and the movement sent my own hand to my hip, which in turn caused all his men to level their halberds at me.

"HOLD!" the huscarl bellowed. Every man froze. I'm not ashamed to admit I stood among them, his voice of command rang so strong. Turning back to me, he said, "We have been down to the beach and inspected the wolf's head that now adorns your vessel. My own man assures me that it is the beast that ravaged these parts. King Hrapp dispatched me to test the truth of these claims and, if I found them honest, to deliver a message to you."

"And that message is?"

"King Hrapp bade me tell the wolf-slayer there is an infestation of trolls my lord would not mind your assistance with. He promises a seat in his hall for as long as you want it along with ten thick rings of purest gold, nine delicately wrought rings of lightest silver, and eight stout rings of hardest steel."

I thought about this offer, considered this new destiny of monster slayer. My life might be short, but my name would be long in this world, possibly all the way to Ragnarök. My father would hear of it in his hall and proclaim, "That is my youngest son of whom you've heard tales. Reaver of wolves, slayer of trolls, and destroyer of all manner of gruesome and monstrous things." It was a good destiny.

I relaxed my stance, and a sigh of relief blew from the huscarl's men. They had been prepared to fight me, but with hearts full of trepidation after seeing the head of the beast I'd slain. I grinned at them; they smiled back. A cheer went up from the villagers, and they began to sing a loud and bawdy song about Finn Wolfslayer and all the awful and hilarious things he would do with troll skulls.

The huscarl climbed down from his horse and clasped arms with me. "Come, let me get you something to drink," he said. "I'd like to hear how you tamed this beast."

I laughed and clapped him on the back. "Have you had Rafarta's mead?" He shook his head no. "Then you have yet to live. Come! Drink deep of it, and I shall tell you how I slew the forest-harrower!"

We entered the inn and every fighting man and villager joined us. I had no skald's tongue, but I knew how to tell a tale where I stood as the hero. Much to my own surprise, I was happy. Happy to be alive, happy to be from under Grímarr's judgmental stares, happy to have a place in the world. A place that would bring me glory.

If the Norns themselves had told me then how fleeting this happiness would be, not one ounce of me would have believed them. But I was young, so perhaps I could be excused for being a fool.

5. The Folly of the Wise

I rose the next morning in an ill humor. I could thank the previous night's carousing with Hrapp's men for the pounding in my head. The day stretched before me full of long, bumpy roads on the backs of ill-tempered horses surrounded by the noise of arms and armor jouncing along. Just thinking about it made me want to vomit.

I exited Rafarta and Valgerd's inn as ready for the long road of travel as I could be and ran into a cluster of men. I vaguely recognized most of them from my few days in town. Even if I hadn't recalled them from this village, I would have known their type from everywhere. They were the kind of men always hanging around a village but never doing anything useful. Here you had a man with the red-rimmed eyes of the too-often drinker. There you had a man who carried a hoe, but awkwardly as though unsure how to use a tool of proper work. Mixed in were men missing as little as a finger or two and as much as an arm to the elbow. Some tottered on a makeshift wooden leg. To a man, each of these held tight to a weapon notched and pitted with age in their unharmed hand. What I had found were the had-beens and never-would-bes and wished-they-weres of Klibo. I couldn't imagine what they wanted with me.

"Oh, by Loki's dangling balls. What fresh doom is this?"

The men shuffled their feet and avoided eye contact with each other or me. My head throbbed and the pale rays of of early morning sunlight stabbed through my eyes like daggers burying their points somewhere between my temples. This failed to cultivate any of my patience or understanding.

"If someone in this motley band doesn't speak up and explain yourselves, I'm going to have to start yelling. Yelling will make my head hurt worse. Then some of you will die horribly." My voice dripped quiet menace. Which was a good thing because I meant every single word.

As one, they looked to an older man standing among them. This leader of the moment had lost most of his right arm. The wound was old enough that it had healed to a clump of puckered scars at the end of a stump. In his left hand he held an out-sized axe easily, despite how obviously it had been crafted for double-gripped wielding. The arm attached to that hand was a mass of ropy muscle connected to a lopsided wad of sinew, thick and powerful on the left side of his chest. But on his right those muscles were stunted and weak.

Steel-gray hair, still shot through here and there with dark black, grew upon his head. He wore it long and scraggly so it fell limply to frame a face as hard and cleft-ridden as the cliff his village overlooked. Simple clothing, homespun and often patched, hung upon his rangy frame. I took him for a former raider who had sailed the whale's road one too many times in the name of pillage and booty. He'd probably spent every intervening year wishing he'd died on some far shore with a sword in his hand. If such had been his fate, then his reward would be Valhalla rather than the pity of other warriors.

This man still stared at his own feet, yet the weight of our gazes must have grown too much to bear. He looked up, met my icy glare, but refused to flinch away. Eyes the color of chipped flint held a sadness, though his voice rang with the clear note of hope.

"Don't judge us too harshly, wolf-slayer. You can see we are not the best Klibo has to offer. Some of us have simply been lazy and refused honest work. Others have allowed themselves to waste away. Some, like myself, have been rendered useless by previous battles. But there has been talk amongst us, and you've sparked something we didn't realize we had within us. Though no fighting force would have us, we nevertheless wish to see the shining halls of Valhalla." He looked around at the men, all of whom nodded or made encouraging noises.

The one-armed man took a deep breath, grimaced, then spoke again in a rushing torrent of words. "We know we aren't much to look at, but we'd be doing the world a service if we died helping you kill a few monsters. Will you have us?"

I had no idea what to say. What could I do with a group of men like these? As I accounted them, I noted some still showed the down of youth on their cheeks while others had one foot in the grave. Destiny rallied these to my flag? I made a face as if to spit.

But then I looked full into their expectant gazes. I looked at their eyes. Something in those eyes, something strong as steel and more powerful than mere bone or sinew, axe or shield, grabbed my attention. I saw courage and the desire to die a proud death. With such men, I could sack kingdoms and overthrow chieftains. With such men I could storm Asgard itself. With such men I could....

I stopped my racing mind. These men had already told me the most important thing we could do together.

We could kill monsters.

King Hrapp's royal huscarl and his men came shambling outside, doing the same stupefied blinking and grunting I had done mere minutes before. They stopped short, wondering at this group of ne'er-do-wells arrayed across from me. We ignored the soldiers and considered one another.

"What's all this, then?" the huscarl asked, his tone already suggesting what he thought of these men. "Who is this rabble? Need my boys to clear them off?"

The men never took their eyes off me to look at the huscarl. They simply waited with hard looks on their faces and steel in their spines. They waited to see if I would invite them along on my certainly dangerous, likely deadly, probably foolish adventure. The decision was easy.

"These," I said, turning to the huscarl, "are my men—"

The men, *my* men, erupted in a cheer. I waited, a quirked smile on my lips, until they quieted.

"And they'll be bringing my boat along to meet us in whatever dung heap the trolls are terrorizing." I looked back at my men. "You dregs can run a longship, I hope."

"We can, sir," the one-armed spokesman said, a toothy grin splitting his face wider than an axe strike.

"Good. Get down to the beach and cast off. Row like bastards and, if you must port the ship, run like Jötunn with Fenrir on their heels. I'll meet you in..." I glanced back to the huscarl, the question unspoken.

"Haraldssun," he volunteered.

I turned back to my new lieutenant. "You know how to get there?" He nodded. "Then get going..." I paused again, realizing I didn't know his name.

"Dalk, milord," he said, and raised his massive axe in an easy salute.

I nodded. "I will be most disappointed if I beat you to Haraldssun, Dalk."

He nodded seriously. "Of course you will, sir." He turned to the other men and yelled, "You heard the chief, you worthless bunch of motherless curs! We have many leagues to cross and little time in which to cross them! MOVE, MOVE, MOVE!"

At first the men looked at Dalk agog, but when he slapped the flat of his broad axe blade across the ass of a lollygagger, the rest got moving, and fast, without further prodding. Within moments, they were specks in the distance, heading toward the beach.

"What in the name of Hel's icy teat was that?" the huscarl asked, bewilderment in his voice and dismay written across his raised eyebrows.

"That," I said, "was the beginning of something."

This became the pattern of every town I visited. The more my fame grew, the more villagers would turn out to volunteer. I'd refuse any regular, able-bodied fighting man. I didn't need trouble with their king or chieftain, and if they'd been worth anything, a king would have conscripted them already. But every aging warrior, every slackjawed youth who had never been given a chance to wield a weapon, every man who lost an eye or a limb but could still heft a blade, I took them in tow, and we fought monsters. We killed things that had no right to exist in the world of men. We killed monsters. We even killed the *fear* of monsters. We slew *myths*.

As expected, monsters spilled our blood. But for every drop of ours, we spilled a bucketload of theirs. Our legend grew, and it was only natural we'd gain a bit of a reputation. This renown led to my title.

The Myth Reaver.

After six or seven winters of nonstop battle against otherwordly things, that was what everyone came to call me. *Everyone.* My fame, or infamy, went ahead of me until everywhere I went, I was well known as the Myth Reaver.

This fame brought with it a share of frustrations.

When it came to that title, I met only two types of people. First, there were those who dismissed me as charlatan or huckster. They didn't believe I'd faced down a Fenrir pup or a nest of trolls. They didn't believe I'd fought Jötunn.

"Ah, so you're the myth reaver," they'd say before looking me up and down. "And when do you plan to kill a dragon then, my boy?"

"I'm not sure," I'd answer. "I haven't seen a dragon yet. I reckon I'd have to see one before I could kill it."

They'd laugh then. Some would laugh in my face and slap my back as though I'd let them in on a tremendous joke. They'd ask me to tell the stories of how I'd battled these things from across the Nine Worlds and, when I'd demur, they'd laugh all the harder. Some of them even bought me drinks.

These fools were very much the majority.

The other camp were those whom I had saved and protected, or close friend and kin to them. This group also held the kings who had invited me into their demesnes to help them with a problem their own fighting men couldn't face. These people called me Myth Reaver in awe and respect because they knew I killed monsters, giants, and tiny gods.

They welcomed me wherever I went and rewarded me handsomely for my help. They asked me to tell tales of my conquests and victories, and I happily played the skald. They recognized what I'd become, something more than mere Viking or feeder of ravens, something more than a king. I was a slayer of monsters, a vanquisher of giants, a protector of men. Some said I was a hero straight out of the sagas.

I respected these even as they respected me. But the former, the non-believers, their condescension wore thin and scraped me raw whenever I ran into it. And I could have split any of them in two with one stroke. But I refrained; always did I hold back my wrath for my fellow men. Not because I had any special fondness for them, but because it would have been too easy. It would have undermined the name I built for myself. If one is truly a reaver of myths, then there is no profit in killing mundane men.

Nevertheless, I had grown weary of the treatment and set out to prove to all the Northmen in the world that I was once and truly Finn Styrrsson, actual reaver of myths and slayer of all-too-real monsters. I watched with hawk's eyes for an opportunity to prove my mettle in a spectacular way. When I received a respectful yet urgent summons from King Dag the Wise, I knew I'd found my chance.

We made all haste to Dag's kingdom and to the doors of his hall. We found immediate welcome, then the guards led into a banquet feast. The steward leapt up and scurried to us. After he confirmed my identity, his clear, keen voice rang through the hall to announce me. "Finn Styrrsson, Slayer of Wolves and Myth Reaver."

I strode into the hall past bench after bench of strong fighting men who stared at me with a mixture of awe, contempt, and terror. But their king sat at the head table wearing a wide, beaming smile.

Seated above his guests on a high backed chair of intricately carved oak, Dag looked every inch the king. Fine clothing and a wide, purple cloak draped his aging but still sturdy frame. His broad hands had softened from infrequent use of the sword, but I had no doubt the knack would return to him if necessary. A simple circlet of gold wound around his head and through the graying temples of hair otherwise the auburn of deer hide. His eyes shone clear as emeralds, bright with the light of wisdom. He had a care-worn face, and I could see the new lines these tense times had etched around his mouth. But the lines also showed him still accustomed to smiling. He had a look of desperate relief in both gaze and grin. Whatever his men thought of me, their war chief saw me as a savior.

"Hail and well met, Myth Reaver," the king called out. He clapped his hands, and collared thralls ran in to set me a new place directly across from Dag. Clever of him. None of his men had to give way to me, yet I was nevertheless given a place of honor. A wise man chose this act, which only furthered my confusion over how one of understanding and discernment could manage to find himself in such a ridiculous, albeit deadly serious, predicament as Dag.

I took my seat, and my men found benches among the warriors behind me. I watched Dag's men give them odd looks as they noted each of my motley bunch of lesser sons, cutthroats, ne'er-do-wells, and scofflaws. I smiled to myself. It amused me to imagine the shock of these fighting men if they tried to take advantage of my troopers. They would not find my men impossible to defeat, but they would certainly find them impossible to intimidate. I turned back to my plate and the king.

"Hail and well met as well, hall-chief," I said. "I come to you famished for both food and news. If you don't think me rude, I would appreciate it if you'd recount to me your current hardship and how you found yourself in it. My jaws will wag on this gracious meal whilst yours wag on your problems."

The king's broad grin shrank to a pensive look, but he nodded. Without preamble, I tore into the roast boar his servants set in front of me. Dag took many sips of wine and ran his tongue over dry lips several times before speaking.

"Know ye, Myth Reaver, that I fancy myself a good and wise king. I am a generous giver of rings and am well pleased to have men of strength and valor at my disposal. But know, also, that no king before me has ever found himself in so tremulous a position. My hardship, as you call it, is that I find my kingdom on the verge of war with a hall-chief of Álfheimr."

He paused, and I chewed thoughtfully and swallowed before answering. "Then it is as I heard it, milord. This be dire news. The Bright Ones are not well known for the arts of war, but they are said to be swift and graceful as the beautiful and virile god, Freyr."

The king leaned forward eagerly. "But you have fought monsters and giants from across the Nine Worlds. Do you think you and your men can best elves?"

His overeagerness told me something about his desperation. Whatever he thought of my chances, he thought them much better than his own. But something about the way he licked his lips, as though I were a sweet to be savored, led me to suspect he held something back. Yes, some vitally important treasure had been locked away in his word-hoard. I feared he would speak with Loki's own forked tongue until he led me like a ram to the slaughter. After all, many men say wise when they mean crafty. But Dag the Wise would not find me weak of mind simply because I swung a strong arm.

I frowned and made as if to think his question over. "We have bested many monsters and beasts, though I'm not sure elves could be described as either. If you don't mind me asking, what manner of affront could have led you, a man with a reputation for great wisdom, into a cave so dark that the light of diplomacy cannot lead you out again?"

Dag sat back, glowering once again. "I'm no skald to tell a true tale with pretty words and mysterious kennings, hiding an old king's foolishness behind happenstance. Nevertheless, this is no tale of my own idiocy. I fell prey to that which no amount of wisdom can stave off: simple human ignorance.

"My fiefdom is near Álfheimr, the kingdom of the Ljósálfar, the Bright Elves. Before you ask what nearness means when moving from one of the Nine Worlds to another, I can tell you only what my own wise men have said. When it comes to the twists of the World Tree Yggdrasill's branches, nearness is a matter of perspective. Álfheimr may be higher in her boughs than Midgard, where we men make our fates, but her branches shift and grow, as do her roots. So some places that ought not be beside one another nevertheless touch. My lands have, through the World Tree's strange growth, come to rest near the Elf Home. More is my lament."

The king wet his lips from a golden goblet then continued with his story.

"At first, a happy accident had befallen me, as equitable a meeting of two kings as could be hoped for."

"Aye," I said through a mouthful, "but what would any elven king care about a ruler of men, no matter his reputation?"

Dag nodded. "In answering your question, I must ask one of my own. Are you aware of the legends of men, upon their death, becoming elves if they were powerful, wise, and clever?"

I nodded. Everyone had heard such stories, though little evidence backed these tales up. I thought them hollow promises to mundane men of greater glory, and I had split giants and monsters with my own blade. I put little stock in such rubbish.

"King Alvis, for that is the name of the elven lord, claims he's a distant ancestor of mine so raised to a position of elven grandeur." The king sighed and rolled his eyes. "Don't judge me too quickly, Styrrsson. We Northmen are very proud of our ancestry, and of course I was happy to discover a hitherto unknown but illustrious forebear, especially one who had gained Freyr's favor. And for his part, Alvis was pleased to dote on me, calling me his 'grandson.'"

Dag stopped and his shoulders sagged. He rubbed at the bridge of his nose with one hand. The gestures, made with the weight of sincerity, caused him to look unseasonably old. Perhaps he held nothing back. Perhaps he was truly this desperate. I couldn't be sure, so I held my peace and waited for the tale's ending.

Presently the king shook himself, realizing how he must look to a guest. He sat up straighter in his chair, drank deeply of his flagon, and smiled widely again. "All this happened via messengers, you understand. One of my people stumbled into Alvis's realm, did his best to speak cleverly and eloquently, and managed to impress the elven warriors who found him. Taken before Alvis, he spoke highly of me, including my ancestry, which is how Alvis came to decide I was fruit of his loins. We dispatched official envoys in both directions.

"I will tell you no lie, I liked how my hall looked draped around the shoulders of dazzlingly beautiful elven warriors in shining mail and long, delicate blades polished bright as a mirror. I thought happily of skalds singing of the elven glory I imagined adorning my hall and my fighting men. Naturally, we exchanged gifts. Knowing I had no wealth to match anything in the Elf Home, I sent living specimens of stor nøkkerose, a beautiful white flower to which the visiting elven warriors took a fancy and assured me didn't grow in Álfheimr.

"Alvis received the flowers with great joy. I'm told he wept tears of gold at their beauty and insisted he visit the home of so thoughtful a descendant. I sent words of welcome invitation to him and his personal guard. Then I set about readying the hall for his royal arrival."

I looked around. That explained a few things. The hall fairly gleamed still, with fresh banners and shields hanging in rafters supporting thick, new thatch. The stones of the walls had been scrubbed white with lime and the tables all recently made or mended. The hall matched the remarkably clean and well mended town surrounding it. A hall was expensive to maintain at any time, but such undertakings must have cost Dag a fortune. Still, what could he do when visited by Bright Ones but put his best foot forward?

"It is as well-made and well-tended a hall as I have ever seen," I told Dag. "I would say it bests even my father's hall, though it grows e'er brighter in my memory. It is as worthy a hall for visiting elven royalty as any place made by the hands of men could be."

He looked pleased. "You are well-spoken and flattering for a feeder of ravens and slayer of monsters."

I shrugged. "My mother bequeathed to me proper manners even as my father gave me my bear shirt. If a few drops of skald spit blessed my tongue, then I have only Odin to thank. But in this I speak the truth: I cannot see how such an effort would affront even an elven king."

Dag's face darkened again. "It wasn't the effort put into my hall and town, Styrrsson. It was the effort I failed to put into the barrow housing King Alvis's human bones."

I managed to hold my mouth shut, but could not control the broad widening of my eyes.

"I read your mind from your soul-windows, Myth Reaver. 'How could Dag the Wise be so foolish as to ignore any barrow, let alone one so special to a royal visitor?' Know ye that I would never dishonor any ancestor's barrow...if I knew it was a barrow in the first place."

"Ah," I breathed. "That distant an ancestor, eh?" The king nodded. "And this long dead King Alvis didn't take kindly to his barrow having been forgotten?"

Dag chuckled, but the sound held no mirth. In fact, it sounded more like a death rattle than a rueful laugh. He leaned toward me, resting his elbows on the table. He looked me in the eye, his dark brows drawn into a thundercloud. "He didn't take kindly to his barrow being used as my midden."

"By Hel's frosty tit," I said. "And you had no idea?"

The king shook his head grimly. "How could I? Alvis died so long ago that I'd never even heard his name. Flood could have removed his bones far enough away that only Odin on his High Seat could find them, and all before my grandfather's grandfather took his maiden wife to a wedding bed." The king slumped back into his chair again. "Needless to say, Alvis removed himself and his honor guard with all haste. And now my only memento of his visit, of this moment supposed to cloak my hall and line in glory, is a declaration of war. Alvis promises that my kingdom will lie as fallow and forgotten as his own resting place." The king picked up a full goblet that didn't belong to him, refused to notice or care, then drained it in one swig. He slammed it down and crushed the metal cup in his angry fist.

"Tell me, Myth Reaver, can you fight an elven horde? Can you stave off my utter ruination?"

I threw the bone on which I gnawed towards one of the king's hounds, quaffed what remained of my own mead, and wiped my arm across my mouth before answering.

"For riches, for fame, and for the honor of your hall, I'll bring you either Alvis Elfking's apology or his head on a pike."

My men roared behind me. They yelled filthy vows of what they'd do to elven warriors. Their war-bellow bolstered men who feared for their king and for themselves, and Dag's warriors soon joined the din. Dag and I shared a smile with teeth in it, and it looked like a tremendous weight had been lifted from his shoulders.

Now all I had to do was guess how to win a war against tiny gods.

6. The Shortest War

It was a glorious morning to die. These were comforting tidings on a day when my men and I would do just that. I glanced at Dalk, who had grown into my strong right arm since that day near Klibo so many winters ago. This one-armed brute standing as my right-hand man was a joke we never tired of telling. But today, no humor graced my stony face. I held my expression still as a mask to preserve the temper of the men, but I let my eyes speak volumes to my second-in-command.

He nodded grimly. "They're going to split and spit us like pigs on market day, milord."

I grunted and turned back to consider the enemy. Three thousand troops stood shoulder to shoulder, their skin and armor shining in the wan dawn light like tiny noonday suns. The elves lacked thick limbs, but neither did they appear as milk-fed weaklings. They stood tall and wiry, wearing their glinting armor and carrying their thin, dangerous weapons with an easy grace. Truth to it, the whole force marched with a lithesome finesse that barely rattled their mailed shirts.

I looked at my own men, split into three ranks of a hundred each. A rag-tag group armed and armored however we'd been able to afford or scavenge. They stood straight and unafraid though scarred and ravaged by time, battle, or both. They milled around with little discipline, clapping weapons to shields and yelling oaths at the elven army. These men had killed beasts, giants, trolls, and other horrors, all under my command and example. But we'd never faced anything like an army, and certainly not an army of beautiful elves.

That beauty was the most insulting bit. Not only did the Bright Ones appear battle ready and delicately deadly, they were stunningly gorgeous creatures. Looking over the elven army, of this I had no doubt: our deaths would be as ugly as we ourselves while our killers remained pretty even in the midst of slaughter.

My men were mean, dangerous, thick-limbed bastards without a stick of fear between them. I would have counted them a match against men, monsters, and even a dragon. But this regimented army of godlings would go through us like an arrow through a sack of flour.

"Methinks Alvis is not as minor a king of the Ljósálfar as Dag had led me to believe," I mused, surveying the walls of Dag's city over my shoulder. He and his men sat safely behind them, ready to receive us in victory or mourn us in siege.

Dalk gave me a bemused, sidelong smirk. "I'll let the men know they can go to Valhalla comforted by the fact they died at the hands of their betters, milord."

I chuckled without real mirth. "Take heart, Dalk. I'm formulating a plan that might just save your lives and will likely turn Dag's bowels to water in the meantime."

He stared at me straight on then. "You mean save all our lives, milord?"

I couldn't meet his eyes, so I inspected my shield instead. "Something like that, yes."

"And pray, mighty reaver of myths," Dalk chided, "how will you ensure this victory?"

I waggled a finger at him. "I will hit Alvis in his softest spot. I will challenge his pride."

"Ah," Dalk said. "So you attempt to attack him in a field you know all too well yourself."

Our eyes finally met, and the teasing I saw there brought forth a hearty laugh, a sound full of true cheer. It rang out over the heads of my men like a soothing balm but rolled over the elven horde like nettles in a saddle blanket.

My laugh eventually dwindled to chortles. Still shaking my head and smiling, I unclasped my sword belt and handed it and my shield to another of my men. I adjusted my wolfskin cloak with its large, black wolfshead brooch to make sure it draped at a rakish angle. I clapped Dalk on the back and strode forward alone into the breach separating the two forces.

"I'm Finn Styrrsson, Warborn and noble," I bellowed by way of introduction. "You may know me as Finn the Wolf Slayer or simply Myth Reaver. I, on behalf of King Dag the Wise, come to you, mighty King Alvis, in parlay." I let that hang in the air for a beat. "I'm to discuss the terms of your surrender."

A silent pause on the part of the elven ranks stretched around us. I could not see through their glare, but I could swear the warriors glanced sideways at one another. I could almost taste their confusion, almost hear their thoughts.

Our surrender? Is Dag mad? What does this Myth Reaver know that we do not? What will King Alvis do?

I beamed at them as they stewed in their confusion. Even if I died today, this moment of unsettling godlings would make it worthwhile.

Finally, the pause ended with the blast of a horn. The sound, deep, rich, and reverberating, flowed forward to Dag's walls, rebounded from their stalwart strength, then rolled back over the two forces. It signaled the elven army, who split down the middle as though a keen-edged sword passed through it. A palanquin on the back of two golden boars trotted through the rent in the ranks. Gems festooned the bejeweled palanquin and combined with the natural glow of the elves themselves, causing my vision to swim and my stomach to lurch. Pomp and the kind of self-importance only royalty can inject filled the moment. Of course, I had to throw it back in his face.

"Away with you!" I bellowed. "I asked for parlay with King Alvis, not some hanger-on riding a spangled wagon!"

My men behind me guffawed so loudly it was only the elves' far superior numbers that allowed me to hear their delicate gasp of horror. Many of the shining warriors lost their composure, right hands darting to their sides where weapons were sheathed. A sharp bark from huscarls stopped them dead. I maintained my look of annoyance and waited.

"Guttersnipe, you have the deep honor of addressing King Alvis of the Ljósálfar, first among war chieftains of Álfheimr," said a smooth voice from somewhere inside the glittering palanquin. "King Dag's reputation for wisdom must be as inflated as a cow's stomach in summer for him to send a lout like you to discuss diplomacy."

I bowed low at the waist. "Please excuse my accidental impertinence, mighty Alvis. I expected a lord of the Bright Ones to be less...shiny." More snickers from my men. "Regardless of his folly, I am the man Dag has chosen to represent his interests today. Shall we now discuss the terms of your surrender?"

Alvis's laugh chimed through the air like crystal. His men joined him in laughter, their giggles polite and womanish. Eventually the king's laughter took on that forced tone of nobles letting everyone know the jest has gone on for too long. Eventually, his charade ground away the laughter of his warriors so Alvis could again speak.

"Why, manling, would *I* be surrendering to *you*?"

"Did you not understand who I am, you wilting flower?" I roared. "I'm the *Myth Reaver*! I kill monsters with my bare hands! My men slay beasts that would make your elfin warriors wet their mail! You lost this battle the moment Dag's messengers reached me. Now throw down your arms as tribute and we'll let you and your pretty fighters go home without bloodying their shapely noses."

Silence reigned from the palanquin. Clearly I had unnerved the king with the sureness of my words. I couldn't imagine what games of power and politics Alvis played in the Elf Home, but I would have bet my right arm there was no way he could return there with a tale of defeat like this and expect to retain his favored position. I smiled a predator's grin.

When next he spoke, it began with a stutter. It was nearly imperceptible, but I knew his men heard it as well as I did.

"Your force is made of mere men, so-called monster slayer. And rough men meagerly armed and armored as well. *We* are Ljósálfar. Any of my elves is worth ten of your men, and we already outnumber you ten to one. I think you presume far too much."

"Fine," I said quietly. I would have bet a golden ring he leaned forward to hear me. "But I respect the Ljósálfar, if not every petty chieftain who rules them. I will not allow your pride to result in the slaughter of all these beautiful elves. On behalf of Dag the Wise, I challenge you, Alvis, to a battle of Champions." I sneered. "Let it never be said that Finn Styrrsson deprived Álfheimr of more of her sons than strictly necessary."

I still couldn't make out Alvis's features, but the sneer dripped from his voice. "Accepted, manling. Do you represent Dag?"

I swept my arm out to part the great, black wolfskin mantle I wore about my shoulders. The elven warriors closest to me flinched. "I do."

"Then I give the honor of killing you, Myth Reaver, to my son, Eldrim. May Odin fail to confuse your foolishness with bravery. I'd hate for you to arrive in Valhalla by accident."

"I'll make sure Eldrim takes him the message." I turned on my heel and stalked back to Dalk's side.

"What are you playing at?" my one-armed huscarl hissed.

I raised my eyebrows at him while strapping my sword belt back around my waist. "Is that any way to talk to your war chief?"

"It is if I think he's gone simple," Dalk growled.

I took my shield from the man who held it. I thumped it several times to ensure its soundness. Then I lunged in close to Dalk and whispered directly in his ear.

"I'm saving your lives, man. Can't you see? I will fight the champion and, if I win, then Dag can clean his breeches and honor us as heroes. If I lose, then you all can run like Thor's own lightning and let Dag pay this pompous braggart a tribute."

Dalk opened his mouth to speak, but with visible effort he closed it. His jaw popped under the strain. He glowered at me, and I knew for sure that, should I survive the coming battle, I would not enjoy my next conversation with my huscarl. He finally nodded through his scowl.

"Besides," I said loud enough for everyone to hear, "how difficult can it be for me to kill one scrawny elf?"

My men cheered at my boast, and I raised a fist to celebrate with them, to spur on their cheers. I turned to face the elven horde and walked with confidence back to a place between the forces. The shining army's horn called out once again, drowning out my men for the length of the blast. Then, as if he stepped out from between the morning mists, Eldrim strode from nowhere to stand next to his father. My men's cheers died on their lips.

I looked Eldrim up and down. I did it slowly, but it would have taken a while even had I done it quick. He loomed enormous. In every way, save two, he appeared the quintessential shining, handsome elf.

He easily measured fifteen ells tall. The champion sported thick slabs of muscle everywhere he wasn't covered by tightly woven battle tackle. The second deviation from the rest of his kind was much more monstrous. His fine elven head with long, flowing hair and delicate features had a companion, an absolutely hideous head with mottled, grayish skin, two eyes that burned like coals, and a mouthful of teeth as large as the dagger at my belt. I stood agog while a long, greenish tongue lolled from between the thing's fangs.

The lovely elven head wore a shining boar's helmet over the flowing, flaxen locks, twisted into a complicated braid hanging down to the back of his knee. The monstrous face wore no helmet, but the sight of it frightened more effectively than any armor could.

Eldrim's left hand held a shield of stunning size, but once he drew forth his truly breathtaking sword, I forgot all about it. For such a gargantuan elf, it looked a normal size and shape, but the blade stretched a tall man's pace long. Its grip and crossbar were beautiful, black stone shot through with gold and silver filigree twisted into a curly script I guessed to be elven. A heavy, silver knob as big around as one of my fists sat at one end of the grip as pommel. It looked for all the world like it could flatten a stampeding bull. But the blade was incredible. The deadly length of steel shimmered in a pale light so subtle it almost vanished against the backdrop of elf shine. Despite its obvious strength, the blade shone a translucent pearly white. It didn't even look like steel at all, it looked fashioned from...well, from moonlight. Some elven smith had reached up into the night sky and, with eldritch powers unknown to mortal men, snapped off a piece of the moon's glow, then hammered it into a death-dealing shape. Eldrim whirled it around and the air filled with an odd hum. Something about that noise convinced me the blade had been honed sharp enough to cut the actual wind.

"Spectacular, isn't he?" Alvis said. "I dallied with his mother, a most beautiful Jötunn named Öndurdís." The king sighed wistfully. "Alas, our union was not meant to be. But before circumstances forced us to part, she did bless me with a son." From the bejeweled radiance I saw a hand reach out and pat the mammoth arm of Eldrim. The lovely face smiled while the other one grimaced and roared.

I couldn't smile as nicely as the elf head and couldn't roar as loudly as the giant head, so I just spit in the direction of Eldrim and looked mean.

"Think you can take 'im?" Dalk murmured.

I drew my sword. "If a mere elf warrior would have been a breeze, this monster will only be a stiff wind. Besides, I know *exactly* how to handle monsters."

I wanted to say something else brave and pithy, but Eldrim didn't give me the chance. His horrible head roared again, and he broke into a run toward me, his sword raised high over his heads. The roar I might have been able to ignore, but each heavy footfall set the ground to shaking, his massive strides chewing up the distance between us.

My men streamed away from my flanks, making room for the fight. I ignored them and forced myself to wait until the last possible second of the charge bearing down on me. I stared into Eldrim's twin faces, one smiling, one grimacing. Without even slowing his charge, he brought his sword down in a viciously powerful overhand strike. I leaned and took two quick steps away from the slash. The softly glowing, translucent blade missed me by an inch, and Eldrim's momentum carried him past me.

I turned on the balls of my feet and jabbed my swordpoint into the giant's thigh with all the strength in me. The combined force of my strike and my foe's own momentum should have shorn even his massive leg off just above the knee cap. Instead my steel rang off the mail shirt that flapped around his knees. Bright blue sparks flew from where the blade met the battle-tackle, and the force of Eldrim's passing knocked me into the air and threw me ten or twelve ells. I landed hard, the impact sending my breath *whooshing* out of me.

I lay there, dazed and trying to force air back into my battered lungs. But spry Eldrim already turned, light as a dancer. He came running back toward me as I struggled to my feet and braced for the charge.

He met me with another slash, this one coming horizontally toward my neck and head. I hunkered down, dropping my head low, and raised my shield in defense. I felt the rush of air over my head and heard a noise like a gale at sea, but I didn't feel an impact upon my shield. In fact, rather than the weight of a strike, the shield suddenly felt lighter.

I looked up to find the top third of my shield shorn off cleanly. For a moment, shock held me fast. No blade could slash through *my* shield. Each one was specially crafted for me, meant to take advantage of my great strength. Rather than light fir or pine rimmed with leather, I used oak banded in iron. Few men could even lift my buckler, let alone sunder it. Yet I beheld the iron rim glowing with heat where it had been shorn off. And I hadn't even felt a tug at my arm as the blade passed. Nothing in the world could be that sharp.

Nothing in *this* world could. But who knew what weird powers and uncanny techniques elves brought to bear upon their metalcraft?

Eldrim loomed over me, watching as all this sank in. When I met his gazes, both faces grinned at me. If anything, it made the monstrous face even more horrible. I stood up sharply, and the giant drew his sword back to skewer me. I grabbed his trousers at the knee and yanked downward. The breeches resisted, and I feared elven seamstresses to be as superior to mankind's as their blacksmiths. But then, with a tearing sound filling the air, the pants dropped around his ankles.

Eldrim roared in anger and shame and grabbed at the waist of his fallen pants with hands already occupied by weapons. I drew back my sword for a thrust of my own, and the giant threw a quick punch to my face with the edge of his shield. The noseguard on my helm caught the brunt of the blow, but it hurt and brought tears to my eyes. The giant in front of me became a giant smudge as I tried to see him through the tears.

I gave up on the advantage I'd won and rolled sharply away and sideways from the giant. I threw away my ruined shield as I went and blinked tears from my eyes. I saw the giant still fought against his ruined pants. With a battle yell of my own, I charged him with my own sword held high in a mirror of his opening attack.

The frustrated elven face tried to tie the tattered waistband back together, but the gruesome face saw me coming. It roared, but the elf ignored it. It roared louder, but still the elf head failed to react. I pulled my sword downward, putting all my considerable power into the edge of my slashing blade. The monstrous face turned and bellowed in the elf's pointed ear. Just before my cut found the giant's guts, Eldrim fell backward and jammed his shield in front of my sword.

My edge slammed into his buckler with a bizarre cracking clang like a bell made of wood tolling and cracking at the same moment. The shield split and the sword shattered against it. Elgrim's arm broke at an odd angle, and both his faces went pale and tight from the pain. At the same time, a vibration ran up through my arms that clacked my teeth together. It made me bite the inside of my mouth viciously, and I spat blood down into the surprised faces of Eldrim.

Eldrim, who had rolled back and to the side so that his weight teetered on his right hip, threw a kick at me that caught me in the midsection. For the second time this fight, I was ripped from my feet and the breath ripped from my lungs. I hit the ground seven or eight paces distant, but rolled to absorb most of the shock.

I came up in a crouch, gasping. "Spear!" I yelled in a harsh rasp. I stretched out a hand toward a knot of my men, and one of them tossed me his spear. I caught it easily in a solid, two-handed grip. I turned and menaced the giant with the long weapon.

Eldrim jabbed his sword point into the soft earth where it stood upright. He grabbed up the wrist of his broken arm and yanked it out of its odd angle. The sound of bones grinding on one another set my teeth on edge, but with the arm straight, Eldrim no longer seemed to notice the grievous wound. The giant gripped his torn breeches and ripped them free from his legs. He quickly wrapped the tattered rags around his broken forearm and cinched it tight. Using his teeth, he pulled the knot tight. He snatched his sword back up and advanced on me.

The whole operation had taken fifteen seconds. It would have been more than enough time to press my advantage, if I hadn't been frozen in place at the sight of this rugged field dressing. I shook myself and gripped my spear all the tighter.

"All right, you freakish bastard," I growled. "I clipped the hawk's wing even as I got myself a longer tooth. Let's see how you do now that I've evened the reach a bit."

A solid ten paces separated the two of us. He gripped his sword in his unbroken hand and raised it to point the tip at me. The blade never wavered as he spoke from his beautiful face. His voice sounded a liquid and melodious tenor.

"I believe it is *your* reach that has exceeded your grasp, Myth Reaver."

My title twisted his delicate lips into a sneer, and his monstrous face made a horrible *chuck chuck* noise that it took me a moment to recognize as laughter. That made me angry, and the anger tore at the edges of my vision causing it to go a bit red. It looked as if the world bled at my rage. I yelled my defiance and charged.

Eldrim swung his sword in a wide arc that would have shorn my torso from my churning legs. I barely ducked beneath the cut with only a stutter step to break my pace, although that hum of the blade slicing air above my head grated on my nerves. My heart soared in my chest. Eldrim would be off balance and his sword well out of my way, unable to parry me when I stuck him like a pig at slaughter.

But I hadn't counted on just how great his strength and speed were. My spear point came within a handsbreadth of Eldrim before he spun his entire body, allowing the momentum of his missed strike to twist him in place. As he turned, he swept the sword downward so quickly I barely even registered the blur of the blade as it came in line with my knees. And, of course, being at least partly elf, the massive bastard had timed the cut perfectly.

Only my own instincts saved me. Honed by countless battles against brutes and horrors much faster and more powerful than I, I dove over the humming blade and jabbed my spear tip into Eldrim's side. I watched it skitter off his battle tackle even as one of my legs ran icy cold.

My spear thrust carried me past Eldrim, and I landed in a roll that brought me to my feet. Or it would have, except that the leg bit through with bone deep chill buckled beneath me. The icy grip gave way before hot, searing pain flaring across my thigh. I glanced down and saw a thin gash already beading with thick, dark blood. I quickly levered myself upright on my spear. As I stood, I glimpsed a flash of clean white through the wound that could only be bone. Bile rose in my throat as blood wept from the laceration.

Wary of an attack from Eldrim, I whipped my spear around to put the point between us. He was moving toward me again but favored his left side where my spear had slid along the mail. I smiled grimly. I hadn't cut him, but I'd bruised him. The brute could be hurt.

My celebration was short-lived. I took a step toward him, and the pure torture from my leg brought me to a crouch. My knee hit the ground hard, and I called out from the agony that vibrated up my leg. Now it was Eldrim's turn to grin. I had hurt him, but he'd crippled me.

He walked toward me with the grace and cruel playfulness of a cat. "The Myth Reaver is beaten, Father," he called. "How would you like me to finish him?"

"Cut him in twain, my son. I would like both cohorts of my army to have part of him to carry as a battle standard when we go to collect our tribute from King Dag."

The gruesome visage made its husking laugh again, and the elven face smiled smugly at me. In two long, quick strides, Eldrim stood over me. Lifting his axe high, he said, "Good riddance, Myth Reaver."

"Good riddance, bollocks," I growled, and thrust my spear up under Eldrim's mail shirt.

Even without my body behind the strike, my arm carried plenty of power to drive the tip deep into unprotected flesh. I ruined my own joke because I didn't emasculate Eldrim in the first blow. But his pain, coupled with the fear that I might succeed on a second try, drove a screaming and roaring Eldrim away from me. Reeling backward, he dragged the spear from my weakened grasp.

Thinking me totally crippled and armed only with shorter reached weapons, the fool even turned his back on me to rip the spear free and check for damage. I drew my sword and the short hunting knife I always carried and leapt onto his back, roaring.

I should have blacked out from the torment that ran through my leg, but I was the Myth Reaver and I would not be denied. My leap took me sailing through the air, and I landed on his back. The impact sounded like I'd landed on a thick, hollow stump. I buried both blades in his back. The mail hung up my sword, but the thin knife slid in up to the crossguard. His screams and roars rose in both volume and pitch, leaving anger behind and edging into panic's territory.

I let go of my sword grip and snatched at the long, silky braid trailing down from the nape of the comely head. I wrapped my hand in it twice as though lashing myself to the deck of a longship during a squall. Straining against the buried knife and the braid, I leveraged my good leg onto the flat of my sword blade and pushed off.

The push moved me higher up the giant's back, and I yanked my knife free before plunging it deep into Eldrim's shoulder. Once again pulling myself against both knife and braid, I brought my shoulders even with his. I regripped the braid near the base of the giant elf's skull and pulled back hard. The delicate Adam's apple of the flawless, elven throat bobbed in front of my eyes as his screams of agony and terror filled my ears. A final time, I pulled the hunting knife free from his back and plunged it into the quivering bulge in his throat. A loud gurgle instantly replaced the scream.

But the monstrous head had not yet finished with me. It turned in an impossible angle and bit its razor sharp teeth into the biceps of my knife arm. Now I howled, but my cries held only pain. I had no terror in me while my free hand scrabbled at the gruesome face. My thumb found one of its glowing eyes, and I pushed. It screamed like a pig caught beneath a farmer's gate but would not let go its bite. One powerful hand reached up and sought to grab me, but the slickness of his own blood kept Eldrim from gaining purchase.

I pushed my thumb farther and farther into that grotesque face until it could reach no farther. It fell short, not plunging far enough in to kill the gruesome head. I pulled that hand back, balled a massive fist, and punched the empty eye socket. At last the vicious maw opened, freeing my arm from its fangs. With anger as ferocious as any she-bear, I felt none of my wounds. My clenched fist smashed into the ruined eye over and over and over again, until finally only a noisy, moist crunch met it. My fist came back with brain stuff mashed into the knuckles.

The roar of the monster head stopped short, and the body crumpled to the ground with me on top of it. Still caught in the painless grip of my own rage, I ripped my sword from Eldrim's back and hacked at his two necks until both heads fell free from the body. I kicked both of the heads toward the elven army, the two grisly balls rolling right up to the toes of the front rank. My wounded leg abruptly remembered it couldn't hold my weight and buckled beneath me. I fell into a low, painful crouch and screamed my rage and triumph at the Bright Ones until my voice cracked and fell quiet.

Near absolute silence reigned, broken only by my own panting, loud and heavy as a smithy's bellows. Nobody moved on either side of the battlefield. Every warrior, whether elf or man, stayed as still as Eldrim.

7. A Less than Triumphant Return

A few minutes passed this way, then the inevitable crunch of shifting feet on frozen ground and chiming of mail shirts began. I'd have been happy to get up and move on my own, but I knew my leg wouldn't hold me. And maybe I was just too tired. Once the low murmuring started on both sides, I knew the moment had ended.

"Bring me a red hot sword and do it now," I bellowed over my shoulder to anyone who'd listen. The blood from my leg pooled around me, steam rising off it in the cold morning air. It only made me more aware that my life seeped out of me.

Startled by my order, Dalk and several of my men came trotting out to me. They helped me up and dragged me a few feet away from where I'd fallen. One of the men tied a strip of cloth tightly at the top of my thigh, and the seep of blood slowed to a trickle. Dalk put a waterskin to my mouth. I took a long swig of it but spit it back into his face.

"I didn't survive *that*," I spluttered, "just to drink water."

Dalk's face became stern. "Water now, milord, stronger stuff later."

I glared at him. "Is there that much blood over there, then?"

"Aye."

I snatched the waterskin from him and drank deeply from it. It bothered my raw throat and threw me into a coughing fit. I sat up to spit and saw several elven warriors lifting Eldrim's corpse from the ground.

"You leave him where he lies," I yelled at them. They stopped for a moment and I hissed, "Get me up, lads." All the men looked to Dalk, who just looked worried. "Don't look at him, especially when he makes a face like an old widow woman. Get me standing or I'll strangle the life from every one of you."

That got them moving. They levered me into an upright position and then held on to me with only the lightest touch so I could stand on my own...more or less. Good men, very good men.

"King Alvis, I claim Eldrim's blade and battle tackle as victor's trophies. You can have the meat if you still want it, but you'll strip him bare first."

The warriors who had lifted Eldrim looked to their king. I still couldn't see a damn thing for all the sparkles, so I couldn't read how he received my demand. A very tense handful of minutes crept by as Alvis thought it over, and I threatened to bleed out in front of him.

"Will that be the extent of my tribute, then?" Alvis finally asked.

I gritted my teeth. He'd played a trick worthy of Loki's own tongue. Dag would be furious. Unless I reminded him that his options had been this or total annihilation at the hands of Alvis's forces. I had to get him something.

"Nay, war chief of elves. Your tribute will be threefold. First, the sword and mail of your dead son. Second, a promise of peace, forgiveness, and friendship with your descendant Dag who meant no offense to you in the first place." I paused to see if I'd stretched too far.

Another minute passed before Alvis said, "I will make that pledge. And what is the third requirement?"

I grinned wolfishly. "No enmity between you and myself, elf king. Peace twixt us, sealed by a boon to be requested at my leisure."

Laughter barked from the palanquin. Cold pumped the blood from the heart of anyone, be he man or elf, who could laugh while his son lay cooling on the ground in front of him. "You dare much, Myth Reaver, but you never cease to amuse. I seek no further quarrel with you and promise this boon."

The elven warriors, their faces twisted into looks of total distaste beneath their helmets, began stripping the gory mail and helm from Eldrim's body. I watched them, a satisfied smile playing on my lips. The elf-king had called me Myth Reaver and there hadn't been a hint of jest upon his lips. I'd planted my legend as firmly as Yggdrasill's roots. My head whirled and, at first, I thought it spun with victory. Then I realized my wounds had taken their toll.

"Lay me back down, you filthy curs," I growled. "And somebody better have that hot blade ready or you'll be looking for another monster slayer's heel to follow around."

"It's here, milord," Dalk assured me. My vision faded to black, but I felt something that smelled of old leather forced between my teeth. It tasted much, much worse. "Bite on that, milord. I'm afraid this is going to hurt a bit."

A spike of fire was laid across my wounded leg and I bit down on the hunk of rawhide until my teeth met. My tortured throat made horrible gurgling sounds as I tried to scream. The only bits of good news were that that the danger of bleeding to death or of passing out no longer hovered over me. Who, in Odin's name, could sleep through that?

~

My men tried to lift me onto their shoulders. I gruffly told them I'd return under my own power or die trying. They insisted. I demurred more insistently.

Dalk leaned in and spoke in my ear. "They do it to honor you, milord, not because of your wounded leg."

I gave him a skeptical look, but his sincere, cow eyes convinced me. I allowed the men to hoist me up, but on my oath, that decision had nothing to do with the fact that my wounded leg burned like Muspelheimr and wobbled every time I put an ounce of weight on it. Well, almost nothing.

Behind me, one man carried the rolled mail shirt of Eldrim the vanquished elven champion. The deflection of my own titanic blows and the fact that the yards of metal rings could be carried by one stout man said volumes about the handiwork of elven smiths. I had already started calling the sword Moon Sliver. A blade forged for someone three times my height with perfect heft and balance I could manage with a single hand. Two would be needed to make the most of the weapon, but the weight could be carried in one. I carried it over my shoulder, the milky, translucent blade looking for all the world like it had been crafted from moonlight. From what little anyone knew about elves, it likely was.

My men threw open the gates of the mighty walls and, bearing me above them, paraded through the roads and byways of the town, winding their way toward the king's hall. Those oaken doors opened wide as well and my boisterously celebrating men streamed through them. Once inside, they found a wall of stunned silence every bit as stout, wide, and tall as the bulwark of wood and stone surrounding his town. Only then did we, as a group, realize we had been the only ones celebrating in Dag's streets. The silence of the hall strangled our triumphant cries in our throats.

Dag's men stood silent, but their faces told a tale worthy of any skald. A war of emotions flashed across every face. They strained with curiosity to see the man who had killed a giant elf, the man who now carried the downed champion's weapons. I noted grudging acceptance of my abilities, the acknowledgement that I'd earned my title of Myth Reaver. This knowledge fed fires of terror in their souls. My victory should have earned me a reception akin to worship. Instead, I found something more like dread.

If this was what the faces of Dag's men whispered to me, their king's face shouted it. I had come here to etch my legend in stone forevermore, to become celebrated as a hero wherever I traveled. Something had obviously gone horribly awry.

"Hail and well met, King Dag the Wise," I said loudly. My voice filled the silence for only a moment before the stillness swallowed it up. My men set me down, and I slumped into a chair at the foot of the king's raised dais. Dag leaned forward on his throne, his chin cupped in his hand and a look of grim contemplation on his face. I kept smiling. This cattle-raper of a king would not rob me of my triumph. "I would happily kneel to you, my lord, but, well..." I gestured at my leg where the once deep gash glowed a livid, red scar of seared flesh shaped roughly like a short sword blade.

The king waved this away with the hand that didn't hold up his crowned head. "A hero need not kneel to a king when he has saved the kingdom. Even in his own hall, that hero is owed a place of respect."

I nodded. "The honor you give me is to your credit, King Dag. I can think of other kings and chiefs who would not treat me as well once my usefulness ended."

He said nothing, and the silence began to wear upon my temper as the burn on my leg wore upon raw nerves. I spoke to fill it and to give me something to think about other than choking the life from this man in his own hall.

"I hope you found the terms of Alvis's tribute acceptable. We had not had an opportunity to discuss such things. Wise you may be, but I believe neither of us saw how this day, this battle, would go."

Dag sat back in his chair, but his face stayed a mask as hard as stone. "Truly, Myth Reaver, who could have foreseen this?" He shook his head, the great red beard shot through with steel gray waggling beneath his chin. "A promise of peace, forgiveness, and friendship from an elf king who just this morning arrayed a mighty force at my hall's threshold is more than enough tribute. What care I if you enriched yourself in the process?"

Something about that stole the smile from my lips. He *did* care but didn't feel he could say so. I looked around the hall as if for the first time. Dag's men stood arrayed around it with shields at the ready and weapons undrawn but close at hand. A half dozen men staggered themselves to the sides and behind the king's chair on a dais not meant to hold so many guards. To a man, those guards looked at me warily, like men who have discovered a dog in their yard with foam dripping from its muzzle.

I brought my eyes back to the king's. "Have I caused you some other offense, then, my lord?"

Shock flickered across his eyes, but he recovered fast enough I suspect no one but me saw the brief moment of indecision. "None, Myth Reaver."

"Then why," I demanded, "do you have your men staged about you as though you expect me to leap from my chair and go for your throat? Why do you refuse to use my given name with friendship and familiarity as you did last eve? And why, when you say it, does my title of honor sound like something you'd say upon discovering you'd stepped in horse shit?"

The aging king's eyes flickered again, and this time I saw fear. The faces of the men on his dais went stony, and their right hands flexed compulsively as they forced themselves to refrain from drawing steel. The warriors about the edges of the hall shifted in a way that made the hair on my neck stand up, and I heard my own men sidle around in response as hands went to sword hilts. I never took my eyes from the king, but I knew my men wore the grim visages of life-takers while the king's showed only fear and uncertainty. There would be blood on the floor of this hall if Dag or I didn't settle whatever lay between us now. My fury smoldered, and I decided to leave the task to Dag.

Dag's lips bounced off one another and his eyes rolled in his head as he considered his words. "Finn, please, I meant no disrespect. If I have been high-handed, even for a king in his own hall, I beg your indulgence. You have done me and mine a service this day, a service I asked of you. My people are grateful. *I* am grateful. Dine at my table, at my right-hand. I would have other words of apology with you while my men and yours celebrate your victory and our survival."

I glared up at him and let him stew in his pot. Then I raised my hand to my warriors in a gesture of peace. Behind me, steel slid back into sheaths and mail jingled as they relaxed. Dag's men around the room and behind his throne did the same, though a great exhalation of relief accompanied their movements. I expected this to embarrass the king, but instead his face sagged like a condemned man granted reprieve. He suddenly looked much, much older as he spoke.

"Then prepare the feast! Bring forth the kegs and drinking horns! Let there be music and dancing!"

"And wenches!" one of my warriors cried.

All the men, mine and Dag's, laughed uproariously at this. Though we forced the laughter somewhat, Dag and I joined in. Our men began to mill about, mixing with one another, and the sound of idle chatter and manly back clapping filled the hall. Servants brought out boards to make tables, including one on the dais for the king, his wife, his head huscarl, and myself. With difficulty and only by leaning on the long, sheathed blade of the sword, I made my way up the few steps and collapsed into a chair at the king's right hand.

"I hope you spoke seriously about the seating arrangements, my lord. If not, somebody's going to have to carry me to a new seat."

Dag smiled weakly at me. "Of course, Styrrsson. Whatever other reservations I may have, I do owe you for the survival of my kingdom. We would not have been able to repel the force Arvis marched out this morning."

I grunted. "We wouldn't have been able to either. I say this by way of explanation, in case you wondered how I came to single handedly battle a giant Bright One."

He looked at me, then turned to look at our commingled men. "You fought that battle to save your men from the slaughter."

It hadn't been a question, but I answered anyway. "Aye." I shrugged. "Well, mostly."

He raised his eyebrows. "Why else? Surely not to save my kingdom?"

"I swore to do all I could with strength of men and arms to stop your destruction, else I wouldn't have been on that battlefield at all. But I heeded your call for help in the first place so that I might make my legend unshakeable. I did challenge Alvis to save my men and yours. But more than that, I made that challenge so that all men everywhere might know that I am the Myth Reaver and question it no more."

"Ah," the wise king said. "For pride."

"No," I shouted and slammed my thick fist into the table hard enough to crack it. The hall went silent and all eyes turned toward Dag and me. "For *glory*."

The king looked to the musicians, waved to them to play anew. Then he looked to the serving wenches and gave them a "hurry on" gesture. In less than a minute, music and full horns had reinstated the levity I had shattered so casually. The king turned back to me.

"Men call me Dag the Wise, and I would like to believe that I have earned that title. I have spent many years leading men and learned both from my mistakes as well as victories. With the weight of that wisdom, can I offer you some advice?"

I nodded. I had the feeling of a man who wandered onto ice he expected to be thick and strong enough to bear his weight, but instead it has cracked and threatened to shatter beneath him. Angry as I had been at this man moments before, if he could offer a path from this perilous ice, I would take it.

"Worry no more about your name and fame, Myth Reaver. You gained your glory before today and have now guaranteed it for generations to come. This is a thing all Northmen warriors seek, to have their name well remembered when they have ridden off to Valhalla."

"Exactly," I agreed. "I left home with no purpose, with nothing to offer the world but the strength of my right arm and the steel of my nerve. From such meager beginnings, I have made a legend."

"This is the rub of it. You are now as far above the famed warrior as he is above the peasant farmer. You are a legend, like a hero out of the sagas, yet still walking among us. Finn, think about your own men. How do you think they will see you after today?"

I thought on his words. I imagined how my men must have felt as they looked over the Bright One host, how they had steeled themselves to die for my name. Then, as they watched me step out and challenge that elven king, their hearts must have soared in their chests, only to sink into their bellies when they saw Eldrim towering in the morning sun. Then the ebb and flow of the battle, the horrible despair at seeing their commander bested, but another triumphant heart-swell as I stabbed Eldrim's nethers and climbed his back to deal the killing blow. An impossible task, and I had accomplished it with enough strength left in me to banter with a godling king.

"They will see me as something more than a man. Something unattainable, untouchable, unbeatable."

The king nodded. "And if you continue this way, they may even come to see you as a god. You walk among men, Myth Reaver, but, whether you like it or not, you no longer walk *with* us. You are above us."

I brooded over this for several minutes. A thrall brought a horn stand, and I drained the horn I know not how many times as I chewed over the revelation Dag had laid before me. My men had loved me already, but now they would likely worship me.

Then I realized a new and awful truth. Despite a crippling injury, this man, this *king*, surrounded by his hall and his strong warriors, had feared what I might do to him and his people. Knowing that, I understood: no "mere mortal" warrior would face me in battle again. I would have to meet my end with blade in hand against a monster, giant, or elf. To die with sword in hand, to succumb to mortal wounds while in glorious battle, was the only way to Odin's golden hall, Valhalla. Without it, the Choosers of the Slain would never select me. I'd never ride on a Valkyrie steed with arms crossed around its rider's slim waist. I would never see the golden fields of Valhalla. I would not fight in the final battles of Ragnarök.

Dag watched me come to these conclusions with no small amount of pity. As though from a great distance, I heard him inform a particularly lovely and busty serving girl to keep my horn ever full and to attend to any other needs I might have. She smiled at me with a gleam of excitement and expectation in her eyes, but I barely noticed it. I had gained everything I'd ever desired since leaving the despair of my brother's betrayal behind. But the winning of those desires had become like a betrayal in and of itself.

The celebration went on around me, but it was no longer for me. I had risen above it, or so thought the men who exalted my name. The warriors congratulated me. The women threw themselves at me. But none of them seemed interested in Finn Styrrsson. They only wanted the Myth Reaver. But the Myth Reaver desired only to be alone and drink himself back to ignorance.

I did my very best.

8. On the Varangian Way and Back Again

Dag's assessment of how people would respond to my presence after my victory against the elves had been predictably correct. I plied my trade among Northmen a while longer, but blooded Vikings and experienced raven-feeders looking at me with a combination of pants-wetting terror and worshipful awe wore thin quickly. Odin knows my men vexed me enough. I caught a few of them planning a religious feast, a blót in all but name, in my honor. For the first time, I ordered a scourging for some of my mighty men.

The moment left a taste of ashes in my mouth. The northlands had already put me in a sour mood, and the scourging left me feeling wretched in my own skin. My homelands no longer stretched large enough for me. The frozen north of my youth chafed until it seemed taking a deep breath might rip my own skin to tatters. When at last a solution occurred to me, I summoned Dalk immediately.

"We're off on the Varangian Way, huscarl. Ready the men."

"Thank Tyr," Dalk said, smiling from ear to ear. If he'd had two hands, they would have rubbed together as though I had offered him a sumptuous meal. "Softer targets for raiding, warmer climes, and even warmer women."

"Aye, along with monsters, beasts, and gods we've never heard of for the slaying. And maybe some folk who haven't heard of the the Myth Reaver and won't look at me as though I just stepped out of a saga."

But Dalk hadn't heard my recrimination. He already yelled orders at the men outside, delivering the good news. I overheard the cheers and celebration. The Varangian Way was the only paradise Vikings and huscarls could hope for this side of Valhalla. And I had it in mind to sail it all the way to the other side of the world if that was what it took to escape my legend. I'd sack and burn Constantinople and plunder her riches single-handedly to live in opulent anonymity. Right then I had sunk into enough of a grim melancholy that I might even have pledged myself to foreign gods and thereby escaped the threat of cold and misty Hel entire.

And sail we did. My men and I drank exotic liquors heady with spices that stole our wits and sanity. We bedded dusky-hued beauties with mysterious eyes the color of chocolate. We slew things that feasted on the dead, monsters created from bits of other beasts that spoke with the voices of men, and mastered the wish-giving powers of unclean spirits. Among the Rus, we battled Grandmother Winter herself to a standstill. She congratulated us on the draw before departing, leaving only a late but much welcomed Spring.

We raided until we amassed a fortune, ate and drank the fortune away, and started anew. Kings and sultans learned to fear us, and some even welcomed us just so that we might regale them with a thousand and one tales of our mighty deeds. The Myth Reaver became well known again during this time, but just enough mistrust of a foreigner persisted that my reputation never grew to become a legend. I felt happy, and I thought I could grow no happier.

Until I received tidings from home.

Dalk ducked his head into the rooms some sultan or other had set aside for my use. "Pardon me, Finn, but ye've a messenger."

My head still pounded from the tale-telling and spirit-drinking from the night before, so I rolled over on my soft bed and glared at Dalk. "He can wait."

"I do not believe you'd say that if you knew whence he came."

That forced me to think, which made my head hurt worse. "Then tell me where he came from so I can tell you that he can wait."

Dalk grinned like a boy with a secret and said, "This man claims to bear a missive from Styrr Warborn, milord. He brings you word from home."

The pain in my head seemed to bleed away all in a moment. "Send him in."

"As you say, milord," Dalk said, still grinning like a fool. He ducked out.

"And bring me drink and a repast, you sassy old swine," I bellowed after him.

"As you say, milord."

I slid to the foot of the bed, gathering bedclothes around me as I went. We had been on the Varangian way at least seven or eight winters. Truth be told, I'd lost count. But that meant I counted as many as thirteen or fifteen winters removed from my home. And although I had no doubt that my father and brothers had heard tales of the Myth Reaver, I had never received a word from them. I didn't believe it would unman me to admit that my heart beat both timorous and excited in my chest.

Presently Dalk returned with the messenger and a servant. The servant set down a silver, water-beaded pitcher of something that smelled of fruit and spices promising a drink as cool as it was flavorful. He also brought a platter of meats, fruits, and cheeses. My grumbling stomach urged me forward, but for an envoy from home I would master etiquette again...for a moment.

"It is a long haul across the Varangian Way," I said to the old man, and gestured to a seat at my room's small table. "Please, sit. Wash the dust of the road from your throat and sate a belly empty from travel."

The man was pale of skin, hair, and eye, just as we had been when we first arrived. He bore a frame both thin and aging, a huscarl who had likely served my father well in his youth with shield and blade. Now he served best in his uselessness. A man like this could go months without being missed, yet Father held him trustworthy enough to speak in the name of his king and chief. The old man gawked at the finery around us, his mouth gaping. Dalk and I chuckled at his wide-eyed wonder and thought of ourselves years ago.

"Not much like the halls of home, eh?" I asked.

"No. No it isn't, milord," he stammered.

"Don't let it overwhelm you," Dalk said, and slapped him on the back. "From what the Myth Reaver says of old Styrr, there's no more gold here than there is in your hall at home. These fools just have to waste it because they haven't mastered proper roof thatching."

The old man shot a look of disbelief at Dalk, but my huscarl was already smiling and winking back at him. The wink overwhelmed the codger and he broke into a laugh at his own foolishness. That seemed to drain some of his tension, and he sat down. Dalk poured drinks for the three of us. Dalk pulled deeply from his cup and I quickly downed three goblets. Food quickly followed. After a few handfuls of dates and goat cheese without the envoy taking a sip or having even a morsel, I spoke to him again.

"Drink, eat. Then tell me news of my father, my mother, and my brothers. Once I feel as though I never left home, you may tell me what my father has to say that is so important he'd send a man halfway across the world."

My father's herald opened his mouth to protest, but I held up a broad hand. "It has taken you months at least to reach this part of the world and Odin knows how long to actually find me. Father's missive will not moulder for an hour of conversation."

The haggard old man nodded, finally reaching for his goblet and drinking deeply. He introduced himself as Sneggie and seemed somewhat disappointed that I did not recall him from my time in my father's house. We munched our way through conversation for the better part of an hour. My mother stood in good health, my brothers had married good matches that strengthened their lines and the potential political power of my father's kingdom. My sisters had also been married off, securing political riches. My father and the kingdom as a whole had prospered...until recently. With this admission, a cloud descended upon Sneggie.

"Which brings us to the message, I take it," Dalk said.

Sneggie nodded, his lips a firm line and his face creased with worry. "Aye, that's the rub of it. Your father has grown in wisdom, and even as his own battle prowess has waned with age, your elder brothers have more than made up for it with their strength of arms. Between that and wise alliances, our people have lived long, protected lives. But now a doom has befallen us, the kind of curse that kills kingdoms."

I'd been very interested in the catching up and assumed father's message would be important, but not dire. This pronouncement had me practically in a frenzy. "Enough skaldry, man! Out with it! What's befallen our countrymen?"

If possible, Sneggie's face took on an even more dour cast. "We are beset by a sea wyrm."

Dalk and I exchanged glances.

"It's true!" Sneggie insisted. "The wyrm, or at least the parts of it that have surfaced, are longer than twenty longships! Its teeth are like swords the length of halberds! It must weigh as much as twelve—"

"We believe you," I said, cutting him off with a wave of my hand. "You wouldn't believe how many times my men and I have been asked when we planned to kill a dragon. After heading out on the Varangian Way, Dalk and I began to think we'd go to our barrows without getting the chance." I sat back and stroked my beard thoughtfully. "Besides, this isn't the kind of tale I'd expect from Father unless it were absolutely true. I suspect he didn't even believe the tales of my exploits until after the war with the elves." I looked at Sneggie pointedly.

The old man's pale skin colored crimson from beneath his shaggy beard all the way to the tips of his ears. "It's true, Finn, your father used to thunder around the hall with every new rumor or story." Sneggie bristled his beard and dropped his voice two octaves. "'What's that boy thinking? No son of a Warborn would traffic in fairy stories and hokum!'"

I laughed heartily at the impression of my father. "Sooth, it sounds like something he'd say."

Sneggie patted down his beard and spoke normally. "But all that changed when Dag the Wise sent his own messenger to attest to the truth of those tales. Dag's personal skald telling of the Myth Reaver's War with the Elves, well...." Sneggie's eyes shone and he spoke in a hoarse voice. "You can't imagine how pride swelled the old man's chest."

I snorted. "I'm skeptical he believed it even then."

"If it had been anyone other than Dag's skald singing about Dag's hall, I doubt he would have."

We three mused in silence for a bit. Eventually I shook myself.

"Dalk, how soon can we be ready?"

Dalk looked up and away as he thought. "We'll need to check the boats to make sure they're sound for a long voyage. We'll have to get them ready for cold waters again. Rouse the men from whatever dens of iniquity they've lost themselves in, then secure supplies." He shrugged. "A week."

A predatory grin swept across my face. "Put the word out that we're hunting a dragon and I'll wager you a gold ring sized for my thumb against your silver one we're ready in three days."

"I'll take that bet, milord." He smiled and raised a finger. "But only because you gave me odds."

~

I did have to pay Dalk that gold ring, but we still cast off three days shy of his proposed week. The men cast off eagerly. They sang rowing songs extra loudly, and the good natured joking at one another's expense reached new heights of ribaldry. Spirits definitely soared high. In spite of my father's lands being in peril, I couldn't stop smiling. If anyone could help him, we could. And, at long last, we hunted a *dragon*.

After everything else we'd done, everywhere else we'd been, every other monster we'd slain, some might think us silly for getting excited about a sea wyrm. In fact, if Sneggie hadn't described her as large and as fierce as he had, our hearts may not have thrilled in our chests as they did now. But any time a Northman declared himself a hunter of monsters and slayer of fantastical beasts, everyone asked when he'd kill a dragon.

It mattered little that I'd killed a grandpup of Fenrir with my bare hands when compared to the dangers of a scaly, ancient wyrm. I could kill Jötunn large enough to strangle a dragon as easily as snapping a chicken's neck, but they somehow felt small compared to just the notion of a dragon. Perhaps the Midgard Serpent loomed so large in the mind of all Northmen that merely knowing it could break the world loaned a bit of grandeur to all its lesser cousins.

Regardless, it wouldn't matter soon. Several months on rivers, a few short months at sea, and we'd be facing a dragon. Win or lose, it would be a pinnacle to all our lives. We'd be dragonslayers, or we'd be dead. I could hear the skalds now: butcher of wolves, reaver of myths, killer of *dragons*.

And best of all, it would bring me home. No more wandering, no more a-viking, no more spending my strength and warrior's powers in the service of whomever had gold rings and an exotic problem made from claws and fangs. I could return to the bosom of my people and put myself and my legend to work as a proper thane should.

I banged my fist on the prow of the boat as the river's spray leapt into the air around me, surrounding me in a cascading array of colors. Father wanted me home. He *needed* me home. And there was nothing Grímarr could do or say about it. At least not until his own coronation. And I'd make sure the hearts of the people belonged to me before my father went on to Valhalla's shining walls.

My place in the world would be solid again, and for the first time since I had left boyhood. I couldn't even bring myself to dread the very real threat of the sea wyrm.

This filled me with pleasure, and, in turn, it made my men happy. But my father would be most pleased. It was a good day promising to lead into many good days, each of them with nothing to fear but Grímarr upon the throne.

9. Homecoming

The trip home was uneventful and pleasant. The high spirits of the day we cast off had seen us through many months on both river and open sea. We made good time and sailed for the southernmost ports of my father's lands as Sneggie told us the sea wyrm accosted them less. We counted ourselves fortunate as we docked a full month ahead of schedule and without having to fight the wyrm on the high seas. Of course, here our good fortune ended.

Right away I could tell these people had fallen on hard times. The wyrm commanded a vast territory, plowing the entire coast of my homelands, harrying every fisherman, raider, and traveler who dared to put hull to whale-road. Everywhere, people spoke of of dooms and curses, and even of Odin's judgment. Despite my questioning, none could name a fault with Styrr's rule that might have offended the All Father.

Wherever I went, Sneggie followed at my elbow. I grew pensive, unsettled at the haggard people I saw before me, and told him so.

"Aye, milord," the old man agreed. "It has been a hard time since the coming of the wyrm. 'Tis worse than when I left." He looked towards the north, his rheumy eyes tight with concern, his forehead creased in worry. "I think it will not be an easy trip to the seat of Styrr's rule." He shook his head. "Times like these make outlaws of so many..."

I grunted. "My heart bleeds in advance for any outlaw that finds himself between me and my father's side. Methinks he'll be ground to dust by the weight of those stones."

We unloaded our supplies and secured wagons and horses as quickly as possible. As we traveled northward toward my father's hall, the sights and sounds stayed the same. The people looked hungry and spare. Men who had once claimed my father as a generous ring giver now cursed him an ineffective king. Shifty louts, the kind of men I had absorbed into my crew wherever I went, teetered on the knife's edge of banditry. Because of this, children watched the passing of armed men from behind mothers' skirts with wide, sunken, and red-rimmed eyes full of mistrust and fear. Even the young lads, all of whom must have dreamed of serving King Styrr as raven feeders not long ago, failed to come out and make a nuisance of themselves.

We marched quickly, eating our unused rations from our sea voyage as we traveled overland. Even so, rumor ran ahead of us and we heard "Myth Reaver" and "returning son" whispered whenever we passed through a village or town. Even after the word got out, my force went unwelcomed save for these mutterings. Or perhaps my still legendary reputation simply created its own dread. Even the possibility of that chafed at me like sand beneath my armor. My homecoming lacked the close fit of family and duty I had expected.

As if to prove how low my father's fortunes had fallen, Sneggie's prediction bore fruit. For speed, we left the paths between towns for cross country travel. Once off the roads, even armed men could not expect safety from banditry. We fended off no fewer than three bandit raids. I would tell tales of these victories if they had taken more than a moment or had anyone's lives been in danger besides our assailants'. A willingness to hide behind hard times as an excuse for violence didn't make these men very good at it.

That the wyrm had vexed my father's warriors enough for these outcasts to consider themselves safe from kingly justice left me angry and sullen. Dalk, sharing my disgust, suggested the blood eagle torture. We broke their ribs and tore their lungs through their backs as a warning to others who might think themselves safe to prey upon their fellow Northmen. Their screams did much to lighten my dark mood.

Eventually my father's hall drifted into sight, shrouded in morning mist. We marched through his town and to the royal fasthold's wide doors, a tired, bitter, and disillusioned force of death-bringers. We were a far cry from our optimistic day we cast off on the Volga River, but it didn't trouble me. This was more the attitude men should have when they are about to shed blood.

I stepped to just shy of an axe-stroke from the hall guards. "Let the king know that his thane, Finn the Myth Reaver, has arrived."

I watched a torrent of emotions spill across the guards' faces. A flash of happiness mixed with relief then a cloud of concern. Their eyes met and each took on the look of strong men resolved to do a distasteful task. I had no idea what to make of this but gave Dalk my own sidelong look to see if he'd noticed it as well. He looked as puzzled as I felt, but I shrugged at him. We'd come here to fight a dragon, what difference did two nervous maidens in mail make?

Sneggie, tasting violence on the air like woodsmoke, stepped between me and the guards. "What's wrong with you two? The Warborn's son has returned to save us, just as old Styrr hoped. And you hold him out here on the doorstep, tired and damp? Move, you fools, before he moves you."

One of the guards cleared his throat and said, "If I might have a word, Sneggie." Sneggie looked to me, but I shrugged again. I had no wish to kill my father's men no matter how impertinent or stupid. Sneggie and the guard leaned heads together and conferred. Sneggie looked shocked, then his countenance fell. They returned to us, the old man's shoulders sagging.

"Perhaps it would be best if we announced you, Myth Reaver," Sneggie said.

"What's wrong?" I asked.

Sneggie raised a placating hand. "I...I should confirm things for myself before speaking, milord."

I didn't like it, but I held my peace. Sneggie and the guard vanished behind the thick door and stayed gone several minutes. The remaining guard eyed me the entire time with the same strange melange of feelings betraying his inmost and complicated thoughts. If it had been any other king's hall, I'd have split him for his impertinence. Today, though, I didn't believe my father's threshold needed a splattering of blood spilled by my hand.

Sneggie and the first guard returned and stirred me from my gory thoughts. The guard bowed slightly, and stepped aside to allow Sneggie the lead.

"The—" the old man choked on a word, but recovered quickly, "—king will see you now, milord."

My war band and I hefted our weapons and baggage and made for the door, but the guard lifted his hand. "The king wishes your men to remain here while he converses with the Myth Reaver."

Once again I glanced at Dalk, and this time he shrugged at me. I looked back to the guards. "Fine. But my men have traveled halfway around the world with me, the last dozen leagues over hard ground and fighting brigands in the wilderness. They need meat and mead, and they need them *now*. I'll leave it to you," I nodded at the guard who had yet to speak a word, "to see to their comfort while they wait."

The silent guard's eyes went wide and his mouth bobbed open once or twice, but I fixed him with a smoldering glare that pulled him up short. "Yes, of course, milord. I shall see to both food and drink for your men."

I nodded at him, loosened my sword in its scabbard, and followed Sneggie and the other guard into the hall. As I stepped inside, I took in a deep breath through my nose and held it. The essence of woodsmoke that permeated the ancient and venerable walls, the subtle, moldy odor of old thatch in need of replacing, the slightly sour stink from decades of spilled mead. The sights and scents of the place overwhelmed me and took me years back to when I was but a boy.

"Home," I breathed.

"I'm sorry, milord?" the guard said.

"Just enjoying my first visit home in so long, countryman. It is simpler, here in my homelands. I missed it."

The guard only nodded and continued through the long corridor filled with flickering torchlight leading into my father's great hall. At last we reached two more large wooden doors, grandly carved with scenes of Styrr Warborn's greatest triumphs. Two more guards flanked these doors and reached out to pull the gateway fully open as we approached. I entered the hall and noted the changelessness of the great room. Even the mead benches were arrayed just as they'd been the day I left so long ago, the day of my first victory as a warrior and my last defeat as a brother. Everything had stayed as I'd left it...except for Grímarr sitting on the throne.

Seeing my eldest brother seated in my father's place filled my heart with red hot rage and my gut with cold, leaden dread. Me being myself, the anger won out.

"Methinks you should step down from father's throne before he comes in and catches your heavy rear upon it, brother. Shenanigans like this will put the old man in the mood to give a hiding the likes of which you haven't had since we were children."

Many attendants filled the room and a few warriors. All of them gasped at my effrontery. Grímarr merely looked down his nose at me with not a flicker of emotion moving across the mask he called a face. I heard the rasp of steel and looked to see a couple of the warriors pulling their swords free from their hips. I rolled my shoulder as if to loosen it for fighting and glared at them, waiting to see how foolish they might be.

"Hold, men," Grímarr husked. "My youngest brother is unaware of the dishonor he does the king of this hall."

I raised a finger and pointed at my brother. "How can you claim it is I who dishonors the king of this hall, Grímarr, when you sit in his seat?"

The left corner of Grímarr's mouth twitched up just a hair. I thought it might be a smirk, but no one had been able to read his face since he'd slept in a cradle. "Don't presume to bluster at me, *Myth Reaver*." His tone sounded too subtle to be a sneer, but too snide to be anything else. I knew not what to make of it. Jealousy? "None may speak to me thus...not in my own hall."

Realization seeped into my mind like blood on snow. My head drooped on my neck and hung low as I said, "My father is dead."

Grímarr nodded slowly. "And have you returned these short days after my coronation to lay claim to his throne? Are you soon to prove yourself the traitor I always expected you to be?"

My eyes jerked up to meet his. "If I'd come for father's throne, you'd be gutted and gasping for breath like a fish on the dock, brother. Don't blame your paranoia on me. You've known since childhood you were my lesser in combat. If you believed that meant I'd challenge your right to rule, then you chased me away all those years ago for nothing."

"Chased you off?" Grímarr said incredulously. "Is that how you remember it? You left under a cloud and made sure your father's people, your countrymen, hated you as you sailed away with your brothers' well earned booty." He suddenly looked very tired. He sighed and rubbed the bridge of his nose. "If it isn't father's throne you're after, then what brings you at this time of ill omens, brother?"

My eyes narrowed. I still couldn't follow the roads of Grímarr's mind. Did he really recall my departure that way? Or did he merely play a role for his new subjects? Odin alone knew what tales had been weaved around my departure in the years since I'd been home. Had father truly wanted me here? Or had he merely been desperate and sent for me as one would call for a vicious hound when a thief is in the house? I might never know.

"Father sent for me," I said, nodding toward Sneggie. "He sent this man on the errand of finding me at the far end of the Varangian Way. And like a loyal subject, when my king called, I came to assist him and my countrymen."

Grímarr looked at me again, his red-rimmed eyes perched over dark circles. "Have you now?"

His voice took on a thin and brittle tone. It made me give his whole face another look, and the discovery of an aging man there surprised me. The aging in and of itself didn't bring surprise; Grímarr was many years my elder. But we Styrrssons are a hardy breed, and mere age couldn't account for this. He looked like a good blanket used roughly until it frayed around the edges.

"Brother," I said, my voice full of the concern that unexpectedly flooded my breast. I took a few quick steps forward and came close to the throne. "Of course I have. Father sent for me because of my reputation. He said that you and my other brothers had not been able to slay the sea wyrm. He welcomed me home to end its terror." I squeezed my eyes shut to stop the tears that threatened as I thought of my father, cold and dead. "But it seems you finally won the day, although father made the ultimate sacrifice to see the wyrm vanquished."

Grímarr looked at me and his impassive features took on a decidedly chilly cast. "Styrr didn't face his doom in some glorious pitched battle spitting curses at the serpent, you witless child. For two years, his brow creased with worry for his people until his heart gave up. Two. Years. Then he died in his bed." My brother's eyes narrowed. "Apparently waiting for you to come and save him."

The words were soaked in venom and landed like barbed nettles. My face burned hot, but with rage, shame, or some demon's mixture I knew not. I looked around the room and found pained and miserable faces yet graced with glimmers of hope.

"I came as soon as I knew, Grímarr. I could do no better. But look around you, brother. Even after the loss of my father, these people still believe I can help them, that I can save them from the vicious beast, the ocean's serpent. Let me help them."

Grímarr scanned coldly across the men in the room. To a one, they ensured they looked elsewhere when his eyes fell upon them.

I leaned in close to him. "Do not blame them, brother. It has been two years of endless suffering dredged up from the depths of the sea. A thousand years of the worst our people had to offer, including the pinnacle of hate between a jealous brother and a prideful youngest son, given horrible form."

"Aye." The single syllable tore itself from Grímarr's throat. "Sent back from the frigid, black deep to devour us with our own transgressions."

I nodded fervently. "And if the sea serpent is the worst of us, it has also taken the best of us by devouring our father. Though it failed to feed upon his body, it ate away at his spirit until nothing remained to keep even that great king alive." I shook my head, a grim determination falling over me.

Grímarr tried to interrupt, but I spoke over him. "Not again. Not ever again. I wasn't here when my father needed me." My voice sounded ragged, rasping in my throat. "I wasn't here to lay him to rest."

Now none would meet *my* eyes, not even my callous brother. Shame wrote itself across all of their features.

"Styrr Warborn has not yet been honored with a Viking's funeral," Grímarr said, his voice tight.

"WHAT?" I roared and kicked over a mead bench. It flew across the room, slammed into the stone wall, and burst into splinters. "Why has my father, *our* father, not been sent out to sea with gold and fire?"

Grímarr looked at me and, for the first time in my life, I saw true emotion in his twisted features. His face seemed unsure what to do with all the feeling. Rather than hint at what went on in his mind, the look only made Grímarr grotesque with anguish.

"Think, Finn, *think*!" Grímarr stood, descended the dais, and grasped at my sleeve. His twisted fingers clawed at the material. "How can he be sent out to sea while the serpent coils her scales around our shores?"

Rage flooded me like a kettle of white hot iron dumped from the forge. It ran through me and I could have sworn the very hair on my head stood straight up from my prickling scalp. As I looked at Grímarr, pitiful in his shame, long-scarred wounds tore open afresh. I hated him for making me leave, hated him for making me miss these years with my father. And most of all, I hated myself for letting him do these things to me, for being halfway around the world when my family needed me.

"Do my other brothers at least still fight?" I asked. The wrath running through me made my voice as cold as the icy depths from which the serpent first swam.

"They guard Styrr's body where it lies upon his boat."

"You've left him *moldering* out on the beach? While you sit here, on *his* throne? *Playing* at being king?" I shook his hand from my sleeve. "You have always feared my strength, brother, and now I see why. You. Are. *Weak*."

I stalked from the room, and all the warriors streamed out behind me. Wordlessly, I made my way through the halls until I stood back at the front door. I had picked up a score of fighting men on my way. When I came back out into the sun, Dalk looked over my shoulder at the train of guards following me like a maiden's veil. He looked at my face, saw the anger and pain there, and turned to the rest of our squad.

"Let's go gut us a wyrm, boys!" he bellowed. A cheer rose up from them, then the clatter of weapons on shields.

"For glory!" a voice yelled out. And all others yelled back, "FOR GLO-RY!"

"For the Myth Reaver!" shouted another voice. And all other voices shouted back, "FOR THE MYTH REAVER!"

I drew Moon Sliver and held it high over my head then, the sun glinting off its translucent blade. Everyone, be they my own warriors or guards of the hall, fell absolutely silent. The wind blew and in the lull, I heard the hum of it cutting itself on my sword's edge.

"FOR THE HONOR OF STYRR WARBORN!" I roared.

The men of the Myth Reaver took up that battle cry, reaching a thunderous volume that would have made Thor blush and put down his hammer, knowing he'd never match it. The sound of proud warriors honoring one of their own rang across the land, and it shook the foundations of the World Tree. I know my father heard it in Hel, and the thought made me smile.

10. The Sea Wyrm War - Day One

My men and I wasted no time shouldering into our shirts of mail and strapping on our weapons. Many of them had dressed while I spoke to the king inside. Those already attired assisted their battle brethren into their armor. The various fortunes gained and lost in the Far East had left us the richest of paupers. We barely owned more than the clothes on our backs and arms we could carry, yet unlike the ragged band we had been here in the north, the mail, axes, swords, and spears we carried were worth a middling kingdom in their own right.

My men shone in the sun, the light glinting and shimmering from helm, shirt, and edge. They stood like a constellation of stars, pointed and deadly, fallen from the sky in broad daylight. They stood ready to do battle with a beast old as the world and angry as a stormy sea. They did it for fame, for glory, and for a legend. They did it for me. They did it for the Myth Reaver.

And if they stood as cruel and bloodthirsty stars, then I stood a blazing sun before them. I wore a shirt of mail crafted for me from the yards of hard-won tackle once worn by Eldrim, champion of Alvis the Elf King. The elf-crafted armor had been woven tightly as a well-made shirt of cloth and felt just as comfortable. Though not indestructible, I knew my own mighty blows had penetrated the mail but barely. No mortal hand had rent it since the day I killed Eldrim.

A helm rode my head forged from the one that once sat atop Eldrim's enormous skull. Master smiths retooled it into a tight fitting cap with a wide nose guard. Atop it sat a wolf carved from darkest obsidian, its tiny eyes two chips of emerald. The wolf's hackles thickened around its neck, its lips pulled back from miniscule, pointed fangs.

About my shoulders sat my ever-present mantle of wolfskin so black it shone a midnight blue. The bristling fur could turn a blow like the toughest boiled leather. It clasped around my neck with the same bejeweled wolf's head pendant given to me by the grateful village of Klibo.

In my left hand, I hefted a shield crafted from planks of aged and fire-toughened oak tied together tightly and centered with bands of shining steel. Far too heavy for any other man to carry, I held a bulwark of strength covered in silk. The silk bore an embroidered standard, another black wolf's head with baleful green eyes.

In my right hand I carried the sword of the fallen elf champion. The crossguard spread broad and solid. It shone like gold, though its strength to deflect a blow was much more than that soft, lustrous metal. The grip stretched long, made for hands much larger than my own, with silver wire thin as a hair wound about it. The wound-hoe's blade stretched over four feet long, but stood nearly translucent and glowing with a pale otherworldly light. So light was the blade and so powerful my own arm I could wield it one handed.

I could only imagine the red-handed, resplendent beauty of our column as we marched down to the shore. Distantly over the ocean, the sky grew tenebrous and clouds rolled over one another, dark and malignant. Blinding shafts of lightning stabbed through the cancerous vapors, and thunder cracked and boomed above us.

"Thor has come out to watch us kill a dragon, lads," I bellowed over my shoulder. A score of voices answered with the first strands of a mighty battle hymn to the Thunderer. I smiled at their courage and joined them in their song.

We crested a hill to look down on the shore for the first time. I saw a sight that flooded my blood with hot rage even as it swelled my breast with pride. Sitting upon struts to hold it balanced and upright, I spied a well-made longship. Upon its sail had been emblazoned the broken shield standard of Styrr Warborn. Heaped high upon its decks stood piles of bejeweled baubles, intricate trinkets, mail shirts, swords, and spears in gleaming gold and shining silver. And on a bower above that great and kingly hoard lay the mortal remains of Styrr Warborn, my father. I ground my teeth as though I'd crush them into powder at the thought of his shade wandering the Nine Worlds, lost and unsure of his own identity since he had not been properly put to rest.

But arrayed around this failed pyre I saw something as wonderful as my father's rotting corpse was terrible. My brothers, save cold-faced Grímarr, stood as fiery testaments to a thane's devotion to a king and a son's love for a father.

Hallbjorn towered over all others with his rangy arms holding both shield and long-hafted halberd. With his height and reach, Hallbjorn killed men before they realized they'd entered his death circle.

Ruddy-haired Magnus swaggered around with hair and beard bristling like a stiff brush. Short and thick, heavy muscles wound about his pale arms, each as round as my thigh and speckled as a hen's egg. He bore a heavy, two-handed warhammer with broad mallet and hooked spike.

Quick-fingered Osvald bounced on the balls of his feet. Two short seaxes hung from his belt, ready for a draw as fast as Thor's lightning. Always a canny fighter, Osvald would stoop to use dirt, rocks, fists, and teeth if his swords failed him.

The twins, Skulli and Snorri, leaned against one another like two standing stones that had withstood rain, snow, sleet, wind and would continue standing until Fimbulwinter's final cold cracked them. Their crimson hair framed their heads like halos of hero's fire.

And lastly, there stood dark and calm Jorund dressed in leathers dyed to match the shades of the deep forest. He stood with bright hawk eyes that saw everything before them. He held a thick yew bow and wore a quiver of darkly fletched arrows.

Jorund's constantly scanning gaze first took note of us. He stepped apart from the other brothers and called out to them. His hand smoothly pulled a shaft from his quiver, nocked it, and drew the thick bow far enough back it shivered under the tension. He sighted down the arrow at me, and I felt a chill as though someone had walked over my grave. But as he aimed, I saw his bright eye widen with surprise at dawning recognition. He un-nocked and sheathed the arrow just as deftly as he'd brought it to bear. He waved a placating hand at our brothers.

"Hold, sons of Warborn," he said, loud enough I could hear him. "This is no enemy force come to raid and desecrate our king and father's corpse. What you see are the mighty raven feeders of Finn Styrrsson, lost brother and celebrated bane of monsters and godlings."

The others stepped to either side of Jorund and shielded their eyes against the glare of our battle tackle. They looked wary. They looked tired. They looked like men who had been defending the body of their dead father from a monster beyond mortal ken.

I held up my hand to stop the march of my men. I cupped my hands to my mouth and bellowed, "Hail and well met, fellow sons of Warborn. I return to fight by your side and to finally do our dead father the honor his kingly life demands. I come to kill a wyrm."

They remained silent for a moment, and I stored a wary breath in my chest. I felt the force around me do the same. We waited, wondering how they would accept their long lost brother. Finally Magnus broke the silence with a voice gruff as a rock slide.

"By Tyr's blessed scrotum, Finn, it's about blasted time you showed up. I've stood here with these other weaklings for days thinking, 'If only Finn would return. Then the only brother who ever matched me would finally stand at my side so we might end this travesty.'"

Magnus's face split into a broken toothed grin as my other brothers groaned, but I returned his smile and quickly crossed the distance to clasp arms with him. He knocked my outstretched hand aside and drew me into a bone-crunching embrace. As he squeezed all memory of air from my lungs, my other brothers fell in to clap me heartily on the back.

"Now we'll finish this gory deed," Osvald said in his brilliant tenor.

"What kept you, Finn? Did a score of Jötunn need besting before you could make your own father's funeral?" Jorund asked, a smile playing on his lips.

"Ah, pipe down, Jor," Skulli scolded. Snorri finished for his twin brother, "Finn's like as not got a big enough head as it is." Their words chided, but they wore broad grins betraying their happiness to see me.

Only Hallbjorn hung back from the reunion. Magnus finally released me, and I eyed my second eldest brother. He inspected me, his face blanked to a mask nearly as smooth as Grímarr could wear. He leaned casually on his halberd, although I knew his apparent restfulness for a ruse. He reminded me of a poisonous snake, more dangerous when coiled in waiting.

"What brings the mighty Myth Reaver back at this most dire of times?" he asked quietly. "Duty? Or glory?"

I spread my hands before him. "Even as a boy, ever have I sought both duty and glory, honored Hallbjorn. Though always did I favor honor over fame. You know this to be true, for you watched Grímarr hatch his scheme to deny me both. I craved duty as his thane, but he would not have it because he feared my thirst for glory. Yet the glory I lusted after as a raven feeder would have come regardless, for even at that tender age I stalked like a wolf among milk-fed babes." I took a step toward him. "I come to see our father laid to rest as he deserved. If, in the doing of my duty, wyrmsbane is added to my legend, then I will celebrate that as well."

Hallbjorn considered this for a long moment before he let his halberd fall to ensnare me with gangling arms. "You learned to speak as well as you learned to fight, little brother," he said into the nape of my neck. He moved me to his considerable arm's length and smiled at me. "And you are sorely needed here."

With that, my men surged forward to meet my kith and kin. I introduced my brothers of blood to my brothers of battle. A father's pride welled up within me as I surveyed them. Where once my brothers had stood as stalwart individuals overshadowed by the sea's primal might, now they stood as part of an unbreakable company, bonded together in the face of horrors against which men were not meant to win the day.

"All right, lads," I shouted over the racket of meeting. "We can hold hands like maidens when the job is done." Thunder rumbled across the darkening sky, punctuating my words. "I want ten stout men to shoulder that burden." I pointed at the ship that held my father's corpse. "That ship burns upon the whale's road by nightfall or may the sea wyrm take me."

Immediately ten of my men dropped their shields and ducked beneath the portage poles already threaded through metal circles nailed into the ship's hull. As they dug in their heels and struggled to lift the treasure laden ship, Hallbjorn stepped near me.

"Did you think we hadn't thought of that, Finn?" Friendly mocking filled his voice, but also the quiet demand of explanation.

I pointed to the blackened, billowing sky with thick shafts of lightning stabbing downward into the wind tossed, foamy sea. "I cannot begin to kill a wyrm that only swims at the bottom of the swan's way. She wishes to add father's grave treasures to her hoard, yes?" He shrugged in answer. "Then let us bait her into appearing so that I might split her skull and have done."

Hallbjorn nodded and shouted orders to my brothers and men. "Strong flanks, you bastards! We'll make a straight line to the water's edge as fast as can be done. Magnus to the left, Skulli and Snorri to the right. Osvald, you're with me. Watch my back. Jorund, have a flaming dart at the ready. If Finn's brazen plan works, I want that ship a pyre the moment it's at sail."

The warriors took their places. My force, led by my battle-ready brothers, split in twain on either side of the ship. Osvald grinned as though he knew a joke and jerked the two short blades from his belt. He twirled their grips through his fingers, their blades reflecting the nearly constant lightning strikes. Hallbjorn hadn't said where he wanted me, but as the men formed their ranks, it became clear he expected my leadership for the procession. I would have the look at our reptilian enemy I so craved. I drew Moon Sliver and hefted my shield.

"Forward!" I yelled at the top of my voice, and we all surged into motion.

The longship lay perhaps fifteen or twenty yards from the sea's edge, out of the changing tide's reach. As we moved slowly, deliberately, weapons at the ready and nerves pulled taught with the expectation of battle, the strip of sand and shale stretched out like leagues.

"FORTH!" I barked, and swung Moon Sliver to point straight toward the water. As if to answer me, the dark clouds split with a crack of lightning that left a purple slash across my vision. Thunder slammed into us, and before our abused ears could really register it, the world filled with rain falling in sheets all around us. It churned the sand and sea alike into a frothing mess.

But we moved. We slipped, we sank, we shifted, we slid, especially the men bearing the boat. But still, we moved. Shortly we reached the sea's edge. We persevered, the rough waters lapping at our ankles and our nerves screaming in expectation of an attack that insisted on never coming. We waded into knee deep water, and I drew breath for the order to let down the boat when something changed. The water around us began to pulse with sound, felt more than heard. A growl, deep and awful, vibrated the sea.

"Ready yourselves, men!" I yelled, hoping they'd hear me over the rain's din. "The wyrm comes!"

I tensed, shield out front and sword drawn back for a strike. The water's pulsating rumble increased until I could hear the beast's submerged snarl even over the rain's constant drumming on my helm. The hum of my own nerves merged with it, doubled, then tripled before I clenched my teeth and reined myself in.

I grabbed my fear, my worry over my father's wyrd, my pride at my brethren, and forced them behind the curtain of my hot rage. My mind became a sort of seething serenity, and the staccato of my own fretfulness calmed. It wasn't only me, though. The wyrm had gone silent as well. I had only enough time to wonder at it before she burst from the water.

I thought the rain had soaked me before, but the splash and spray as the great serpent's head broke the surface sent up a crushing breaker that nearly swept me off my feet. I gazed up the serpent's long, sinuous body, straight as a scaled column rising from the water, to stare at a fearsome head as wide across as a mead hall. Arm-long hair the sickly green of old seaweed swung from her head and neck. Sharp, black scales bristled across her bulk. Flaming red eyes stared down at me, angry as the storm that beat upon the sea. She flared her nostrils, each one large enough for a grown man to crawl through, opened her mottled black and red maw, and *roared*.

The fetid wind that buffeted me stank like a hundred fishing villages in the hot summer sun. The noise sounded like a thousand ram horns blown all at once by stout men. This uproar meant to announce the end of the Nine Worlds. It brought a din to turn men's bowels to water so that terror's icy claws held them from running. Luckily, I was no mere man. I was the Myth Reaver.

A wordless, guttural battle cry tore from my throat, and I dashed forward, swinging Moon Sliver. I brought the long sword around in a great arc that slashed through ebon scale and into the soft meat beneath. The beast roared again in a higher pitch as battle-sweat gushed from the wound. My upraised shield caught and deflected most of the blood into the ocean, where it hissed like steam upon contact with the water.

I heard other voices join me in battle cries and sworn oaths to Odin, to Thor, and to Tyr. Men rushed forward, swinging weapons into the barn-sized column of the wyrm's massive body. The warriors sounded the clash of weapons upon its scaly hide as blow after blow fell, but the natural armor of the beast turned aside all attacks. Sparks flew, but no point or edge could pierce the soft underflesh. None could scratch that save an elven blade driven by my own titanic strength.

The colossal head rose higher and drew back like a man taking a deep breath. The monster spit a hissing noise I hadn't heard before, but tales of dragons flashed through my thought-hoard.

"SHIELD WALL!" I yelled as loudly as I could. A few men raised their shields along with me, but the noise of rain and battle drowned my warning. Or maybe I was just too late. Heedless of my mad scramble, the beast leaned over us, opened her repugnant maw, and spewed forth a green and faintly glowing liquid smelling like a hundred gallons of horse piss.

That stench persisted until the spray hit unprotected flesh. Then it smelled like charred meat, burning hair, and raw, terrible pain. Men died screaming, their flesh melting from their bones wherever the beast's baleful spew landed. Shields sizzled but held under the onslaught, protecting those of us quick enough to raise them. I stabbed Moon Sliver into the beast several times, but vomiting forth more of the noisome spit seemed the only effect.

I saw small pock marks begin to form on the underside of my shield, and I wondered how much longer it would endure. Then I heard a thrumming bass note, and I saw Jorund's fiery arrow arcing through the air toward the beast's face. I only had a moment to wonder what such a tiny missile would do to such a massive beast before it flew into the great viper's left nostril.

It brought instant change.

The belch of bane-water halted immediately and the creature made horrible gasping noises. Every gulping breath just caused her to retch louder, and her hoary head wobbled on its long, undulating body.

"FALL BACK!" I ordered. Men turned and ran away from the beast. I saw another two dozen warriors shove shoulders beneath the barrow-ship and assist the bearers in running back to safety. I followed behind the men. I pushed them into greater hurry with my shield and righted any who slipped back to their feet before they could drown in panic and shallow water. I tried desperately not to count the faces I *didn't* see.

The monster wrestled itself back under control, bringing her coughs and sputters to a slow halt. Only the absence of this racket allowed me to hear the screaming voice and repeated sounds of dull, reverberating impacts. I looked over my shoulder only to see Magnus, his shorter stature burying him in water up to his chest, still singing the hymn to Thor and forcefully slamming his hammer into the side of the wyrm over and over.

Odin only knew how he'd avoided the bane-water without a shield. Perhaps he'd simply ducked beneath the waves. Regardless, his hammer, made to do the most damage against men in plate armor, hurt the beast now. I watched Magnus drive the hooked tip of his hammer's spike into the center of a scale. The spike went in deep, and Magnus yanked hard on the hammer's haft, the edges of muscles and ropy veins standing out on his thick arms. A mighty yell and a mightier heave ripped the scale free with the sound of tearing leather.

The beast roared louder than even when I'd cut into it, and swiveled her head around to see Magnus fall ass over elbow. My brother slipped beneath the waves, then bobbed up like a cork, beaming. He held the hammer over his head, brandishing the scale, still stuck to the point of his hammer spike, like a trophy. He didn't see the wyrm look down on him, her crimson eyes narrowed in pained anger.

"Magnus! MAGNUS!"

He heard me. Even through the driving rain, even through the growls, clicks, and snarls of the wyrm, he heard me. But he only looked in my direction, smiling wider, jabbing the hammer at and yammering excitedly. I pointed at the dragon, but the smiling idiot nodded and kept jabbering. I ran towards him then, sluggish in the knee deep water. For the first time I noticed the frosty coldness of the ocean when my numbed feet scraped and slid over wet sand and shale.

I saw the beast focus intently on Magnus, the way a man might target a tiny fly before trying to swat it, and I knew I wouldn't be fast enough. I threw aside my shield and forced tired and aching muscles to churn harder, to pour on more speed. The beast arched her twisted, sinuous body and dove her head downward toward Magnus. I screamed "No!" and dove toward my brother, Moon Sliver outstretched in front of me.

The black head flashed past my vision and Magnus vanished behind the beast's jaws. I had already leapt, and my momentum carried me sword-tip first into the fleshy, unguarded corner of the wyrm's mouth. I dealt a glancing blow, certainly not a mortal wound. But the gash tore soft, delicate flesh and it must have been searing agony.

A screaming roar sliced through both air and water, and the partially submerged head of the wyrm yanked back in pain and surprise. Magnus's face, pale and slack with terror, flashed back into view. I tackled him, and we went under the waves. We rolled in the froth and came up spluttering. I wrapped my hand in his battle harness and hollered in his ear.

"Head for shore, you great, heaving lummox!"

He nodded dumbly, his eyes still wide and unfocused with shock. He moved toward shore, but either because of his recent brush with death or the searing cold of the sea, his steps were wooden and slow. I frantically looked toward the shore and saw that the longship had been replaced in its struts and man-sized silhouettes stood around it tensely watching the drama that played out between Magnus, me, and the wyrm. I couldn't see if Dalk was there. I couldn't tell if any of my brothers had survived.

I looked up wildly at the beast towering over Magnus and me. We'd never make it to shore before she attacked again. I'd gotten lucky once. I might wound her again if she bit, but it likely wouldn't be lethal, and I'd probably die in the attempt. And that was only if she bit. We wouldn't survive another burst of bane-water. I decided I would die either way, but I might save Magnus.

I changed course and ran toward the wyrm again. She looked down on me, angry but wary. Her head drew back, and I saw her neck bulge the same as it had before she spat out liquid death upon the heads of my comrades. I ran harder. I reversed my grip on Moon Sliver and grasped the hilt in a loving, two handed embrace. The wyrm's mouth opened. I saw a flash of pale white flesh amongst the night-black scales where Magnus had torn a swatch of snake-leather free. I threw myself at it, and brought Moon Sliver down with all my might.

The opalescent tip sank into the pale, velvety flesh all the way to the hilt. Over four feet of hard, sharp, elven steel lodged in the monster's belly. Even this could not kill the titanic beast. No, she would not die. But she would *hurt*.

The thing's gargantuan scarlet eyes widened in shock, and she screamed, spewing her load of noxious bile a hundred ells into the sky. The droplets rained down, burning and stinging me where they landed. But that shower was the least of my problems. The beast, tired of having a nail driven into her side, writhed and thrashed to dislodge me. She threw her head upward until a hundred ells of its bulk rose up and over the sea. I hung a dozen of those ells above the waves myself, praying that Moon Sliver's sharp edge would not rip the flesh further and drop me back toward the water. The long serpent coil then twisted inward and flung itself back to land flat on the surface of the ocean.

The shock and the noise put the thunder crack that had heralded the storm to shame. The impact shook me loose, and waves submerged me. I rolled and tumbled beneath the water, my mouth and lungs filling with the icy, brackish water. I held on to Moon Sliver and tried to keep from impaling myself on it as I bounced and skidded along the ocean floor, each of the collisions bruising. I thought they should have hurt, but the cold leeched the strength and feeling from my limbs. Oblivion's sweet embrace came over me, and I expected to open my eyes on Valhalla.

Instead, I opened them to the blasted rain pelting my face, Dalk, and my brothers looming over me.

"Thank Odin," Dalk breathed as soon as my eyes fluttered open. My brothers echoed his sentiments. Magnus offered me a hand, and, when I clenched his forearm, he hauled me up to a standing position. Forced to bear my weight, every muscle in my body screamed. Though I had scrapes and many, many bruises, my dousing left me mostly unharmed. Hallbjorn handed me Moon Sliver in my sword belt. I took it and clasped it on. While doing so, I looked out over the sea.

The wyrm cavorted angrily out there, diving and slashing her way through the waves. She roared and screamed at us. Every now and then she swam into the shallowest water that would support her bulk and spewed the bane-water at us. It landed a few paces shy of where we stood, near the newly replaced struts holding the longship out of harm's way.

"What now, Finn?" Hallbjorn asked. I looked at him, a little surprised. To my memory, he'd never taken second place to anyone but father or Grímarr. But there he stood, waiting to see what the Myth Reaver would have him do against this bitch beast from legend.

I looked at the exhausted, haggard, and wounded force that stood around me. They had become a shadow of the army we'd been this morning in both numbers and strength. I turned back to the monster that kept my father from being laid to rest.

"Send somebody back to the hall for the rest of our gear. I'm going to need another shield, and I'm sure others will need replacement weapons for our next foray."

"*Next* foray?" Skulli said, dismay painted on his face.

I felt my features take on a grim cast, my mouth a hard pressed line as I glared at the sea wyrm.

"Of course. The beast still lives, doesn't she?" I pounded my fist into my open palm. "We nearly had her that time."

11. The Sea Wyrm War - Day Two

I had gone into the first day hoping to put my father to rest before dealing with the sea serpent. My first attempt ended as near an utter failure as it could be without totally wiping out our war band. I had lost many, many friends and comrades in arms in a matter of minutes. Only for the grace of Odin himself did I not lose any of my brothers or Dalk. We spent the rest of the day slipping and sludging in the pouring rain, testing the defenses and commitment of the serpent. Though my brothers assured me we had done more damage and come closer to putting our father to rest in that first offensive than any previous try, it seemed we would die to a man if we made another straightforward attempt.

The sun set behind the dark clouds still thick and heavy with rain. I called to make camp before losing what little light we had. I took Hallbjorn and Dalk aside.

"The beast lives at the bottom of the oceans. I suspect the darkness of night is no challenge to her whereas we are in fifty times the danger should we attack now. No, we will dry out as best we can. We will rest. And tomorrow, we will try something else."

Dalk nodded and smirked. "Does the mighty Myth Reaver have a plan more clever and subtle than yelling 'attack' and walking into the sea?"

I felt my cheeks go red at the chiding. In front of my brother, the heat of embarrassment overtook me. I shrugged and smiled uneasily at the two men. "Surely you've noticed by now how rarely I've needed another plan."

Hallbjorn threw his head back and laughed from his belly. He clapped me on the shoulder. "Indeed, little brother, we've heard. Still, I can't fault you for the attempt. We've lost more men than you did today, and several boats as well, without ever blooding the creature."

I nodded. "Whatever else befell us today, we've learned she has weaknesses. I think her desire for Father's grave hoard is a larger soft spot than the one Magnus made with his hammer."

Hallbjorn's bushy brows raised in disbelief. "You have a scheme to exploit the mind of a sea wyrm?"

I nodded again. "Come morning, I plan to go fishing. We can easily get ropes and anchors for hooks. But I will need bait."

Dalk looked thoughtful. "What did you have in mind?"

"Something I'm afraid only my eldest brother can give," I said and spat in the sand.

Hallbjorn wore a suspiciously blank face when he said, "Anything I could ask him for?"

I spat again. "We're going to need some gold. A lot of it. And he probably shouldn't expect to get it back."

~

Sometime in the night, the rainstorm broke. We woke early to breakfast and dry clothes and bodies we had thought would be damp until we died. With our deaths looming not far in the future, little comforts like hearty food and warm, dried clothing felt especially sweet. Having this moment, the time before the battle, with my brothers again was also precious. It stirred my heart, and I unlocked my word-hoard.

"Brothers," I said as I stood from breakfast. "And I call you *all* my brothers. For it is shared blood that binds men as brothers, and we have shared the blood of a dragon." A small cheer of agreement answered me from every mother's son.

"Soon we will find ourselves in another pitched battle against an ancient and terrible thing. The viper makes her life in the bowels of the frigid sea. She is a terror of the deep and a cold-blooded hater of men. It is not for us to question the Norns that they would bring such a doom and judgment down on this people, or why they would consign my father to so ignominious a fate. I know not why this gruesome beast came, but I know now why she stays." I gestured to my father's graveship. "Her serpent's heart longs for my father's grave goods, his death spoils. But we will not let her take these riches!"

Another cheer, this one louder.

"We will not let her have them, because Styrr Warborn deserves better than to suckle at the cold teat of Hela. Though we cannot change that wyrd, we can at least give him honor and a memory of his identity while he walks that mist-shrouded and chilly land. We kill this beast today for Styrr's suffering people! We slay her for glory! We deal her death that we might become *legends*. And maybe, just maybe, make Styrr one with us." I drew Moon Sliver and raised it over my head. "Who's with me?"

The answering cheer might have come from a thousand raven feeders rather than a mere hundred. Every man leapt to his feet, slamming weapon into shield and raising a clatter sure to awaken the ire of the scaly peril whose humps I saw breaking the shining surface of the swan's road.

"Then get to your posts! And let's go fishing!"

Another cheer, but this one more diffuse as the men scattered to their positions. They readied equipment, most of which consisted of ten long, stout sailing ropes, expertly knotted to a two horse cart harness at one end and hooked to an anchor at the other. A fortune in gold and silver wound around each anchor. A king's ransom as bait. I thought of dead-faced Grímarr and smiled at the thought.

Short, stout Magnus and his hammer, the only weapon besides my own elf-smithied blade that had shown itself able to damage the beast, stepped next to me. We traded the grim smile of the warrior who goes to his doom, to his glory, or both. We walked out knee deep into the pounding, frothy surf.

"Hooks into the water, lads!" I ordered.

Stepping to the edge of the water, the lead man on each rope whirred the anchor over his head and pitched it high and far out to sea. We'd put the strongest men at the lead of the rope to make sure the bait landed deep. We were not disappointed when each anchor splashed into the whale's road ten or twelve ells away from us. The men held the ropes loosely, but their constantly scanning eyes betrayed their apprehension. I glanced over my shoulder, and the others manning the ropes and the horses looked just the same. Hallbjorn had thrown a rope, and he couldn't resist asking the obvious question.

"Now what do we do, Finn?"

"Haven't you ever been fishing? Mostly you wait."

Some time passed and the sun climbed higher into the sky. I began to contemplate the distasteful notion of using my father's barrow-ship as further bait for the monster when I saw the creature's hump off to the side.

"Haul them in," I yelled. Each man hauled the rope in hand over hand. Though not quick, they remained steady. I had no doubt the anchors stirred the muck of the ocean bed, allowing the early morning sun to glitter along the strands of gold we'd enmeshed with the anchors.

The shimmering motion must have caught the attention of our prey, because the low rushing sound of the surf that had numbed our ears for the last few hours split with an angry, roaring cry. The humps undulated faster and faster with a staccato rhythm until the beast swam perhaps a half a league away from our end man. The graceful serpentine motion took on a fevered pace that stirred the waters into foam where, until then, it had not created more than a ripple. The scales flashed out of sight, and I yelled out a warning to my far man.

"Rodmar! Brace yourself! She's coming for you!"

Rodmar had just enough time to nod and set his feet before the rope pulled taut in his fists. The horses dragged furrows in the sandy ground as the serpent's strength pulled them toward the water. Rodmar's squad reacted quickly, most of them hauling back on the rope while one man whipped the horses lightly and yanked on their bridle. The draft animals heaved against the ropes and there existed a moment of perfect tension where they strained one direction and the beast tried to swim out to sea.

"Olaf," I called to the next man in our ragged line. "Drag yours in faster; get her attention."

Olaf gave the rope a series of sharp tugs sure to stir up the baubles and set them to glinting beneath the clear, blue water. He was in the middle of one such tug when his rope pulled tight so suddenly that he lost his footing and fell face first into the water. He came up spluttering, but his muscles nevertheless strained against the rope. His squad also sprang into action, and now two teams of horses dragged against the serpent.

And she knew it, too. She vaulted out of the water, roaring and shaking her woolly head against the two lines embedded in her mouth. I shaded my eyes with my shield and squinted toward the monstrosity as she pulled and reared and threw herself around. I fretted that the anchors would tear loose, or that they had been swallowed but had not hooked upon anything. But even at this distance I could see that the ropes had been well and truly swallowed down the beast's gullet.

Even if she tried to cough them up, as she must at her lair, the anchors would hold fast. But I reckoned the longer the tugging war went on, the angrier the wyrm would become and the less likely to give up. I glanced over my shoulder to the shore. The horses did an admirable job, but they had already lathered and their sides heaved. We needed more hooks in her.

"The rest of you lazy bastards, reel them in!" A flurry of rapid, hand over hand pulling of the ropes answered my order. Through sheer luck or the Norns' heavy hand, the speed of Hallbjorn's pulls caused the glittering anchor to break the surface of the water. The sun glanced off it in the way only warm sunlight can gleam from Freyja's tears. It had an instantaneous effect on the serpent.

She stopped fighting the two lines hooked in her craw, the scarlet eyes narrowing upon Hallbjorn's bait. She looked at the flashing anchor in something like awe for a moment before diving down into the water and swimming furiously toward it. Shock stole our senses for a moment. Nothing so large should be able to move so fast.

"Hall—" I started to say, but it was too late. Thankfully, my brother had seen what came and steadied himself. The viper ran aground near us, cutting a furrow deep into the shale bed where we stood. The fiend threw muddy salt water thirty feet into the air, but I flung my shield in front of my face to ward off the wave of ocean and earth sweeping over me.

I looked over the edge of my shield just in time to see Hallbjorn's anchor vanish down the gaping maw. I could see right down into the belly of the beast. Her throat muscles undulated sickeningly, forcing the treasure, and the hook, deep down the recesses.

I started to yell orders at the other rope-throwers, but four of them saw their opportunity without my aid. Their shining boat hooks shot into the rippling gorge muscles of the sea serpent only to vanish into the depths. My men knew their parts well, and all five of the new ropes immediately pulled taut. I heard the shrill, screaming neighs of horses join the grunts and cursing of men. The wyrm jerked forward a half dozen feet, dragging her furrow further into shallow water.

A cheer went up as my compatriots unable to get a hook into the wyrm's mouth dropped their ropes and joined their fellows in the tugging war. The war band took up their favorite hymn to Thor again, and the bass rumble of the song gave rhythm to their heaving and hefting so that every man and horse pulled as one.

The wyrm's baleful eyes grew wide, and she roared in defiance. She wriggled backward, hairy tentacles flapping around her head, muscles rippling beneath black scales that shone darkly in the sun. She gained a few feet, but the next all-as-one pull regained the lost distance and more. For once, men controlled this force of nature. The wyrm knew this, and she feared us.

In panic, the monster began a frenzied spasm that jerked the men sideways. Though they fought to retain a grip, the wet rope slipped from their grasps. Only the horses kept it from being a total loss, the knots affixed to their yokes creaking under the strain so loudly I could hear them even over the tumult. The horror's hysterical bid for freedom ruined the rhythmic pull when men fought to regain their grips and failed to match the wyrm's writhing. The time for cleverness had ended; now was the moment for battle.

"MAGNUS!" I yelled over the rising pandemonium. My squat brother nodded at me, grim determination turning his face to angry brows and bristling beard. We advanced on the viper's snapping jaws heedless of its mouth daggers. I swung Moon Sliver at the monster a few times but failed to score anything other than glancing blows. The mere nicks I gave her didn't even register on the fiend's frantic brain.

But Magnus and his hammer had no need of a blade's subtlety. He roared a challenge to the sea-horror as he ran toward her, spun on his heels, and brought the hammer around in a complete circle. With the sound of a full charge running into a shield wall, the heavy head of his weapon slammed into the tip of beast's nose, landing right between its flaring nostrils.

The effect on the monster matched that of a bucket of cold water in the face of a panicked man. She stopped thrashing with a pathetic whimpering noise and went stock still, staring dazedly down her muzzle at Magnus. I grabbed one of the hairy, tentacle things that fluttered around her head and leapt at the same time I hauled myself upward. I landed amongst the wyrm's mane, which roused the horror from her stupor. The wyrm shook her head the same way a dog shakes water from its coat. But I held fast, a grip like that of thirty men the only thing keeping the monster from slinging me off her neck.

Magnus swung the hammer again, this time bringing it into contact with one of the serpent's long, curved front fangs. The tooth snapped off at the root, and the creature roared, rearing up and away from Magnus's assault. Even in shallow water, the column of muscle pulled itself straight. The wyrm's rearing dragged the screaming horses backward. I heard wood snap and the harsh whip crack of a rope no longer under tension. It hit something with a wet, meaty slap followed by a pained groan.

The wyrm struggled less now, using height to distance herself from Magnus. Although she had won the tugging war, the wyrm made no attempt to wriggle back into deeper waters. Whether anger, greed, or an animal's burning desire for revenge against the warrior that hurt her, something had shifted her from flight to fight.

Past time for me to make my move.

While I swayed dozens of feet in the air, the serpent's relative calm gave me seconds to act. I clambered the last bit of distance to the top of her mane with handholds of the weird, slimy hairs. Upon reaching the flat top of the beast's head, I leapt to my feet. I ran a half dozen steps down the other side of her head and jumped, twisting in the air. I passed her gargantuan, crimson eye and noticed, for the first time, a thin, black slit of a pupil running down the middle from top to bottom.

I stabbed Moon Sliver into the wyrm's pupil like a key in a lock. The blade slid easily through the thin, leathery membrane covering the red orb, and my weight pushed it deeper into the eye socket until the hilt rested against the ruined sphere. I whooped in victory, thinking I'd pierced her brain and won the day.

I was a fool.

The monster screamed. She rolled her massive head around, trying to see what had attacked so tender a spot. Moon Sliver's edge rode the leather surface of the ruined eye until it rested on the lower edge of the socket. I clung there, my blade constantly threatening to tear loose and drop me a distance far enough to break every bone in my body. The beast screamed again in renewed pain and terror, and I agreed with her. My heart fluttered in my chest. My final gambit had failed and here I would die...

But I had not accounted for my brethren.

Hallbjorn took over yelling orders to the remaining rope teams. They took advantage of the wyrm's confusion and regained their footing as well as control of the horses. They hauled and fought and dragged the wyrm's head nearer and nearer to the ground. Jorund rained fiery arrows down on the side of the the monstrosity's head opposite me, threatening her good eye. The creature stopped rolling her massive skull around and focused on protecting what remained of her sight.

The wild whipping of the wyrm's head had settled into something more akin to a longship bouncing on storm tossed waves. As a Northman and a Viking, I knew how to get around on that. I snatched at the eye's edge with my left hand, and grasped the scaly shelf below the ruined orb. I pulled against it and Moon Sliver until I could rest a knee alongside my hand. I tore my sword free, and a cascade of effluvia gushed from the hole, deflating the eye and soaking me in gruesome juices. I stood with my feet braced in the socket.

Using the hair, I clambered to the top of the the viper's head. I heard Hallbjorn's calls and the repeated smack and ping of Magnus's hammer on her scaly hide. I felt the monster's head lurching lower, but indecision caught me. What could I do against a fiend so massive? Where inside did she inter her vitals that I might stab my blade home and end this nightmare battle?

I heard a familiar tearing noise and a triumphant call from Magnus as he tore another scale free from the wyrm's carapace. I heard shouts and the noise of drawn weapons as several men chopped, stabbed, and skewered at the new soft spot. Perhaps men could do nothing against such a horror but tear it apart piece by piece.

The wyrm must have decided something akin to this as well. I felt muscles coil beneath me, then a sharp jerk back. The head tilted downward so that I could see Magnus beating against her side and the men stabbing into her weakened flesh. She opened her mouth wide, and I heard a hissing sound etched upon my memory of the previous day.

"SHIELD WALL!" I bellowed, but no one seemed to hear me. "Magnus, get out of the way."

I missed my chance. The hissing gave way to the spray of bane-water. The noxious fluid hit Magnus full on and the flesh melted from his face and hands like wax from a candle. He didn't even have time to scream. His body fell into the waves, and the monster turned her murderous spray fully on the other men. They died just as quickly and just as horribly as my brother.

A red mist came over my vision, and I heard a voice twisted with inhuman rage. A small part of my mind realized it was my own. I let loose of the hair and slid down the length of the wyrm's scabrous muzzle. In a moment, my legs hovered over nothing but the spray of bane-water and the screams of the dying. I curled into a ball behind my shield and landed inside the mouth of the monster. The shield, so massive no man but I could lift it, blocked the spray almost entirely.

The shield hissed beneath the onslaught, holes and pits forming on the underside almost instantly. I felt droplets of liquid fire land on my face and hands, but they only fed the wrath within my heart. In a berserker rage, I swung my long sword over and around the edges of my shield, slashing the wyrm's mouth to ribbons. I must have hit whatever spewed forth the bane-water, because the spindrift of burning doom slowed to droplets.

I roared my triumph and threw aside my ruined shield. I continued to hack the tender flesh of the monster's mouth, severing sinew, cracking teeth, and cutting deep into her jaw. I lost myself to my frenzy, and time slowed so what must have only been seconds felt like hours. I cut, I hacked, I slashed, I stabbed. I stomped the forked tongue into mush. I broke most of the teeth in her head with my gauntleted fist.

The world went sideways and the floor of the monster's maw no longer claimed me. I hung weightless for a moment, then tumbled toward the rear of the her jaws. In my battle madness, I didn't care. I ruined whatever part of the fiend I found nearest at hand, never realizing what was happening until I slipped past the horizon of her throat. Daylight shut away, and I plunged into darkness.

Thus ended the Myth Reaver, swallowed by a dragon.

12. The Sea Wyrm War - I Am Told of My Victory

My eyelids fluttered open and it took a moment to focus my vision. I looked up to a thatched roof. It confused me. The last thing I remembered was going down the throat of a sea serpent. If I hadn't been blinded by rage at the time, I might have expected to awaken to the golden roof of Valhalla. Or at least to a beautiful Valkyrie ready to take me to Odin's Hall. It would have been good to see Magnus again.

Magnus. I squeezed my eyes shut to hold back a torrent of feeling for my dead brother. But he had died gloriously. His praises would be sung for generations, and I knew he sat in Odin's presence now, awaiting the final battle of Ragnarök.

I regained control by focusing on my surroundings. I lay in a spacious room, warmed by a large fire I heard crackling to my right. A clean and fresh smelling roof hung above my head. I lay in a bed large enough to fit my frame and filled with soft feathers. Wherever I was, they had wealth. I thought I heard voices downstairs, and I definitely smelled something cooking.

The smells of food preparation drifted into my nose, down to my belly, and squeezed. I needed to relieve myself and eat, in that order. I moved to swing my feet around the side of the bed, expecting to be hurting and stiff. To my surprise, I moved with ease. Pulling my legs from underneath the embroidered bed clothes showed my own well-muscled and unscathed legs stretching out from a sleeping shirt. Looking at my hands and arms, I found them nearly unwounded. I had burns and pockmarks in the process of healing, but nothing more severe than that. Bringing my hands up to inspect my face, I found similar wounds there. My beard actually had fared the worst under the flood of bane-water. The assault left the hair patchy enough I considered shaving it all off and starting fresh.

I rose and dug beneath the bed for a chamber pot, then made use of it. I walked to the window and threw the shutters open wide. I recognized the view immediately. This had been the room in the top of my father's mead hall I shared with several of my brothers as a boy. I dumped the pot, replaced it under my bed, looked for clothes, found none, and decided I didn't care. I headed out and down toward voices.

I went downstairs into a space that had been used as a communal room during my childhood. This had been where the family came together without the presence of father's warriors, subjects, or visiting dignitaries. It sat near the kitchens, staying always warm from the ovens. The smell of fresh bread and delicious stews permeated the place. I breathed in these smells of childhood and felt something I had not felt in many, many years.

I was home.

As I neared the bottom of the staircase, I overheard voices speaking, and I stopped to listen.

"—most amazing thing I ever saw," said a voice I thought to be Skulli's.

"Most frightening, you mean," answered Snorri.

"You two shut it," intoned Hallbjorn. "I don't care if you do think of him as a fresh faced man-child with more strength than sense. You've heard the tales about him, he's obviously moved on from the boy we knew." I heard the shifting of a body on a chair. "Dalk, you've been with him since almost the beginning of his...career. Have you ever seen anything like that?"

I heard Dalk clear his throat, then take a drink of something, then clear his throat again. "Well, nothing exactly like *that*. But I've seen him do all kinds of amazing things. Horrible things, when he gets angry enough. And we *have* spent the better part of fifteen winters killing things that most warriors would wet their mail over."

Soft voiced Jorund broke in. "I wouldn't have denied it after Dag's skald came to us, but I'm not sure I really believed it either. After what I saw yesterday." I heard a pause and a murmur of agreement from many throats. "Well, I believe it now," Jorund finished.

Osvald piped in, high and a bit loud. "But he was barely scratched. Why hasn't he risen?"

I stepped into the room and proclaimed loudly, "Because doing incredible things is exhausting work, Osvald, and nobody saw fit to offer me any mead."

Dalk and all my surviving brothers, save Grímarr, sat around a table. They turned to stare at me. Osvald and Jorund moved quickest, coming to their feet and clapping me on the back. Dalk and Hallbjorn hung back but traded small, relieved smiles. Snorri pointed at Skulli and said, "Told you it would only be a day! Pay up!" Skulli dug into a purse and dropped coins in his twin's hand, grumbling all the while. I accepted all of this with happiness and embraced each of my brothers and Dalk before settling in at the table.

Dalk, as much my servant at times as a comrade in arms, set a flagon of mead in front of me, then went to lean against the wall while my brothers sat. Hallbjorn saw it and shook his head. "No, good Dalk, you shall serve no one in this mead hall, not even our little brother. Not today, not ever." He leaned his head into the kitchen and bellowed, "We need another chair, a cask of mead, and enough food to fill men who kill dragons."

I heard a flurry of activity as Hallbjorn walked Dalk to the table and bade him sit. Maids scuttled into the room with a chair for Hallbjorn, rolling a cask in front of them. As soon as they set it upright in the corner and tapped it, they scurried out.

"Tell them to wait on the food, Hallbjorn," I said.

He smirked at me. "This was your father's hall. Now your eldest brother's hall. *You* tell them. Besides, aren't you famished?"

I nodded. "I am as empty as that mead cask will be in a quarter hour. But as much as my belly needs filling, my memory needs it more. I would hear what happened after it swallowed me."

Hallbjorn nodded, stood to walk to the kitchen door, yelled to keep the stew hot, then came back to the table. He sat down and everyone in the room stared at me. I drank my mead in one long draught, setting the flagon down, only to find them still staring at me.

"Well?" I asked. "Isn't anyone going to tell me why I'm looking at you sorry lot instead of a ravishing Valkyrie in Odin's hall?"

They chuckled and drank from their own cups. Jorund refilled my mug, then said, "I will tell it as I probably had the best view from the beach." He sipped at his cup again, slowly, as though he stalled, then began.

"What I tell you now I cannot believe you don't recall, for I will go to my doom never forgetting it. It was as though I watched a saga come alive, like something from a legendary time when men had not yet learned to be lesser beings than elves and Aesir and, in their ignorance, comported themselves like the gods."

He took another slow sip and continued. "From the beach, I watched you cut out the wyrm's eye and did my best to assist you by harrying her other eye. I saw you battle your way to the top of her head and I wondered what you pondered there while Magnus, brave, strong Magnus, tore yet another scale from the great fiend's hide with his hammer. I watched the beast draw itself up and make ready to rain down a liquid death upon Magnus. I heard your proud voice shout out a warning, and I saw our brother die."

Skulli raised his cup, and said, "To Magnus Dragonfoe."

We all raised our cups together, and said in unison, "To Magnus Dragonfoe." We drank deep from those cups and smashed them to the ground in Northman fashion. Before the tinkling sound of broken pottery had ended, maids ran in with replacement mugs, already full, then departed just as quickly.

"Aye, I recall all this," I said. "The death of Magnus and our other comrades is what caused my berserker rage. I remember ruining my shield to take away the wyrm's bane-water, and I remember being swallowed when the great monster's throat hid the sun from me. But from there, nothing."

Jorund nodded. "We thought ourselves ended. Hallbjorn called for a retreat, and every man ran back to shore, expecting the beast to murder them just by rolling over. I watched as the half-blind monster growled, whimpered, and twitched. If you have never seen 2,000 ell of nearly beached sea serpent twitch up and down her entire length from nose to tail, then there are no words I can use to explain. The movement nearly dragged the horses into the sea until their handlers cut the ropes. My heart broke as they did so. I knew this ended you and our attempts to lay Styrr to rest. He had died because of this creature. So many of our own fighting men had died. So many of yours had died. And finally, the Myth Reaver had perished. Surely our entire people would follow suit.

"But then the wyrm stole back my attention. She had neither escaped back into the sea nor snatched up the fleeing men to fill her tortured gullet. Instead, the wyrm made horrible rattling noises in her throat. She opened her mouth as if to roar, but hacking coughs were the only noise made. Dark blood flowed from her nose and flew from her mouth with every wracking fit. Everyone else still ran for their lives; I alone held a vantage point from which to see that these were not the noises of a beast about to crush our hopes and spirit. Only I saw that the great monster writhed in death throes."

He went again to sip from his cup and noted its emptiness. This reminded me that I had not touched my own cup since Jormund resumed his tale. I cleared a dry throat and found myself not alone in doing so. My brothers and Dalk all took long draughts while Jor refilled his cup. The others waited patiently, but I could not stop the drumming of my fingers on the table. What could have happened to the wyrm?

Why am I not drifting on the ocean's endless motion as dragon scat?

Jorund watched me fidget with a small amused look on his face for a moment. Snorri broke in and said, "Ah, get on with it, Jor. You're having too much fun at Finn's expense."

Jorund laughed. "You're right I'm sorry. The monster was dying, hacking up blood by the cartload. She reared up again, fully two thirds of her length raising into the air like a tower. She made one last massive cough, expelling blood, bile, and who knows what else high into the air. Then she crashed down sideways, throwing up a mighty wave. The noise deafened, and it took us a moment to realize what had happened, to realized the ancient wyrm had fallen dead. We stood on the beach, silent and staring at the carcass of the dragon who had plagued us for so long, at the fiend who had taken a father and a king from us.

"Then we heard a noise, even over the endless thunder of the swan's road. It sounded a little like a butcher halving cows. Or a little like a man shoveling wet dirt. But it also had a hollow sound, as though it all happened in a mine or a cave. To a man, we inched towards the carcass, unsure of what we would find, or even what we looked for. And then, as we drew within an ell of the corpse, your elven blade slashed through the wyrm's skin. Only it cut from *the inside.*"

"We backed away in fear," Jorund said. ("I didn't," Skulli said quietly. "Shut your hole, Loki-tongue," Snorri snapped. Hallbjorn glared at them until they quieted. They looked into their cups rather than meet his cold glare.)

"All of us backed away in fear as the blade cut a wider and wider slit in the side of the corpse. Until finally, with a roar that chilled my spine like a blast of Hel's wind, you burst free from the dragon's innards. We beheld you, a terrible sight. Wild eyed, screaming your own bile while covered in the dragon's blood, spleen, and viscera. You stank like a thousand miles of fish buried and left to rot for a thousand years then dug up again as a plague on the world. You stalked towards the wyrm's head, your voice ragged and chest heaving. You swung Moon Sliver over and over and over until, finally, you had freed the head from its sinewy, scaled neck. Hallbjorn moved to help you, but I held him back, afraid you would not recognize friend from foe.

"Then you did two things even more stunning, if such is possible. You threw Moon Sliver aside and levered yourself beneath the hoary head of the wyrm. You rolled it toward father's barrow-boat, then heaved it up and stuck its dripping neck onto the front of the boat as a gory trophy for Styrr War-born to take into the afterlife. A final gift to a dead king from his son, the Myth Reaver.

"With that, you lashed one of the broken ropes to the boat and all alone drug the whole thing, longship, grave-hoard, wyrm head, and our father's corpse, out to the sea. When you reached waist high water, you pulled the boat toward yourself and pushed it finally out to sea. Then you turned, and even at that distance I could tell you looked at me by the shiver that ran through my limbs. You stared at me until my arms realized what you needed, though my mind had not yet seen it. I pulled out my bow and my thickest arrow. I slung a small jar of whale's oil to the tip and lit it on fire. Then I shot it into the air.

"It arced high and long, the farthest shot I've ever taken. But my precision left no doubt where it would land. The arrow hit father's corpse, the shaft splitting his mouldering heart. The jar of flaming oil caught the boat alight quickly. The licking tongues of wood's bane reached the wyrm's head in seconds, and something, perhaps the vestiges of the beast's poisonous spit, joined with the flame to create a pyre the likes of which has never been seen.

"Having finished your grisly work, you strode back to the beach, stalked back to the spot we'd made camp, lay down, and fell into a deep slumber. The boat burned for an hour before it sailed away over the horizon to run aground no man knows where. We stood mesmerized by it, only shaking off the spell of the moment when it vanished from sight. Finally we looked to you but feared to tend you that you might not recognize us, and, in your madness, kill us as you had the wyrm.

"I admit it was not our bravest hour. Indeed, some of us," Jorund looked to Skulli and Snorri who turned a bright red above their beards, "volunteered to gather your sword while the rest tended to you. Hallbjorn, being the bravest of us, poked you with a spear haft. When you failed to rouse, we lifted you and bore you to the mead hall. Here, we stripped you of your stinking clothing, unclasped your heavy mail from your shoulders, and removed your helm from your troubled brow.

"We washed you carefully, with an eye toward finding and tending any wounds that you might have gained in the slaying of the wyrm. But we found you nearly untouched. We saw only the burns on your hands and face, gained in stifling the bane-water. Yet even these were found to be minor."

"Sigurd's blessing," Osvald whispered. Nobody acknowledged him, but it sent my mind to racing. Sigurd, the hero who had killed a dragon and bathed in its blood, thus making himself invincible. The thought...troubled me.

"Surely," I began slowly, "surely we can attribute my state of health to the fine elven armor I wore."

Jorund's mouth became a firm line. In a voice devoid of tone, he said, "It is true, the armor had barely even pitted or been stained by its trip into the dragon's gullet. And Moon Sliver, once polished, looked as lovely as a blade ever has."

I could tell he didn't believe it. Or that he didn't know what to believe. I looked around the table and saw the same conflict going on behind the eyes of everyone at the table, including Dalk. I had become a hero before, a legend from the sagas. What would this tale make me? I couldn't care yet. Not while I had greater concerns.

"What of the rest of my men?" I asked. Dalk sighed loudly. "Dalk?" I said, turning to him and making his name a question. "What is it?"

"Aside from your brothers you see here and myself, only ten of your men survived the wyrm's final death torrent. They are receiving a hero's treatment elsewhere in the town."

"At any rate," Jorund cut in, "once we cleaned you and declared you unharmed, we brought you up to our old room to rest. We stayed down here to attend to you and to guard you."

My brows knit in confusion. "Guard me?"

But then I remembered my confrontation with Grímarr. I had yelled at him, called him weak. I had challenged his ability to rule if not his actual right. And my surviving allies must have heard about this almost immediately upon returning from the victory and funeral. Of course they'd had to guard me. My stomach churned as I thought of Grímarr's burning anger. I cringed as I thought of his vengeance.

Hallbjorn put a hand on my shoulder. "Things have been...tense since we returned. But come, you can see for yourself. Let us eat and catch up. Tomorrow we'll have to comport ourselves as befits triumphant raven feeders and dragon slayers. Grímarr will want to..." his eyes refused to meet mine, "...to honor us."

13. Grímarr Honors Me More than I Can Stand

We ate, my brothers, Dalk, and I. We laughed as Skulli and Snorri told ridiculous stories about the years since I went away, complete with equally absurd voices. I listened as Hallbjorn and Jorund told me how the kingdom had been faring all this time. Osvald told of his time riding the roads with father's bandit patrols. I told Osvald he needed to get back to work on that and where he could find the blood eagles we had made.

My brothers avoided studiously all talk of Grímarr. It seemed they felt that they travelled in a rough patch, this expanse between my eldest brother and me, believing there was no victory either way. I understood. And I worried what this would mean for them. Could these loyal thanes live at odds with their king and brother?

Even with the unfortunate discussion of banditry and the obvious hole created by Grímarr, it was both wonderful and sad to hear what I'd missed these long years. Wonderful because I had often lain awake nights wondering about my family and their fortunes. But sad because I'd never get back that time, never have those moments with them.

Of course they were anxious to hear about my adventures. Naturally, they'd heard them all before, but not "from the horse's arse," as Osvald put it. Dalk and I also told them a hint of our times on the Varangian Way. They listened enthralled, of course.

At one point, Hallbjorn excused himself only to return a few minutes later with my aged mother. I rose and went to her, tears threatening to stain my cheeks. The dew of sadness already tracked her weathered face. We embraced, and I winced to find her so thin and frail.

"Mother," I breathed.

"Finn, my boy, you've been missed," she said into my chest. After a lengthy embrace, she finally pushed me backward to arm's length. "Come, boy, let your mother look at you."

She tutted about my wounds and beard as she had done for torn clothing and muddy footprints. I tried to look contrite and swore I'd shave my beard smooth before my audience with Grímarr in the morning. She soon tired.

Hallbjorn sent for a maid to see her back to her chambers. While the maid waited, Mother clasped me close to her again.

"Your father was always proud of you," she said quietly into my ear. "He died proud of you, convinced you alone could save his people. Thank you for proving him right."

I wanted to say something, but the too-large lump filled my throat. I could only nod to her. After mother left, we drank and talked until we had burned several candles to the nub. Finally, when even I who had slept more than a day yawned, my brothers took it as an excuse to turn in for the night.

Hallbjorn lingered until even Dalk had left, then he clasped me with more strength than mother had, but with just as much tenderness.

"It is good to have you home again, little brother. I hope you can stay this time."

I wanted to ask him what he meant, but before I could, he walked away.

~

The morning dawned bright, crisp, and clear. I opened my window and heard something I had not been blessed with since I had arrived in my homeland. I heard the sound of happy people talking in the streets.

I went downstairs, breakfasted, and returned to my room. Inside a stout trunk at the foot of my bed I found rich clothing as well as my clean and nearly flawless armor and helm. My sword belt and sheath had been ruined in the wyrm's stomach, but someone had seen to it that I received a new one. I dressed and prepared to face Grímarr and whatever he planned to do to...honor me. That nagging worry, that I might have tied a millstone about my own neck as well as those of my brothers and comrades, would not stop gnawing at the back of my mind. It left me standing in the room with a moment of indecision. Somehow, despite my battle tackle and the fine clothing, I felt vulnerable A knock on the door saved me from further contemplation.

"Come," I said, and Dalk entered. He carried a thick, rolled bundle of black fur so dark it shone a midnight purple.

"I thought you'd need another wolf's cloak, milord." He draped it around my shoulders where I pinned it with the wolf's head brooch. The brooch looked somewhat the worse for wear after going through a dragon's guts. Still, with my cloak, I felt fully clothed again. Dalk stepped back to admire me.

"You ought to be careful with this one, milord. It's the last wolf's cloak you have."

I looked at him in surprise. "Really? All those ells of wolfskin have finally been used up?"

Dalk smiled. "Well, when your idea of a battle plan is to kill a dragon from the inside, things are going to get a bit tattered."

We laughed together as though we didn't have a care. But when we finished, I looked Dalk in the eye. "What do you think of my brothers, old man?"

He frowned at me, and his creased face looked older. He took a breath, and said, "The men who stood with us against the wyrm are some of the finest men, the bravest raven feeders, I have ever had the good fortune to know."

"Aye," I agreed. But the question I really wanted to ask had been left unanswered. "But what of Grímarr?"

He paused a long time. "I can't say anything of King Grímarr, milord. I have not been given a moment with him as yet."

"But you know something. My brothers have said something while I slept."

"No, milord, they haven't said anything. It's mainly what they haven't said."

I raised an eyebrow. "And what haven't they said?"

"They haven't said how worried they are, even though they have the look of men who carry great burdens whenever their new king is discussed."

Worry turned down the corners of my mouth. I opened it to say more, but another knock on the door interrupted me. Hallbjorn stuck his head into the room.

"Ah, Dalk, good. I'm glad to have found you here. It's time for Grímarr to receive his conquering heroes. Everyone else is ready outside."

We made our way down to the family rooms and exited the back of the mead hall. My father's stated purpose for these back doors had been that servants and children could enter and exit without interrupting whatever important business went on in the main hall. But he had been a crafty man in many ways, and I knew that he had often used them himself to vanish for a bit with his wife or children while leaving courtiers, visitors, and hangers-on unawares. Another wave of memory overcame me as I recalled him doing just that in order to train weapons with me as a boy. My heart ached bittersweet again to be back in my father's house. My worry and curiosity over Grímarr's plans vanished, swallowed up in the feeling of pleasant memory.

To the side of the hall, we found my surviving brothers and warriors. Just like me, they wore resplendent and polished arms and armor. It wouldn't do for us to enter Grímarr's hall looking like anything less than triumphant warriors and courageous dragon slayers. We had become, in every way, heroes of the kingdom.

Grímarr's kingdom. Grímarr's hall. My stomach turned at the thought of it. It wasn't that I begrudged him as Styrr's heir. He was the first born and anything other than a clear succession would cause endless bloodshed. None of us wanted that, least of all me. If I'd been unsatisfied with that destiny, Grímarr would never have been able to manipulate me into leaving all those years ago.

And he left no doubt as to his qualifications. He had been wise and crafty enough to outmaneuver father, and that would make him more than a match for any of the neighboring kings. It wasn't that he had a weak sword arm or thin courage. My other brothers assured me he knew the arts of war well and had, until Styrr's collapse and death, led the efforts against the sea wyrm.

No, my feelings were entirely personal. I didn't like Grímarr, never had, even as children. And the feeling had been mutual, likely since I fell from between my mother's legs. He must have feared that rivalry would treble when I began to display my preternatural strength and gift for battle. Gifts like mine would leave him broken and dead rather than on a throne. He never saw, even for a moment, that my loyalty to our father and our people would outstrip any dislike or ambition.

And now, after months of believing I'd be welcomed home by Styrr and given the opportunity to bring my legend to his court, allowing it to serve as I'd always wished it to, Grímarr sat on the throne. I hadn't let it concern me overmuch. Though utterly committed to seeing my father's corpse laid to proper rest, I hadn't entirely expected to survive the battle with the sea wyrm. And *of course* I'd flown into a rage and called Grímarr a weakling in his own hall, in front of several of his own men. That could not go unpunished, even for a hero to the realm. That left no way my hopes of warm welcome and proper thanehood could come true now. I had only to wait and see how Grímarr the Crafty managed his revenge.

The dour faces of my brothers told me they felt the same way. None of my men, save Dalk, truly understood why I had left home or what machinations went on even now. But they felt the dread rolling off my brothers, souring their day of triumph. They stood as mighty feeders of eagles and slayers of an ancient serpent. They deserved better. Whatever else might happen today, they would receive the honor due them.

I locked away in my thought-hoard these considerations of ill omens and coming vengeance and forced my face to break into a wide smile. "By Ymir's frosty breath! Who are these avenging warriors that I see before me? I'd heard I'd be meeting my own men, all of whom are worth a brace of any other warriors. But these before me are worth a brace of my own. 'Tis a sight truly marvelous." I turned to my brothers and gestured expansively toward the ten warriors who had traveled with me to the known edges of Midgard and back. "Behold, the ten most dangerous men to walk the Nine Worlds since the ancient times of the sagas. Tyrr and Thor might quake at the sight of them."

My brothers seemed to understand my purpose, and they changed their demeanor to one of celebration. My men who had only moments ago lived under an iron sky, unsure of what would befall them, now looked like men soon to be honored. We had readied ourselves as much as we could.

"Come, my good and faithful friends. Let us meet King Grímarr with honor and discover what manner of ring giver he is."

The men, gleeful looks on their faces, looked to Dalk and Hallbjorn. I looked at them also and found mischievous grins on their faces. I suddenly felt as though a great joke would soon be pulled on me.

"The men have crafted a gift for you," Dalk said. "Well, they commissioned its crafting."

"Magnus had planned it as a gift for you before he died," Hallbjorn said. "He told us all about it, and we," he gestured to everyone standing there, "thought that it would honor both you and him to see it done."

Hallbjorn took a bundle from Osvald. The gift was hidden beneath rough wrappings, but as he offered it to me, the wrappings fell away. My eyes went wide with wonder. I took the gift from Hallbjorn and rubbed my hands over it.

I held a dragon scale, but no longer merely a dragon scale. It had been fashioned into a shield. The scale itself made up the core, but thick bands of iron wrapped it now as well. A stud of polished steel sat in the center. I turned it over and saw the stud housed a handle expertly wrapped in fine leather. I looked up at Hallbjorn before my grateful eyes swept over all of them.

"It's...beautiful. Thank you." I could say nothing else.

"It's made from the first scale Magnus pulled off the wyrm," Hallbjorn explained. "He somehow dragged it back ashore after you saved him."

Dalk cut in. "He said the hole he'd pounded into the center reminded him of an unfinished shield. That's when he had the idea to turn it into one."

Osvald spoke. "At first, I think he meant to keep it for himself or add it to father's grave hoard. But by the time he told the rest of us about it, he planned to give it to you."

Jorund spoke up. "He said something like, 'The flesh of a legendary beast turned into a legendary shield for a worthy warrior.'" He looked embarrassed. "That's what Magnus thought anyway."

I hefted the shield and found it heavy, but not as heavy as my usual shields. Somebody besides myself could use this, though the thick iron bands would make that difficult for them. I realized Dalk had left me shieldless purposefully, and I looked happily at the men around me.

"What will you call it?" Dalk asked.

Dalk spoke true, of course. Any gift such as this, let alone a gift for battle, required a name. I thought for a moment before it came to me. "The serpent took my father from me. And now it will protect me as I make widows and orphans. Therefore I name this shield Fathersbane." A general murmur of appreciation arose from this. "I regret that I have no gift to give to you, to any of you, that is as worthy."

"The hell you don't," Snorri said.

"You already gave it to us," Skulli agreed. I looked at him quizzically. "We're still breathing and that bitch of a serpent isn't. That's gift enough for a lifetime."

Everyone murmured their agreement.

"Then I'm only sorry I couldn't have given that gift to more of us," I said, thinking of Magnus.

We stood in silence a moment, but the ever responsible Hallbjorn broke the spell. "I believe the new king has been left waiting long enough."

We could do nothing but agree. I was ready to face Grímarr and whatever the Norns had woven for me. We made our way around to the front of the hall singing the hymn to Thor quietly. The villagers thronging around the entrance to the hall saw us coming and raised a cheer that drowned out our quiet song. We pushed our way through, the crowd's hands outstretched to brush us as we passed. Blessings and well-wishes showered upon us from every mouth. We basked in the adoration due warriors as mighty as ourselves.

When we reached the wide doors of the hall, two guards stood vigil. Some formal words may have passed between them and Hallbjorn, but I couldn't hear them over the noise of the crowd. The two guards solemnly opened the doors for us, and the already deafening noise reached a new pitch. We wended our way through the receiving passages with more cheering people lining the walls. As we progressed, their clothing and jewelry became more and more fine, though their demeanor remained just as rough and just as celebratory as the peasantry outside.

At last we made it into the hall proper. More benches had been moved in to accommodate the guests worthy or rich enough to have such a close seat to the festivities. Despite the massive assemblage, a thin column of empty floor ran from where we entered to the foot of the dais. Upon that dais sat a single table with empty chairs enough for me, my brothers, and my men. Amidst those chairs sat a throne carved whole from a single mighty oak and festooned with gold and jewels. I remembered well my father sitting upon that chair, dispensing judgments and orders and making his word law. Now Grímarr sat upon it, wearing the finery of kingship, and with the gold and iron crown of our father resting upon his brow.

Grímarr's usually stoic and unreadable face split in a wide smile as he clapped and cheered along with the people he now ruled. This, I must admit, unnerved me more than anything else he might have done. Grímarr never smiled. Grímarr never cried. Grímarr never got angry. Grímarr's face was like a mask, unmoved and unmoving. When I met his cold, calculating eyes and saw that the delighted smile never reached them, I realized that this happiness hid as much as his usual impassiveness.

The noise of flagons and fists pounding the tables, the thrum of the hymn we sang mere minutes ago upon the lips of a mob, and the racket of swords upon shields from Grímarr's men-at-arms filled the place to bursting. I expected the roof to tear free at any moment. This went on and on for some time before Grímarr began gesturing for silence. Two of his warriors stepped forward, raised horns to their lips, and blew them as loud as they could. I didn't hear them at all. But the gestures continued, the people began to quiet down, and the horns could eventually be heard, though the faces of the men blowing them glowed red and sweat drenched them from the effort.

All through it, Grímarr's smile never faded.

Finally, when the glorious hall grew reasonably silent, Grímarr turned that Loki's smile upon us and spoke.

"To brothers, both those who share the blood of Styrr and those who have shown themselves worthy to do so with mighty, nay, unbelievable deeds of heroism: I *welcome* you. Nay, I *honor* you. For you have released my people and my rule from a doom the likes of which Midgard has not seen in an age. You have avenged my father and seen him laid to rest with all honor due him."

The cheer began again, but as though he'd expected it, Grímarr began making his gestures and appeals for silence almost as soon as the praise restarted. The horns joined him in his appeals. The people begrudgingly settled down again.

Grímarr began again. "What rewards can I give you worthy of these feats? How many golden rings is a wyrm worth?"

From the rear of the hall came a loud voice, "A hundred!" An answering call yelled, " A thousand!" Another bellowed, "Tens of thousands!"

Grímarr's smile never faded, he only nodded more emphatically as the numbers grew. "I agree wholeheartedly. No reward I am able to give today can match this mighty deed."

The crowd crowed noises of grim disappointment, yelling catcalls and jeers bordering on the treasonous. I shot a glance sideways at Dalk, but the noise drowned out anything other than worried looks. I found myself surreptitiously loosening sure Moon Sliver in its scabbard. Truly, my senses screamed danger, but left me unsure whom I meant to battle.

But wise and well-loved Hallbjorn's clear voice rang out over the rebellious noise. "Your brothers who have lived in this hall all their lives raised their weapons against the wyrm in loyalty to first our father and then to you, King Grímarr. We ask only that you give us the opportunity to do so again."

Grímarr nodded. "Noble Hallbjorn, I would expect no other sentiment from you and the brothers who have served our father all these many years." Grímarr's eyes didn't move to me, but I felt each word as a blow nonetheless. "Your service is not a reward to you, but a gift to me. Stay here in my hall and know that the honor accorded you will be without limit."

"But what of the Myth Reaver?" a voice asked, its tone ragged and a little angry. "And what of the Myth Reaver's band?" another, similar voice bellowed. The hall took up the hue and cry. Dalk and my men looked ashamed to cause such a furor in a king's hall that was not their own. I feared for them. I feared for myself.

Swords rasped out of sheaths and clamored on the shields of Grímarr's fighting men. The rancorous and rebellious talk died down once again. Once silence reigned, Grimmar spoke, this time wearing the sorrowful look of a disapproving father.

"You misunderstand me, my people. Noble Hallbjorn, stalking Jorund, quick Osvald, and riotous Snorry and Skulli pledge their loyalty to me anew, and therefore give me the rest of their lives to repay this deed. So I give the same offer to Finn the Myth Reaver and his retinue. I cannot repay them today, so I ask that they become my thanes that I might repay them *forever.*"

Dalk and my men, useless ne'er-do-wells and wandering reavers all of them, looked shocked at the offer. These men had never dreamed their service to me might one day end in anything other than a noble warrior's death and a welcome in Valhalla. To men who had never enjoyed noble title, lands, or the protection of a king, these things held a worth greater than the weight of all the gold in the Nine Worlds.

And for me, a welcome back to my people as a legend and a hero was my longest held dream. The dream had died down to embers until my father sent for me, his message rekindling it to a blazing inferno. To receive the same offer from hard-faced and hard-hearted Grímarr, even under duress and only offered so as to appease his people, was a wish too foolish to consider.

My war band looked to me, the question written plainly on their faces. I looked to Hallbjorn and my other brothers with the same question. They each nodded to me, looking more pleased and satisfied than I had seen. I looked to Grímarr.

"Well, youngest brother," he said to me. "Will you return to the hall of your father? Will you, and your followers, take your rightful place at my table today and forever?"

I felt my men at my back. I felt their loyalty, their camaraderie, their friendship. Normally, these things gave me strength and held me up. Today I felt only the weight of responsibility. I felt the weight of desires so beyond the comprehension of these good and true men that they had never allowed themselves even to wonder at them. A king to serve, a people to protect, and a welcoming place to call home were the true desires of their hearts. They were the true desires of my heart as well.

And yet. The matter of Grímarr still hung over me. I had insulted him, I had challenged him in his own hall in front of his personal guards and retainers. Rumor and gossip moved faster through Northmen villages than plague. My transgression could only have been more public if we'd had it out in the town square. No matter what the service, no matter how glorious the deed, Grímarr did not forgive anyone, especially me.

But all eyes turned to me now. They required a decision, and I could make only one in this moment. I chose to save tomorrow's trouble for tomorrow.

"King Grímarr, on behalf of my men, we accept your offer. We pledge our loyalty to you as thanes even as you promise your loyalty as our king." I turned to the teeming hall. "The Myth Reaver has come home!"

The noise we'd heard when we entered was a mooncast shadow to the jubilation that roared through the hall now. The very walls shook and dust rained down on us from a roof that rumbled under the onslaught of the noise. My brothers clapped us all on the back and embraced us. I'd never been happier. It lasted for all of a minute. I made a mistake. Beaming with pride and happiness, I looked back to Grímarr.

His face returned to the inscrutable mask I was used to, but his eyes betrayed him for the first time in my life. Those normally passionless orbs now blazed with a murderous fury.

And those eyes never left me.

14. Betrayals Abound

We spent the rest of the feast at Grímarr's table, arrayed to either side of his throne. I sat at his right, Dalk at his left, then the rest of my warriors spread evenly on both sides. Finally, on the far flanks, my brothers. Outsiders no longer, we received seats of the highest honor. Grímarr gifted each of us with a drinking horn decorated in gold and silver, our names and a blessing etched upon them in ancient runes. Exquisitely carved sea wyrms studded in emeralds and with two rubies for slitted eyes stood in relief upon the stands holding the horns. And the horns never ran dry as the feast went on.

Extraordinary congratulations continued throughout the day long feast. Men and women in rich clothing came to toast and salute us. Some of them I vaguely remembered as esteemed men from my much younger days. Others I recalled as playmates.

Though they gave high praise for each of the dragon slayers, all eyes looked at me in that worshipful way that had once chased me out of the North and onto the Varangian Way. Knowing that these were my people I'd come home to, I couldn't imagine leaving again. The day was perfect save for one thing.

Grímarr's piercing and hateful gaze rarely left me. And every look of adoration from his subjects sharpened his enmity for me to the keenest edge.

I now knew what I had before only suspected. The offer of hearth and home might have been made sincerely for those who rallied to my banner, but Grímarr proposed the reward to me entirely under duress. He feared the whispers of his people if he didn't honor me even as he'd feared my disloyalty in our younger years. His concern about me was unjustified, but rebellious whispers at a king who refused to honor the savior of his kingdom were likely far more substantial threats.

I did my best not to care. I had arrived home, most of my brothers welcomed me, and my best friends and stalwart warriors surrounded me. What did the disdain of one small-minded brother mean to me? What was the hatred of one petty king?

The revelry wore on until only the head table still drank from their horns. Eventually, all of my men save Dalk retired to Frigga knew where, many in the company of maidens anxious to assist their acclimation to the court. More time passed, more mead sloshed inside us, and the evening grew very late indeed.

Eventually, Dalk passed out on the table along with Osvald. Snorri and Skulli would come to blows in another moment if their loud voices indicated anything. Jormund sipped at his horn quietly and calmly. Hallbjorn and I matched horn for horn. Grímarr sipped as quietly as Jormund. His face betrayed nothing, but his eyes remained unclouded by drink as he stared at me. I had grown the worse for the mead, and having some idea what whirred behind Grímarr's eyes wore me down.

Hallbjorn sensed this and, noticing the twins headed toward blows, stood and clamped a meaty fist on each of their shoulders. "All right, boys, that'll do for that. We've fallen comrades to see to." He gestured at Dalk and Osvald. "Snorri, see to Dalk. Skully, to Osvald." Both twins opened their mouths to protest, but Hallbjorn interrupted them. "And I'll see to it that you do right by them." He glared down at the identical warriors until they closed their mouths and set off, supporting Dalk and Osvald while still grumbling. Hallbjorn turned to me, gave me an unsteady wink, and headed off after them.

Jormund turned his attention toward his eldest and youngest brother and sat very still, almost as though he hunted a flighty prey. Just as I began to grow uncomfortable, he unfolded himself from his crouch, and, without a word, left the hall. I sat with only Grímarr left as company for three breaths before I'd had enough. I rose, saying, "That'll do for me as well then."

"I would have words with you before you retire, thane." My brother spoke with a voice cold as Ymir's blood, but I refused to do anything but hope for the best. I waited, not seating myself or saying anything. Grímarr rose and came to stand next to me, his sharp features dancing in the dying firelight.

"I did not know that father had sent for you."

I still didn't look at him. "And did father always tell you everything he did?"

I saw Grímarr tilt his head in the corner of my eye. "Almost everything. He groomed me to be king, after all."

Finally, I looked him full in his dead face. "And why do you think he didn't tell you this thing, *King* Grímarr?"

"Because I wouldn't have approved."

"Because you don't trust me," I said through clenched teeth.

Grímarr clicked his tongue. "And here I thought you'd blame my weakness."

"You don't trust me *because* you are weak. Weak in your character. You imagine yourself in my place and how it would chafe you. You ponder how honor and loyalty would not be enough for you. How you could grab everything in the Nine Worlds if only you had my strength."

"Ah," he said, his eyebrows going up the tiniest fraction of an inch. "So I am treacherous."

"You are."

He nodded once. "You are right about one thing, brother. I *am* treacherous. But that is not why I don't trust you." He paused while I seethed. "Tell me, if I hadn't chased you away while still too young and stupid to realize your full potential, what would you have done?"

Without hesitation, I answered, "I'd have been the greatest thane father ever had. Then, when the time came, I would have been the greatest thane you ever had."

Grímarr considered me for a moment. "By Tyr's bloody stump, you actually believe that, don't you?" He chuckled, and my eyes goggled. I could not recall the last time I'd heard sounds of mirth or melancholy from Grímarr. I'd heard it said he didn't even make them in his crib.

He shook his head at me. "You great hulking idiot. What do you think father's enemies would have done once they heard about you? They would have banded together and attacked him. Despite any other differences, they would consider you too great a threat."

"I would have beaten them."

"All of them?"

"Yes."

"Alone?"

"If I had to."

"Goodness, you actually believe that too." Grímarr sighed as though he spoke to a particularly tiresome child. "What, then, do you think father's allies would have done? Hmm?"

I didn't answer. He leaned in closely to me and hissed, "They would have become his *enemies*. And much smarter ones than the last batch. One of them, at least one, would have been as treacherous as I. And you would have died in your bed, poisoned beyond even your vigor to survive. And then we would have been weakened, alone...defenseless."

"So you chased me away for my own good, then? Is that it, Grímarr?"

He chuckled again, walking away from me and toward the fire. When he turned back to me, its dying light glowed like a halo around him. It glittered off his gold and iron crown. "Absolutely not. I chased you off, you great oaf, for *our* own good. If you gained anything from it, then we've merely had a happy accident."

"Your people must be glad father didn't agree with you. Otherwise, they'd still be menaced by that wyrm. And you'd be king of nothing but a barrow."

Grímarr shook his head at me again, and turned back to the fire. He picked up a stray branch of kindling and poked it into the ashes, causing them to flair and pop.

"Please don't be so dense, Finn. Of course you have your uses. You can do impossible things simply through the determination to do them. But what happiness has this brought you? Are you loved or feared? Respected or worshipped? Could anywhere other than some foreign land of heathen mad men accept you as you wished to be?"

I didn't have an answer for that, but Grímarr let it soak in for a while anyway before continuing.

"You are cursed by greatness, Finn. You always will be. You can't *help* doing these things. If you'd met a boatwright rather than a monster plaguing a village, you probably would have knocked together a fleet of ships and discovered some far off, never-before-seen continent." He sighed. "And you'd be just as miserable when you returned."

"But I'm not miserable, Grímarr. Don't you see? I've come *home*. I will do anything to protect my homeland and my people. I will do anything to protect my king. And if you are so devious and treacherous, then you will be able to protect me while I protect you."

Grímarr dropped the smoldering brand into the fire. He turned to face me again, his head tilted in that familiar, considering posture. "Perhaps." He paced toward me then turned on his heel to pace away again. He repeated this a few more times, murmuring the word "perhaps" under his breath the entire time. Hope swelled in my breast. He stopped his thoughtful walk and looked up into my face.

"No," he said, and shook his head as curtly as he'd nodded before. "It simply won't do."

"Grímarr..." I couldn't help the catch in my voice, and it shamed me even as I begged. "Please."

My eldest brother peered at me, something like pity in his eyes. It galled me. "You are as wild and terrible a danger to our people as the sea wyrm, Finn. That you cannot see it makes you doubly so."

The hope that had buoyed me mere moments before drained away, leaving me emptier and hollower than I could have imagined.

"You can't make me leave," I said. But it lacked heat, held no strength. "The people won't have it. I'm their hero. What will they think if you make me leave?"

"Oh, I won't make you leave, Finn. You'll leave of your own accord. It will be entirely your choice."

My anger flared, but it was a small thing. Small as the coals of the fire. "Then I choose not to leave. What will you do? Poison me in my bed?"

"Of course not, Finn. You are a hero, a champion, like one from the sagas. I would never stand for you dying ignominiously in your bed. It would be too large a blow to the people." He shook his head in that tight, economical way again. "No, it wouldn't be *you* who died in your bed."

"What do you mean?" I croaked, my throat suddenly dry.

"There are eleven other men once sworn to your banner, now sworn to mine. Each one more dear to your heart than even your own blood. Perhaps the poison will find the one-armed one...Dalk wasn't it?"

This time my anger flared to raging life, hotter than any smith's forge. I threw aside the mead bench that separated us with a casual flick of my hand. Before he could move an inch, I had Grímarr by the throat. I lifted him until his feet left the floor.

"And what if I simply kill you here and now, fiend?"

Grímarr's hand moved subtly and something flashed in the firelight. I looked down to see a small blade poking me between the ribs, pointed directly at my heart.

"I've bathed in a dragon's blood, brother," I growled. "That blade won't stop me."

I didn't know if I spoke truth, but it didn't matter to Grímarr. He croaked out an answer. "Then you will prove me right." My fingers tightened. "Loyalty," he choked, "honor...mean nothing...to a...a legend."

My anger flared again and it made the muscle in my arm spasm. The thews that had choked the life from a giant wolf, that had shoved a spear into a giant elf's nethers, that had hacked their way from inside a dragon, ancient and terrible. Beside these things, my brother's throat would hold no more challenge than old straw.

Which was exactly his point.

I dropped him, and my once but past king fell to the ground. He held his throat and sucked air in gulping rasps. I stalked to the rear exit that would lead to the kitchens, family commons, and, eventually, my room. I stopped at the threshold, my back still to Grímarr.

"As soon as is seemly, brother, I will gather my men and go."

He choked out a harsh laugh from his tortured windpipe. "Sweet, trusting Finn. *You* will go, but I'd bet this hall your men do not. As ever, the Myth Reaver walks alone."

His hoarse words echoed in my head all the way to my room. They continued to nestle into my brain like a worm or a wasting disease. I lay for a long time, unable to sleep, harried by the sharp edge of Grímarr's words.

I saw sunrise before slumber won out. It was the first dawn I'd seen in my home since childhood, and it was...beautiful. Sleep eventually took me despite the disquiet of my mind, and I carried the beautiful image of that aurora with me into my dreams.

I awoke to a twilight glow, having lost the day to fitful rest. The dream of the dawn had given me a feeling of warm and protected bliss that waking memory shattered into a million jagged pieces, each cutting my soul as deeply as any blade could my flesh. Grímarr had given me no timetable for his ultimatum. It chilled me enough just knowing he planned to kill those most beloved to me if I didn't leave. Would he stop at Dalk and my men? Or would he continue on to the brothers we had in common? I couldn't begin to know. Regardless, the day had worn on too long to depart now. And I needed to speak to my men before I could do so.

That thought brought back Grímarr's final words to me. They rattled around my head like old, dry bones in a cup.

Whatever else I needed could wait. Right now, I *wanted* a drink. Many drinks.

I dressed, leaving off sword, shield, and mail, then stole down the stairs quietly. On my way past the kitchens, I grabbed a loaf of bread to throw to my gnawing hunger. If any of the kitchen maids saw, none of them had the temerity to speak to me. I left from the rear door, hoping constant mouthfuls of bread would keep any others from accosting me.

I didn't need conversation. I needed strong drink, fetching young lasses serving it, and a room of rough hooligans to get pleasantly drunk with. A fight with bare knuckles and nothing at stake but a broken nose or unhinged jaw also sounded appealing. All these things together meant a tavern. The realization brought a savage smile to my face.

I stalked through the village, but even my full mouth and grim demeanor couldn't stop people from hailing me. I nodded and pressed my way through the incessant barrage of friendly greetings.

The map of memory led my feet directly to Rovfugl's. I remembered the tavern well from my youth, and it didn't seem to have changed a bit since. Wide front doors thrown open to the street spilled the raucous noise of laughter, yelling, squealing, and fighting out into the evening. The sign that creaked as it swung overhead might have had a new daub of paint, but it still bore the same old design: a wide-eyed owl staring at a serving maid's generous figure. It was precisely the place I needed. I went inside, and dealt with the flurry of "hail and well mets" before settling in for a drink.

Another drink followed that one. Another ten drinks followed the second, and another dozen followed those. Before I knew it, hours had passed and I'd sunk deep in my cups. Jests had been told, fights had been had, maidens had been pinched, and I felt much, much better. That's when Dalk and Hallbjorn found me. I instantly felt much, much worse.

"We've been looking all over for you, Finn," Dalk said. He sat down at my table and made a gesture with his single hand to the barkeep.

"Aye? Not quite all over. I've been here all night." Despite a slur, my voice had an edge to it. I bounced the pretty maid off my knee. She gave me a cute pout before heading off. It didn't matter. I reckoned I wouldn't be having fun much longer.

"It took us a bit to realize you weren't at the hall," Hallbjorn said. He looked decidedly uncomfortable in the taproom. Not out of sorts...more out of place.

"Oh? Must I now and forever only get drunk and throw up on Grímarr's floor? Can I only knock out the teeth of his guests? Can I only dally with his women?"

My questions went unanswered until I finally looked drunkenly into the faces of my brother and best friend. They stared at me, eyes wide and jaws hanging loosely.

"Pardon my sharp tone, but I'm in no mood to hear what Grímarr needs or desires of me. A new scheme needed hatching, and I couldn't think beneath his roof."

Hallbjorn looked at me pointedly and then around the common room. "It doesn't look like you've been doing much thinking here tonight."

Dalk broke in. "And whatever you've been up to, we would've gladly done our share if you'd stayed with us at the hall."

The mention of the hall set my teeth on edge. "Grímarr's hall is no place for me. He made that clear to me yestereve."

Through a haze of drink, I saw Hallbjorn go pale. But Dalk didn't seem to notice.

"When did this happen?" he asked, grinning. "Before or after he made us his thanes and promised to show his gratitude all our born days?"

"After. Not long after he threatened to kill you. Which happened right before I threatened to kill him."

A dangerous silence invaded the common room.

Hallbjorn leaned in close to me. "Bad business discussing the murder of a king in the town surrounding his mead hall."

Dalk looked confused. I probably just looked angry.

"You're right, Hallbjorn. We should have this talk privately."

Hallbjorn started to stand, muttering something about "finally some sense." But rather than following him upright, I raised my voice so all could hear. It wasn't hard in the uncomfortable quiet.

"Three of your king's thanes would like to have a private conversation."

No one moved or spoke.

"Now."

Chairs scraped across the floor, drinks were raised for quick draining, and the tavern's clientele took a quick, corporate step toward the door. The barkeep looked confused for a moment but finally shrugged, dropped his rag, and joined the mob headed outside. As they trailed out, I stood and walked to the bar. I refilled my flagon and drank from it while they left. Refilling it again, I came back to the table and sat down. I kept drinking.

Dalk broke the silence first. "Finn, what's going on? What's all that talk of death threats? And why did you have to empty a tavern rather than step outside with us?"

"I'll let Hallbjorn answer the first two. I'm still drinking."

Dalk looked at Hallbjorn, his face a mixture of amusement and concern, as though he couldn't decide how seriously he should take all this. He'd seen me in dark moods before, especially after a victory. But something about Hallbjorn's unwillingness to meet Dalk's eye, the uncomfortable shifting and throat clearing, put my huscarl's hackles up. No, I reminded myself. Not my huscarl anymore. Grímarr's.

"Hallbjorn..." Dalk trailed off. He looked at me. "Finn?"

"Fine," I growled, looking up at Dalk. "I thought my brother had arrived and would talk straight, but apparently one of my tittering sisters came to the tavern instead. Grímarr thinks I'm dangerous to the kingdom. I used to think it only jealousy filled his heart, maybe mistrust that I would challenge his position as firstborn and heir. But apparently there's more to it than even that. He wants me gone. And badly enough to threaten your life." I looked at Hallbjorn. "All your lives."

Hallbjorn's face grew hard. "Watch what you say. That's my brother and my king of whom you speak."

I snorted. "What about your brother and fellow dragon slayer? That worth anything?"

Hallbjorn sighed. "More than I'm probably willing to admit."

Dalk's head had waggled between us as we spoke. "But...but...we're heroes. Especially you, Finn. You're the reason he still has a kingdom."

I nodded. "Aye. And that's why I've been given the chance to leave rather than simply getting a thin knife between the ribs while abed."

Dalk's wavering expressions settled into forced amusement. He chuckled, but it sounded like a death rattle in my ears. He waggled a finger at us. "You two. You're putting me on. Don't think I can't whip both of you, one arm or not." When neither of us returned his smile, his forced cheerfulness wavered. "You can't be....you're serious?"

Hallbjorn nodded. "Finn has most of the right of it. As boys, Grímarr martialed the lot of us as though he were the general. But Finn would have none of it, he refused to follow Grímarr's lead. And when Finn grew up and his...talents became obvious—"

"He chose to mistrust everything I stand for," I spit. "Everything Father ever stood for."

Hallbjorn shook his head. "It isn't like that." I glared at Hallbjorn until he looked away. "Not entirely like that."

"Would he really do it?" Dalk asked, looking pale. "Would he kill me, kill any of us, to get you to leave?"

"He would," Hallbjorn and I answered as one.

"That's how I know it isn't *all* about pride and connivance," Hallbjorn said, rubbing his hand through his hair. "Grímarr has always been willing to do whatever it takes to safeguard the kingdom. Whether father approved, whether *anyone* approved." Hallbjorn looked pleadingly at me. "He truly does see you as a threat to our stability."

Dalk drew himself up, his back straight and his voice stern. "The Finn Styrrsson I've followed all these years would never threaten the kingdom of his people."

I gave Dalk an appreciative nod before turning my attention back to Hallbjorn. "And you, brother? What do you think?"

Hallbjorn's face became stony, his eyes calm. "I think you are a true hero, undaunted by any danger. I think you are stouter of heart and stronger of arm than the rest of us combined, including father. I think you would never willingly do anything to endanger us, that you would risk yourself first and forever." He looked away from me. "But Grímarr is king, father's chosen heir. And the bastard is rarely wrong about these things."

I wanted so badly to be angry with Hallbjorn. I wanted rage to overtake me so I could flatten my flagon against his head with a clear conscience. But I could not. He believed every word he said. He made me want to believe them. And, just like that, I realized I did. I put my hand on his shoulder.

"These are all things I needed to hear from you. Whatever kind of Loki-spawn Grímarr is—and make no mistake, he is a prince of liars—*you* are true. And though you do not trust his character, you trust his judgment. Thank you for that."

I caught Hallbjorn up in a warm embrace.

"I will be sorry to see you go again, my brother," Hallbjorn said as we separated, his voice thick with emotion. "Are you not more unhappy? Where will you go? What will you do?"

"Ah, well, that brings us to the scheme I've hatched. And the lesson I sought to teach by emptying the tavern." I waved around, allowing the echoing space to demonstrate my point. "I came in here to drink and fight. Do you think if I'd strolled in with Moon Sliver on my hip that anyone would have traded blows with me? Even a friendly scrap with nothing to show for it but scuffed knuckles and a crooked nose?"

They gave only the hemming and hawing of grown men when they're too early in an argument to concede anything.

"Yes, yes, I hear you clucking, hens," I said. "The fact of the matter is, no, if there was even a chance a brawl could escalate, I wouldn't have found one here. Or anywhere. And if I can't find a simple brawl, then I may not be able to find a battle."

They both snorted almost in unison.

"Are you seriously worried you won't find some Northmen spoiling for a fight anywhere?" Dalk asked. A broad, exaggerated smirk demonstrated the sheer ridiculousness of the idea.

"No, that is not what I'm saying. Go down the street anywhere and you can find a Northman willing to fight. But I don't think I'll find one willing to fight *me*."

Again they made noncommittal noises, although much less stridently this time.

"You two are nattering old women. Dalk, do you remember what it was like before we went on the Varangian Way?"

"Aye," Dalk said.

Hallbjorn wore a bemused smirk. "And what was so terrible, little brother, that you felt chased to a warm land of dusky hued ladies and fat purses?"

Dalk shook his head. "It was no laughing matter. Finn had become a living legend. *Everyone* had heard of the Myth Reaver. Everywhere we went, everybody met Finn with a mixture of awe and terror. We never knew if we would be received with open arms or a closed and barred gate." He looked at me sharply. I nodded grimly.

"And now you see. Those who welcomed us did so guardedly while those who politely asked us to move along always did so from behind high walls. It never occurred to anyone to *attack* us." I snorted. "And they acted like this when I only killed massive wolves with my bare hands and fought giants in front of besieged cities. How do you think it will be now that I've killed a dragon?" I spat onto the ground of the tavern. "How do you think it will be for any of you?"

They didn't understand and their lack of understanding upset them. The clouds of anger darkened their countenances. At last they stood ready to hear my ill tidings. At last they would ask the right questions.

"So we will be mightily feared! Dreaded by our enemies! Is this not the hope of all Northman raven feeders?" Hallbjorn demanded.

Dalk slammed his meaty fist on the table, cracking the wood with the strength of his one arm. "If none will stand against us, then we will be the greatest thanes who ever lived! Who could stand to King Grímarr? He may well forge a kingdom of the whole world, built on the backs of nothing but our reputations."

I drank the last of my flagon and slammed it to the ground, shattering it. I knew my eyes flashed dangerously, my face a thundercloud. I stood up, knocking over my chair, and pointed a finger in each of their faces in turn.

"And what happens to you, Dalk, or you, Hallbjorn, or any of the men when you win this kingdom without sword or spear in hand? What of you mighty men during this golden age? I'll tell you. You *die*. In your *beds*. Of old age. With fat grandchildren arrayed around you."

I breathed hard now. My soft words for Hallbjorn of only minutes before were swept away by a torrent of rage. I *knew* whom I really ought to hate. I *knew* who owned responsibility for my endless restlessness. The tension wound tighter and tighter within me, and I couldn't wait to tell my brother and best friend.

"And when the great-grandmother closes your eyes for the final time, where do you think you'll wind up? Helgafjell's sunny mountainside? Is a quiet, restful peace any place for fighting men? For dragon slayers? Or perhaps you'll curl up in Freyja's bosom at Fólkvangr with the women and fighters who can't be trusted to stand at Ragnarök." I snorted and spat again. "Most likely, you wind up in Hel's frosty embrace, building a ship of your hair and fingernails, waiting for the end of the Nine Worlds, dreaming of past and finished glories."

I picked up my chair and cast it across the tavern, shattering it to splinters against the wall. I roared a guttural, wordless yowl of despair. When my voice croaked and my lungs ached, I came back to myself enough to speak a final thought to them.

"We have shackled ourselves with cumbersome glories that will drown us in eternity. This is the wyrd the Norns have saddled us with. Yes, *us*. Not just the Myth Reaver, but all men who fought beside me and won."

All the color had faded from their slack, staring faces. I could only nod as I watched each new horror sink in.

"Dag tried to warn me years ago. I thought I'd heeded his wisdom, but my folly won out. The invitation home enticed me more than I could bear. Now I've doomed the rest of you with me."

Dalk, ever one to follow my lead, asked the next, most obvious question.

"What must we do to stave off this wyrd?"

"My friend, it is as obvious as the crooked nose on your face. If men will not fight us to end our days, then we must fight *gods*."

"What?" Hallbjorn spluttered. "You would have us assault the Aesir themselves?"

I nodded once. "Aye. And in their own halls."

"Madness!" Hallbjorn exclaimed.

"Nay, brother. Madness is to contemplate the dull fate that awaits us—powerful raven feeders, slayers of dragons—if we don't take this fight to the All Father." My hands and face were open as I asked the question. "Is it not mighty Odin's wise rules that have consigned us to that wyrd? Should he not be forced to answer for that? Or kill us himself, thereby removing the Norns' yoke from our necks?"

Hallbjorn rose in anger and stalked across the room. His shoulders heaved and he shook his head now and again, as though he refused to let my words penetrate his ears. Dalk merely sat, his mouth working soundlessly.

"You both know I speak the truth. You *know* it. Grímarr doesn't deserve the power we can give him, not if he can't wrench it free with his own grasp. And we don't deserve a death so much more shameful than our life. Let us ascend to Asgard, let us challenge the Aesir in their gardens. And when one of them puts us in our place, as we know they will, then we will not have far to ride"—I curled a fist in front of my face—"to Valhalla!"

Hallbjorn turned to me slowly. I expected his eyes to be agleam with zeal. Instead, they became empty orbs, flat and dead in his face.

"No. No, brother, I will not join you in this madness. I will not allow Osvald, Skulli, Snorri, or Jorund to follow you on this blasphemous fool's errand. It is not for us to question the All Father, especially not with steel and hate."

"I'm surprised," I said, my words holding a sharp edge of ice. "Although I shouldn't be. My brothers have never, not from the first day we sailed out together, been a boon to me. They have never borne my burdens or suffered wounds on my behalf. Not unless they meant to add to hardship and hurt later." I turned to Dalk. "The bonds of true brotherhood have always been forged by the men who chose to follow me."

I came around the small table and knelt in front of my oldest friend. "What say you, Dalk? Will you and the others stand with me against hopeless odds one last time? Just as you have so many times before? Even to lay siege upon the gates of the All Father if need be?"

Dalk's unfocused eyes came to rest on my beseeching face. "Do you understand what you did for us? Can you understand? You took those of us thought used up, or, worse, worthless from birth. You gathered the weak, the broken, the wounded, and the lazy. You gave us a leader and an ideal to follow. You made us into indomitable warriors simply by being an invincible champion before us."

I beamed at him, and my heart swelled. But then a sobbing croak came from his lips, and he looked away from me. The betrayal stabbed a spike in my chest, each word hammering it home.

"But now, we wasted and worthless have a home, a people, and a king. You cannot ask us to leave this behind for your mad quest." He squeezed his red rimmed eyes shut tight. "You cannot ask this of us because, if you do, we will follow you. And we will hate you for it."

I froze inside. Cold and dead. There was nothing else for me here. Without a sound, I stood and walked to the door. Hallbjorn took a halting step toward me, his hand outstretched.

"Finn, wait. This...thing you go to do, it is too terrible, too large for any single man, even the Myth Reaver. You cannot do it alone."

Hallbjorn's words stopped me, and I half turned to him, framed in the doorway. Grímarr's damnable voice rang again in my head, but now I understood his words as a gift. He had shown me something about myself I wouldn't accept because I understood it only as a curse. In this moment, I knew it to be a blessing. The realization brought a cold smile to my face, the last thing Hallbjorn and Dalk saw of me before I left. I called my new revelation to them over my shoulder as I vanished from their sight.

"The Myth Reaver always walks alone."

15. The First Faltering Steps toward My Destiny

It was late into the night and there weren't many out and about, but I headed toward the sea regardless. Docks always have some life about them no matter the time of day or night. When I reached the docks, I checked berths by flickering torchlight. Now that I knew I'd go alone, I had no reason to dally. And I had in mind a way to make myself ready that would leave a bitter flavor upon the tongue of my eldest brother.

Since the destruction of the sea wyrm, the ports in Grímarr's capitol had re-opened. Servants had been sent south to collect my ships and had returned with them. The longships under my banner now waited for me in newly liberated berths. I looked over the ships that once held hundreds of men who fought in my name. They bobbed up and down on the waves, now empty. Most of the men who had sailed them would never ride the whale's road again. The few who remained would never do so with me. It seemed fitting.

My eyes eventually strayed to my own longboat, the flagship of this tiny fleet. Everyone knew the Myth Reaver, and everyone would have recognized this as my ship. The giant, mummified, and now, rather ratty, wolf's head lashed to the prow saw to that. It was the very same boat I had sailed away within the last time my brothers had turned me out. This also seemed fitting.

"You," I shouted at a loutish sailor loitering nearby. "Do you know who I am?"

He glared at me through one squinted eye for a long moment. I watched him track me upward, noting the lack of weaponry, before he reached the silver wolf's head brooch that held my wolfskin cloak in place. His head whipped towards the ship I stood nearest, then whipped back to me. His eye widened in shock and he nodded his greasy head vigorously.

"Gather up some men, I have work for them. They don't need to be shipwrights, but they should know how to manage a hammer and saw. Skilled thralls will do. Conscript freemen if there are some available. There's a gold ring in it for them, so roll them out of bed if necessary. Then find me a fast runner. I have a message to send to the hall."

At first the lummox didn't move. I made an exasperated noise in my throat that sent him scampering like a hare. In short order, thick-limbed men milled around with sleepy eyes and heavy tools at hand. I took a breath to start bellowing orders when a youth with downy patches on his face tugged at my sleeve. I glowered down at him.

"I'm Agdi, milord," he said, and tugged his forelock clumsily. "I heard you need a fast man, milord, and there's none faster for leagues, milord."

I grunted, but he had the combination of youthful nimbleness and long, clumsy, coltish legs that meant he probably wasn't exaggerating. Much.

"You'll do, Agdi. I want you to run to the hall as fast as you can. Bang on the door until somebody answers. Tell them Finn Styrrsson sends word to the king's steward." His eyes widened a bit at my name, but he didn't interrupt. "Insist they get the steward himself. He'll be the man who looks too weak to hold a sword but is dressed finer than a Saracen whore. Tell the steward that the Myth Reaver wishes his weapons, clothing, booty, and a few weeks supplies bundled up and delivered to this dock by midmorning. Tell him that if it isn't here by then, I'll be around to ask him about it personally. Is all that understood?"

"Aye, milord," Agdi replied. the boy made no complaint at all I asked of him. No, his mouth twisted in a grin, and his eyes shone. It was the Northman's way. Any burden could be justified if it might bring enough glory, and a night's work would leave the boy such a story to tell his friends tomorrow. I decided he needed a token to prove the tale.

"Good. You should also tell the steward that I said this quest deserved a man's reward. Tell him you're to have the ring on his left pinkie for your trouble."

His eyes went even wider. I worried they might fall right out of the sockets.

"What if he's not wearing a ring, milord?"

I grunted again. "You've obviously never met any stewards. Shouldn't you be halfway to the hall by now?"

Without another sound, Agdi became a flurry of knees and elbows leaving a faint trail of dust. I turned to the men.

"All right, listen up. I'm Finn Styrrsson. I'm going to tell you to do some very odd things to my boat. I don't want a lot of questions because I've been very drunk tonight and it's starting to wear off. It's leaving me surly."

Exactly the kind of grumbling and murmuring you'd expect from tradesmen awoken in the middle of the night to ridiculous requests bubbled up from the crowd. They all recognized my name, so they realized it wasn't really a request. But much like Agdi, they deserved a reward, preferably one that would send my eldest brother into a fit.

"You'll just have to trust that what I tell you will work because I've done it once before. This time I want it done *well*, which is where you come in. I will explain it to you once and then I will go to sleep far enough away your noise won't awaken me. If you manage to do an adequate job without waking me up, then the king's shipwright will owe each of you a gold armring."

That changed the grumbles into interested mutterings. So I told them how to rig my longship so I could row it single handedly. They all traded dubious looks amongst themselves, but, to their credit, nobody interrupted me with questions. I then stumbled away and found a pile of hay more or less outside of earshot from the docks. I fell asleep as soon as I laid down my head.

~

I pulled my cloak off my face around midday. I stumbled back to the docks, stretching my limbs and grumbling all the while. I felt pleasantly surprised to discover everything finished to my satisfaction. My personal cargo had even been loaded onto my ship, including Moon Sliver and Fathersbane. The boat, at least, was ready to go.

The men had done exemplary work. The oars had been refitted and rigged so that I could once again row a twenty man ship all on my own. I grinned to myself as I imagined all of the workers demanding payment from Grímarr's shipwright.

I had all the pains and kinks one earns sleeping drunk in a haystack, but I figured nothing would work them out like a good day's worth of rowing. I found someone willing to sell me a warm loaf of bread and a skin of water for a ridiculous price. Then told them to see Grímarr's steward to collect. I watched the old woman's eyes account for the inflation she could get once I no longer vouchsafed the price. Grímarr's coffers would be hard hurt by my departure.

That knowledge was a small sliver of warmth against the aching cold of the many betrayals stacked around me. The ache reminded me I no longer had any reason to stay. The time to put my back to the work of dying gloriously had come.

The quiet of the docks had given way to their usual bustle and noise. Despite myself, I looked to see if Dalk or Hallbjorn would come to see me off. Had they told the rest of my war band brothers I planned to leave? Probably not. They wouldn't want any of them to try and stop me. They certainly wouldn't want any of the others deciding to join my sacrilegious scheme. No other lives than my own needed to be ruined by Grímarr's conniving.

Grímarr. Just thinking my eldest brother's name stoked the fires of my fury high enough to boil my blood in my veins. There the snake sat in his great mead hall, the center of a kingdom our father had carved out with blood, sweat, and gold. I imagined him rubbing hands together in glee that another sinister skullduggery had borne fruit. I pictured him celebrating with men who had once been my own thanes in all but name, enjoying their friendship and comfort while I turned to an empty, desolate road, alone. Again. I set my jaw. At least this time I would not be alone for long. The Aesir would see to that. I only had to find one and spit in his eye.

My plan was simple. The only way from Midgard to Asgard was a fiery bridge called Bifrost, a legendary structure crafted of rainbows. Even alone, my preternatural strength could move my longship at fantastic speeds. I would simply look for a rainbow, of which there was no shortage in the cold, rainy north. Then I would row toward it like Fenrir himself nipped at my heels. It would be no problem for me to catch every rainbow I set my eye to and, eventually, one of them must be Bifrost. If I needed incentive, I had the emptiness of true betrayal to spur me on. If I could find a god, challenge him, and die with sword in hand, I'd join the endless brotherhood of the Einherjar in Valhalla. After the treatment of my brothers and men, nothing could be better.

Sadly, my simple plan rested upon a loose foundation. The chilled rains, frigid sleets, and frozen snows rolled nearly endless in the North, so I had nearly endless rainbows to chase. But even though no boat could outrun my own with me at the oars, rainbows proved faster still. No matter how mighty my pull of the oars, I never grew nearer to one of them. This frustrated and angered me, which allowed me to row all the harder and faster...at first.

I rowed, portaged, camped, rowed, portaged, and camped again. This went on for days stretching into weeks. The drudgery of it wore upon me. I had managed to forget the hole torn in my soul with the hooks of treachery by focusing on an immediate goal. But the longer I failed to attain that goal, the more my forsaken status ate away at me.

I lay one night looking at the stars through slitted eyes in that in-between space between wakefulness and sleep. That was a place of inspiration for me. I cast my thoughts out, seeking wisdom to set my course. I thought of Dag, a king well-known for his judgment, and how he might look favorably upon me with advice again. I thought of Dag's misfortune and how not even wisdom could save one from the capricious Norns and the wyrd they set. How alike were Grímarr's perfidy and Alvis Elvenking's, both rulers cloaking their treachery in the boon of friendship. I drifted off to sleep and dreamed of visiting an elven court. When I awoke, I knew exactly what had to be done.

I rowed toward Dag's own country like a man possessed. I pulled into his docks and made straight for his hall. We greeted one another with honor and affection. He asked me to stay for the night. I accepted his kind offer and begged his indulgence and advice. He acquiesced and met with me privately. He allowed me to tell of my problem and my goal at length.

"So? Am I as mad as Hallbjorn and Dalk think me?" I asked him.

The old king stared at me from a craggy face. The years had done their violence to his body, but his eyes remained undimmed by age or dementia. I trusted the sharpness of his mind. His hands steepled beneath his chin as he considered me. At last he took a wheezing breath to speak.

"Were it any other man, Finn, I would call him a blasphemous idiot. But I beheld the Myth Reaver and your impact on the world. And I mark how the actions of your brothers and men-at-arms have left you...different. Hollowed out like an old log left to rot. Yours is a mad dream, one I cannot believe will be as clear a path as you hope. Yet for all my vaunted wisdom, I cannot fathom a better course for one such as yourself."

I breathed out a chest full of air I hadn't realized I'd held. "Thank you, wise one. I accept fully that the plan may be ridiculous, even insane. Yet I was otherwise at a loss."

He drummed his fingers on the arm of his chair as he considered me. "You are not one to rely on another's counsel often, Finn. And neither are you one to require the sanction of any mortal man or blessed being to set on a course for action. I believe my hearing of your plan is simply an explanation for the true purpose of your visit."

I nodded. "Your reputation for piercing discernment doesn't begin to do you justice. I need to see King Alvis."

Those gleaming eyes showed no surprise. "You would have me introduce you formally to his court?"

I shook my head. "No, I fear a formal connection between you and my battle plans would not bode well for you and yours. But I need no introduction to Alvis. You may recall he owes me a boon. Nor do I need an escort. I simply need directions to where this world draws near his own. I will, as ever, make my own way once I know which direction to travel."

Again, the venerable king considered me and his eyes bored straight into the center of me. After a time, he seemed to see whatever he'd been looking for and his face hardened. He nodded once decisively. "You shall have it. But tomorrow. Tonight, you will dine with an old man and tell him tales of the Myth Reaver on the Varangian Way."

How could I refuse?

~

In the morning, Dag presented me with a detailed map. As I studied it, I suspected some of the spidery writing on the thin parchment had been written in the ruler's own hand. My eyes stung from tears at this valuable and kingly gift. It was a testament to my belief in Grímarr's cunning and understanding of politics that I didn't immediately swear fealty to the old man right there. Instead, I offered him my boat and everything on it save my arms, armor, and the clothes on my back, as tribute.

He graciously accepted, then gave me two horses, a charger and a pack horse. The pack animal had been laden with a month's worth of supplies at least. He probably thought he had evened the scales between us. A tiny ember, the only bit of happiness I could still feel, flared in me as I thought of his face when he discovered the riches I'd carried with me. The Varangian Way had been very good to me. But in his way, Dag had been much better.

I set out on the two-day course Dag laid out for me upon the map. But restless energy filled me now that I had a workable goal. With the moon near full, I traveled later into the night than I would normally chance the animal's footing. So it passed that early on the morning of the second day, a subtle shift came over the land. The morning sun took on a more golden hue, the plants seemed more vibrantly alive in their verdancy, while the dappled shadows seemed even deeper and more malevolent.

I slowed and breathed deep. The air tasted sweeter, smelled more fragrant. A warm breeze that had not been there moments before tickled my arms and neck. The lustrous light shone similarly warm on my skin. Everywhere I looked, things appeared more beautiful, more brilliant, more alive. And beneath that, there lay a perilous hate that raised the hairs on the back of my neck and made my right palm itch as it did just before a battle.

"Álfheimr," I breathed.

"In case you didn't realize, mortal, that means 'Elf Home,'" said a voice from my left. "You trespass in the lands of King Alvis. Turn back."

I turned to see two elven warriors, resplendent in mail and helm. They sat astride warhorses that dwarfed my already impressive steed. They held in their right hands long pikes with shimmery blades. Their left hands bore shields painted in gold and green lines curving out from the center. They didn't look angry, exactly. They looked more bored. Or perhaps annoyed that I interrupted their boredom.

"King Alvis? Then Dag's map led me true," I said, dismounting.

"Oh, good," the quiet guard said, chuckling. "More of Dag's mongrels come calling."

My face grew hard. "You'll watch your tongue when you speak of Dag the Wise. You'll watch it, or I'll tear it out for you."

The two elves shared a look, but said nothing.

"Before you make a rash decision you'll come to regret, you might want to ask who I am," I told them.

They shared another look. Then one of them sighed and said, "And who are you, then?"

"Finn, son of Styrr who is called Warborn. Wolf Killer, Dragon Slayer, Butcher of Elven Champions." I leered at them. "The Myth Reaver."

They shared a third look, but this time obvious meaning passed between them. Vexation. Unease. Worry. While they dithered, I unhitched Fathersbane from my saddle and drew Moon Sliver from its scabbard.

"Perhaps you recognize this blade? The craftsmanship is elven, yet it is made for one who would tower over you or me. This is the blade of Eldrim Alvisson, your one time Champion. And if you don't lead me to your king's hall right now, I'll give your guts an even closer inspection."

The worried looks changed to determination. Either they didn't believe my identity, didn't care, or had orders to stop anyone coming from Dag's court. They leveled their pikes at me, spurred their horses, and charged.

I dodged to my left, taking myself out of harm's way from the rightmost warrior's long hafted blade. I held Fathersbane up high and swung Moon Sliver. The pike's blade slid off the dragonscale, and my sword bit deep into the legs of the warhorse. My strength and the horse's momentum met at the unnaturally keen edge. With little more than a sharp tug, I sheared all four legs right from its body. The legless beast and its rider fell to the ground in an awkward tangle, its animal screams ringing in my ears. I stepped toward the writhing mound and kicked the elf warrior in the face. His form went limp and still.

I turned to face the other warrior as he wheeled his steed around. His eyes widened at the gruesome scene, but he mastered his shock. His horse trotted sideways as he considered how best to attack me.

"I came here with no quarrel, elf," I growled. "I came seeking the boon owed me by your king. *You* attacked *me*. But your cohort isn't dead, and neither must you be if you simply lead me to Alvis's court now."

He yelled something unintelligible in his highborne tongue, spurred his steed, and lowered his pike. The beast's hooves pounded like thunder, the warrior's cry rang high and vigorous. I settled myself for his charge. A small smile played across my lips. The killing was no longer a means to an end, but instead had become merry fun all its own. My mind had twisted bloodsimple, and I was too far gone to care.

~

Sometime later I kicked in the broad, oaken doors of Alvis's hall. They flew open wide, slamming into a few benches and scraping them along the floor until the overextended hinges screamed a tortured squeal and finally dragged the doors to a stop. The revelry I'd heard muffled through the great wooden doors faltered and died to silence. I stepped into their midst, a gore splattered specter of grim death.

"King Alvis," I said in a hoarse whisper, "The Myth Reaver comes seeking his boon."

A clatter of metal and at least a dozen elven warriors materialized between me and their king. It was good to see even fair-haired elfin bastards knew a guard's duty. They stood ready to defend a king who still only stared, agog.

I leveled my blade at the warriors. "No more of your men need be slaughtered, Alvis. Your men chose the battles already fought, not I."

The air rang with the rasp of steel freed from sheath. The royal guard advanced upon me.

"Alvis," I said. The name hung in the air, both threat and question.

At last the goggling king spoke. "Stop! Let him speak!" His warriors stopped moving, but they never relaxed their guard. Nor did they stop pointing their swords at me. "What is it you want, Myth Reaver?"

"You remember me! After the reception I've received from your subjects, I thought I'd been forgotten in these shining halls. Or did you order them to kill me on sight? Perhaps to assuage your own shame? Or merely to leave your promised boon to me unfulfilled?"

The beautiful king pointed a finger. His face twisted in rage just as lovely, in its way, as any other countenance an elf lord chose to wear. He spoke, his voice harsh and spittle flew from his lips. Even that somehow looked graceful.

"Do you dare charge into my hall and accuse me of these things? In front of my *guests*?"

I shrugged. "I introduced myself to your men, milord, and still they attacked. Are the rules of hospitality so different in the Elf Home?"

"What are they to think when an aimless mortal wanders the byways of Álfheimr, slaughtering them like swine?" He lowered his pointing hand. "How did you find your way to my hall, anyway, Myth Reaver? Mortals are not well known for their ability to navigate elven roads."

"Dag showed me how to reach your demesnes, milord. As for how I found your hall proper..." I unhitched a sack from my belt and threw it at the feet of his warriors. The neck fell open and the head of a male elf rolled out of it looking embarrassed. "I had heard elves were undying folk, but did you know your heads could keep talking even after removal from your shoulders? That surprised me."

The king glared at the blood-soaked head where it lay, a pool of gore puddling beneath it. Despite the head's lack of neck and shoulders, it rolled its eyes wildly, avoiding the furious king's gaze.

"Do not think he gave me the route to your hall easily, milord," I assured the king. "I had to persuade him most...vigorously."

The king spluttered, and his golden hued face turned a ruddy color, like burnished copper.

"I will have you gutted and on a spit for this," the king raged.

"Or you can give me what you owe me and I'll be on my way. Honestly, I'd have preferred it that way. I came to suffer a warrior's death, but your elves aren't up to the challenge."

My mention of a death wish cut through his fury and sparked curiosity. His color did not change, but his look became more shrewd.

"The boon you crave is a warrior's death?"

I barked out a laugh. "In a roundabout way, though not at the hands of you and yours. Which is my good fortune. As I said, I'd have been sorely disappointed."

The line of warriors between myself and their king bridled, their glares turning even more murderous. But their king merely considered me.

"If I weren't about to have you executed, I'd hear the tale of what stole the Myth Reaver's zest for life."

"Maybe you should hear the boon first. On your oath, you *do* owe me. And I guarantee it will take me away from your hall and your guests."

The shock was wearing off, and Alvis regained some of his control. His color returned to normal and he seated himself on his throne. He leaned back and steepled his fingers beneath his chin.

"After all this chaos, Myth Reaver, I owe you more than that. Not to mention the bad taste of wielding that sword in my own hall. Perhaps I will grant you this boon before I have you gruesomely murdered. Speak it."

"I seek passage to Asgard."

The king snorted rudely. "Do you now? Why invade my realm? We are not so close to Asgard that riding burning Bifrost wouldn't have been a shorter way."

Then it was my turn to snort. "If the Bifrost bridge is anything other than a prank perpetrated on men, I wouldn't be able to prove it. No, despite the length of my journey, I think you'll sponsor it, Alvis."

His eyes narrowed at my familiarity. "Boon owed or not, I think I will not. Asgard is not a place for mere mortals."

I glanced pointedly at the elf blood splattering my clothing and at the disembodied head doing its best to not get noticed. "I think it's obvious there's nothing mere about this mortal. And I'm willing to prove it by slaughtering your court. The gold I would owe for their lives, the...elfgild, I suppose, should balance well with punishment for reneging upon your solemn promise. A kingly ransom for a broken kingly oath?"

He glared at me and the color began to rise in his face again. "It might. Or my warriors may slaughter you where you stand."

"They might," I said, nodding grimly. "But not before I kill several score of them. But before I do even that, O King, my first cut is for you. I'll leave you blooded, scarred, and ashamed. Forever." I looked meaningfully around the room at his guests.

We stared at one another, king and reaver, for a lengthening moment. My gaze never wavered and neither did my sword arm. The king, to his credit, never relented from his scowling glare, even when he finally spoke.

"Warriors, stand down." The troop turned to look at him in shock, but he ignored them. Instead, he gestured at the thralls and servants who cowered in the doorway to the kitchens. "You! Clean up this mess and set a place for our"—he looked back to me—"guest. Serve him from my own plate as a sign of friendship."

I sheathed my blade and let Fathersbane dangle from its shoulder strap. Servants frantically scrubbed blood from the floors at my feet as I removed my helm and stepped over them. Dodging those servants who scrambled to set a place for me, I climbed stairs to sit down at the king's own table. I greeted the elf lord with a nod.

The glare had faded, but his stare stayed cold and unfriendly.

"Welcome to my table, Myth Reaver. You will stay within my hospitality until I can teach you the way to Asgard. Then you will leave my demesnes with as much haste as mortal limbs can manage."

I inclined my head toward him. "You are most gracious, mighty King Alvis. I expected no less."

If anyone enjoyed my jest, they didn't show it. For myself, I set to the repast before me. Killing elves is not hard work, but like any light task repeated often enough, it still left me famished.

16. Thunderstruck by Trickery

Three nights I stayed a guest to Alvis's hospitality. It was a nerve-wracking time. A nation of godlings had nearly declared war against me. How could I possibly trust the pinch-faced bastards? Especially when I only desired my just, promised reward. I began to think of Alvis as a prettier Grímarr, and he grew easier to manage. But it was difficult, this only drinking from his goblet, only eating servings from his plate. I checked beneath my bed every night and slept with an ever-present grip upon Moon Sliver.

Each evening Alvis, his steward, and I retired to his study whereupon they drilled me on maps, distances, and landmarks. These sessions never ended until the wee hours of the night. They stressed to me the dangers of Álfheimr and further impressed upon me that it was a world not made for mortal eyes and ears.

"The very land will twitch and shift, boy," Alvis admonished me one night. "If you don't leave this hall with every step of your journey committed to memory, and with your will steeled never to deviate from it no matter what your senses tell you, then I will have given you no boon. And no hall-chief will thank me for a mislaid, red-handed berserker loose in his lands. So focus!"

Despite his antipathy for me, the warnings' sincerity rang true. And dying of old age while wandering lost in elven lands got me no closer to Valhalla than it did in the world of men. So I focused, I studied, and I committed my route to memory based on mountains, ancient trees, and mighty, rushing rivers.

"Things even an elf's capricious nature cannot dislodge," the steward said. As though these words made any sense at all.

So I found myself shooed from Alvis's hall with a combination of distaste and well-wishes from the king. I cannot attest to whether or not the fastidiousness of my training had been warranted. Since I paid no heed to paths, trails, roads, or landmarks other than the ones taught to me, everything I saw on that journey might have stood a thousand years or the space of a breath. Sooth, the trek bored me and deadened my mind. No elf, beast, or monster accosted me. I wondered if Alvis had laid some charm or geas upon me that his world might leave me unmolested.

Then, just as it had been when I moved from Dag's lands into Alvis's, I noticed changes at once subtle yet profound. The slender pine and yew of the Elf Home forest became thick, stalwart oaks. Roiling columns of clouds ranging from steel gray to pitch black obscured the clear, glittering sunlight. The sharp tang after a storm replaced the warm breeze. And beneath it all, the place had a weight to it, as though made of substances more...solid. More real.

I had reached the goal of my quest. I had arrived in Asgard. But as I took in my surroundings, I realized that, even in this, Alvis had stirred the pot with a crooked finger. I didn't merely stand in Asgard, I had stumbled into Thrudvang.

A streak of lightning as big as the world split the murky sky, leaving a flashing purple line across my vision. The thunder that followed drove the breath from my chest and filled the air around me until I wondered if I could inhale through the noise. The pack horse's lead jerked from my hand as the animal screamed and ran from the light and din. I cursed, but immediately wrestling the reins of my steed stole all my attention. Thankfully, though the racket spooked the stallion, I rode a trained and battle-tested warhorse. It responded to my strength and sure touch without flinging me to the ground and trampling me.

I patted the horse and clucked to him, soothing my own rattled nerves as much as his. The oaks, the clouds, and the thunder and lightning crowded in around me. I had *definitely* arrived in Thrudvang, the Fields of Strength. These lands belonged to Thor the Thunderer.

"Hel take you, Alvis, you Loki-tongued bastard of an elf," I said. "You certainly threw me from the cradle to the battlefield."

My heart raced, the hair stood up on my body, and every nerve tingled. I hadn't been this frightened since that first battle alongside my brothers all those years ago. I gripped Moon Sliver's hilt until my knuckles turned white then took deep breaths and willed my body to relax.

"This is what you came for," I reminded myself. "Alvis did you a favor. No wandering around looking for an Aesir who can best you. He brought you right to Thor, right to your doom."

"To your doom for certain, trespasser," said a deep, rumbling voice, "but not to Thor."

A new voice followed the first, only this one held as much growl as it did words. "You tell him, Magni."

From amongst the oaks ambled two very large red-haired men. But the red hair only demonstrated the differences between them. These had to be Modi and Magni, Thor's sons. Everyone on Midgard knew the tales told of these two and understood they exemplified Thor's two greatest assets, his strength and anger. I was a little intimidated to stand before them. At first.

The more muscular of the two I took to be Magni, the Thorsson named after his father's great strength, and the owner of the first voice. His hair and beard were the color of burnished copper, matching his shirt of mail and the head of his massive, two-handed hammer. Every step he took shook the ground. He swung the hammer lightly, as though it weighed nothing more than a child's toy.

The other man had to be Modi, so named for his father's great rage. Modi stood nearly as large as his brother but leaner. His hair and beard were flaming red and fashioned into spikes held fast with lime. His eyes slitted in anger and were surrounded by a face contorted with rage. His mouth twisted into a gash full of teeth filed to points, flecks of foam and drool speckling his lips and beard. He wore no arms or clothing save a ragged, sleeveless shirt of bear skin that hung nearly low enough to be decent. Disdaining weapons, his massive hands flexed convulsively in front of him, as though he imagined what it would be like to wring my neck.

I had never liked bullies, not since the day I toddled up to two of my brothers and broke their bones with my tiny, bare hands. I shouldn't have been surprised, but Thor's sons were bullies. Just the tone of their voices, the swagger they carried themselves with, told me the two things I needed to know about them.

First, they needed a thrashing.

Second, I was just the one to give it to them. My death could wait a bit longer.

"Say that to my face," I said. I dismounted, hefted Fathersbane, and loosened Moon Sliver in its sheath. "That is, if you can stop kissing each other long enough to repeat it."

My tiniest insult brought instantaneous action. Modi, already a slave to his heart-hate, threw his head back and screamed his fury to the storm clouds above us. With a snarl that blew anger-foam from his lips, he broke into a dead run toward me. I set myself behind my shield, digging in as though I readied myself for the impact of a siege engine. Modi saw this and churned his frenzied legs even faster.

At the last possible moment, just before Modi's clawing hands snatched at my shield, I stepped to the side. I kicked at his heel as he ran past me. He tripped and slammed headlong into the oak I'd had at my back. The impact shook the tree, causing whole branches to cascade down around Modi's dazed form. He stumbled and then slid to the ground, a massive purple welt already forming on his forehead. I laughed.

Magni rushed me, bringing his hammer down toward me in a powerful overhand swing. I didn't believe I could swing a hammer that size at all, so he was obviously strong. But he lacked celerity. I took a very small step sideways and turned my body just a bit, and the hammer head whistled past me close enough to flutter my hair. It pounded into the ground with a deep, hollow tone. The ground shuddered beneath it, then cracked.

"Nobody treats my brother that way," Magni said, his face inches from my own. He didn't sound angry or even indignant. The statement held more fact than bluster. Having seven brothers myself, I began to understand.

I stomped my booted foot down on his instep and ground my heel as hard as I could. His eyes bugged from his head and his face turned a bright red beneath its coppery beard, but he did not cry out. I leaned in closer to him, putting more weight on his anguished foot.

"Oh? Does Papa come around and make the other children play nice?"

Near us Modi swore, his voice pulled thin like a child throwing a tantrum. I moved away from Magni, and Modi rushed me again. He moved slightly more carefully this time, coming at me in more of a lope than a dead run. I whipped my sword up, merely meaning for the sharpened tip to bring him up short. He shocked me by slapping it aside with his bare arm, leaving a deep gouge running from his wrist to his elbow. He didn't seem to notice, and it left me so perplexed that I couldn't defend myself from his broad, meaty fist clouting me in the nose.

I heard a sickening crunch, and my nose flattened against my face hard enough to crack something in my cheek. My broken nose and face burned like cold fire while my eyes filled with water and my world with pain. I fell backward, Moon Sliver slipping from my grip. Modi came down on top of me, pinning me to the ground beneath my shield. Pure luck or the intervention of Norns saw that we landed with my shield protecting me. Otherwise he'd have had all the time he needed to tear my throat out with his teeth. As it stood, I felt his hot spittle on my cheek with every lunge, but the shield between us kept him at bay. Barely.

"Hold him, Modi," Magni said in his quiet, solid way. "I'll break his legs for you."

The world began to return to focus, the harsh throb of my face falling into the background behind my own anger and battle-lust. I roared back into Modi's face, and pushed up against my shield with all my strength. He laughed at me, the noise like a dog's cough and his breath rancid like meat left in the sun. But the idiot hadn't counted on my own unnatural thews. I bucked and heaved, throwing him off me like a sack of flour. Modi made a startled sound as he hurtled away from me, hitting his charging brother with full force. The two of them went down in a pile of cursing, punching limbs.

I rose and gingerly reached my fingers up to my face. The bones in my ruined cheek ground against one another like sand on stone, and my nose felt huge and angry. But I'd had my nose caved in before. I grabbed hold of it with thumb and forefinger, wrenching it into place. The pain blinded me and tore a scream from my throat, but something in both the ruined side of my face and my crushed nose shifted of its own accord, and the agony faded to nothing before I'd even finished my yell. I found myself screaming about nothing, so I snatched up my sword just as the two brothers leapt to their feet, ready again to kill.

I held up my sword in a guarded gesture. "Hold it right there! I've decided which one of you I want to fight."

On the face of it, the statement was so ridiculous that the brothers froze and looked at one another in confusion. I left my face a mask of sincerity, though inwardly I shook my head at their stupidity. Definitely bullies. True warriors did not act this stupid even in the Aesir. I knew this because I'd met a few stupid warriors and they were invariably young and soon dead.

"Don't pretend you didn't recognize me," I said when their confused silence had drawn on for a bit. "Surely even in this out of the way mudhole you've heard of the Myth Reaver. And heard that he had come to Asgard."

"We've never heard of any Myth Reaver," Magni said slowly.

"And Thorssons wouldn't care if they had!" Modi snarled at me. "We fear nothing, not even Ragnarök!"

I did my best to look dismayed. "Never heard of the Myth Reaver?" I shook my head. "It never occurred to me I'd arrive in such a backwater that you wouldn't know who I am. Famed wolf killer? Feller of giants? *Dragon* slayer? No?" They shared another look and shook their heads. I sighed. "Well, regardless, I heard tales of your prowess. Both of you. Having heard, I wished to fight the greatest of Thor's sons. I came to test you and see which that is. And I've made my selection."

"Then prepare yourself, *Myth Reaver*!" Modi shouted. "I will rip and tear you! Then wear your flesh like a hat!"

I *tsk tsked* and said, "That won't do. If I wanted to fight mad dogs, I could have stayed in Midgard. My strength is easily as legendary as yours. But it may not be as legendary as his." I pointed at Magni. "I'm here to test grips with him, pup, not you."

Modi's eyes shifted to Magni and narrowed. "You think my brother a more powerful opponent? You think him more dangerous than me?" His voice fell quiet but no less murderous for the softness. He raked furrows in the ground with his clawed fingers as he spoke.

Magni shifted away from his mad brother, slowly raising his hammer.

"Modi..." he said soothingly, as much a warning as a call to remain calm.

"Shut up, brother!" Modi shrieked. "Everyone thinks your thick arms make up for your thick head! I'll show them anger is more than a match for strength!"

Magni took a few steps further away from his brother, but he maintained a strong defensive posture. "Modi..." he said again. This time his voice held more warning than mollifying tones.

Just like that, they forgot me. Magni screamed at his brother, and I clapped my hands over my ears. It didn't help. The scream went on for what seemed like hours, Modi's eyes bulged and the veins and sinews in his neck stood out by inches. His mouth yawned wide like a cave to Hel. The shriek held an intensity as terrible as the earlier thunderclap in its piercing way. Unlike the thunder, though, it went on and on.

Through the din, I looked at Magni. He stood unfazed by his brother's antics. At one point, I thought he might have rolled his eyes, but the racket of the scream shook my own in their sockets, making detail impossible to discern. I could be sure of nothing beyond Magni's stalwart stance.

Finally the wail ended and Modi charged. Even through my tortured ears, I could hear the beleaguered sigh escape Magni's chest-bellows. The berserker ran toward his brother, who waited with a bored expression on his face. At just the right moment, Magni swung his massive hammer around in a wide arc, grunting lightly with the effort. The broad head met the side of Modi's broad head. It had the air of a well practiced, oft repeated maneuver.

The noise of the hammer blow rang like a deep, melodious bell. Modi fell to the ground like a house collapsing. No sound came from him, no cry of pain nor even a groan of discomfort. The berserker, knocked wide of his target, simply ran a few more dogged steps before his own weight pulled him over and buried his face in the ground.

Magni watched the scene, his shoulders sagging with pity. He slowly turned toward me, saying, "You'll pay for tha—"

He never finished. I interrupted him with an overhand sword stroke I'd started while he'd still had his back to me. He raised his hammer in both hands, the haft crosswise above his head, to block the blow. But I'd expected this, wanted it. I brought the blade down with all the might that pulsed through my thews.

A loud crack sounded, like a frozen limb snapping from an ancient tree in silent midwinter. A bright flare rose up where my sword met Magni's hammer and an unseen force threw us both backward a dozen ells. I sat up, dazed. I blinked spots from my eyes and shook a thick blanket from my skull. I found Magni doing much the same. He held a short hafted hammer in one hand and the rest of the haft, now a club, in his other. I glanced down at Moon Sliver, worried I'd shattered it against such a worthy weapon. But I found only a notch the size of the nail on my smallest finger in the otherwise polished and flawless blade.

Magni and I both rose slowly, testing our bodies for injury. If the Thorsson felt like I did, soreness ruled him but left no lasting wounds. In sooth,

Magni looked at his broken hammer in much the same way I would look at a broken limb. His mouth took a sour twist, his brows knit tightly together. He opened his mouth, but I silenced him with a gesture.

"I know, I know. I'll pay for that as well. But tell me...are you so sure of that now?"

Magni didn't speak an answer, he only tested the heft of his now single-handed hammer and padded toward me warily. I shouldered my shield between us and held my own blade at the ready, approaching him with the same vigilance. His hammer had become ill-weighted, clumsy to wield with a shortened haft and the strength of only one arm, while I remained well protected behind a shield and the tip of a long blade. He'd clearly underestimated me, but just as clearly wouldn't do so again.

We circled one another, drawing nearer and nearer. Our eyes darted, looking for an opening in the other's guard. Now and then one or the other of us feinted one direction, only to find the gambit ignored or a swifter defense already deflecting. We prodded and tested one another though we still remained outside weapons' reach.

To his credit, Magni seemed willing to wait forever while I grew impatient. Finally, with a cry, I lunged at him, pointing Moon Sliver's tip toward his guts. He sidestepped deftly and brought his hammer down toward my sword arm. But the overbalanced maul made him slow, and I blocked it with my shield. It rang an odd note upon impact, but I otherwise felt nothing from the blow. We skipped backward from one another, and circled again.

Modi groaned loudly, and I flicked a glance in his direction. I'd made all the mistake Magni needed. In that split second, he threw himself upon me, raining blows down on my shield one after another in rapid succession. I stepped back over and over, faltering beneath the power of each pounding strike.

No damage transmitted through Fathersbane, but neither could I get my feet beneath me enough to bring my sword to bear. At any moment I would trip over a branch or root and fall, leaving myself unprotected for a death blow.

I stumbled to the side with purpose. I angled toward a Modi who still moaned wordlessly but had managed to pull himself up to his hands and knees. As I moved sideways, a hammer blow unbalanced me. I stumbled and fell, rolling away from my attacker. Magni pressed the advantage, landing a solid strike against the boss of my shield. My fingers went instantly numb and threatened to let loose the shield, but I gritted my teeth and held on despite a weakened grip.

The rapid strikes and measured retreat brought me alongside Modi. Just where I wanted to be.

"Modi, look out!" I yelled, feigning a maiden's terrified squeal.

Modi looked up, his eyes foggy and unfocused. But even through a haze, he saw his brother, full of fury, arm stretched backward, ready to deal a killing blow. I watched panic race through Modi's dazed mind. He reacted predictably.

"Modi, no!" Magni yelled at his brother as the berserker rose from his crouch with a snarl. Modi threw his shoulder into his hammer wielding brother's midsection. The air left Magni with a *whump,* and the two of them bowled over into a wad of flailing limbs and furious noises. Magni's hammer flew wide of the battling pair.

They rolled this way for twenty ells until finally Modi pinned Magni to the ground, his knees in his brother's shoulders. I knew even the rage of the berserker would not hold back the power in Magni's limbs for long, but Modi didn't need long. His claw-like hands grasped at the forest floor and found a large stone. Raising it over his head, he brought it down over and over, until nothing remained of Magni's face but a ruin of blood, snot, and cracked teeth.

Modi roared his triumph to the heavens. I cut short his celebration when the three ells of elven steel sprang from his chest. He gurgled once, then slumped forward to cover his brother's smashed face with his own body. His fall pulled him from my sword. I bent to wipe its blade clean on his bear shirt.

"I knew Thor had two sons he named Strength and Anger," I said to the two corpses. I shook my head at them. "Good thing for me he didn't have one named Bright."

I laughed at my own jest. My whole body filled with the joy of surviving a life-or-death struggle. I laughed until my sides ached and tears streamed down my face. The battle-joy made me foolish, and I bellowed to the roiling clouds overhead

"I have bested your sons, Thunderer," I yelled. "There is no man, beast, elf, nor even god that can stand before the Myth Reaver! Least of all you, Thor!"

The sky answered my challenge with another blinding fork of lightning and another deafening clap of thunder. This brought another flash with thunder, and another, and another, and another, until the whole world had filled with nothing but thunder and lightning. Somewhere in this symphony of light and noise, the clouds let loose their rain-hoard in a mighty downpour. The rain instantly soaked me to the skin. So thickly fell the drops I could see nothing else. So loudly roared the cloudburst I could hear nothing else. But I understood the message well enough.

Whatever I believed about my superiority to the Thunder Lord, Thor came to prove me wrong.

17. Storm Breaker

The pounding of rain upon my helmet, of thunder upon my ears, and of lightning upon my eyes besieged my senses. Yet somehow, even through all that, I heard the roar of Thor's coming. Even through the sheets of cold, sleety rain, I could see massive trees knocked aside, their thick trunks cracked as they fell over out of the way. I heard a rattle of cart wheels that dwarfed the blasts of thunder. I heard a voice, deep and resonant, coming from everywhere and nowhere all at once. It cursed me as a son-killer, a reaver of children. It swore vengeance upon me so severe I would wonder why the Norns had hated me to give me such a wyrd.

Then the massive hammer flew past me. It moved so fast the wind and rain fought to get out of its way. It made a high-pitched whistle that cut through my skull like a hot spike driven in my ear. It flashed past me, and the air of its passing blew me backward so that I had to wheel my arms to maintain balance. It hit an oak tree three or four ells past me, and lightning struck the tree's high boughs at the selfsame moment. The venerable oak exploded into shavings.

Before I'd even realized it sought me, death in the form of Thor's hammer, Mjölner, had missed me by a hair's breadth. Mjölner that never missed its mark. I knew that, had its master wished it, I'd have been dead already, flattened to a smear on the countryside.

The hammer rebounded from the blackened stump and stabbed toward its owner fast as lightning. He reached out a broad, guantleted fist and plucked with a loud, clear clang of metal upon metal. I beheld the fist of the Thunderer. He rode in a cart pulled by two immense and evil-tempered goats. The cart hurtled toward me, coming to a rattling halt so close I could feel the goats' hot breath.

"WHO DARES?!" demanded the Storm Lord, mighty Thor himself.

Thor's voice boomed, the most intense thing I had ever heard. It didn't enter my brain through my ears as much as crash upon the shores of my hearing like pounding ocean swells. In the same way a pretty girl lights up the room with her presence, Thor brought noise. The very air rang, hummed, clanged, and clamored. Where Thor walked or rode, there went a cacophonous din of celestial proportion. It seemed as though sound existed solely so that Thor could own the lion's share of it.

Somehow, Thor even *looked* loud. His presence assaulted my eyes as hard as it did my ears. I'd fought giants, gargantuan warriors writ immense as mountains and obviously far larger than even mighty Thor. But standing in the shadow of those behemoths had failed to overwhelm me as Thor's presence did.

Nor was it merely a question of strength. My mighty thews pulsed with power, more than any other man's I'd ever met. Even as an unproven youth, it had been said that I held the grip of thirty men in each fist. Since then, my sinews had grown adamantine, unbreakable as a cliff and relentless as an avalanche. But seeing Thor's thick slabs of muscle grinding over one another like millstones held together by tendons thick as cables, I felt puny and weak.

Hands the size of hams wore stout iron gauntlets that I feared would set my own arms to creaking beneath their ponderous weight. The armored gloves had no purpose other than protecting the wearer from the haft of Mjölner, which glowed constantly red hot from the lightning bolts occasionally striking its wide head. A broad belt of finest make encircled Thor's middle. It contained him barely, like an otherwise robust dam besieged by a raging river swollen past its banks. Tales said this belt doubled Thor's already incredible potency. A tremor ran through me at the thought.

When I had screamed to the sky that I could kill anyone, anything, even the Thunderer, I had believed it. But the Thunderer's arrival robbed me of that confidence utterly. The wolf had been nothing. Eldrim had been but a morsel. Every monster or monstrosity I'd faced along the Varangian paled to nothing before Thor. Even the ancient wyrm, essence of timeless power and hatred for all things warm blooded, couldn't match the anger that bristled Thor's dark auburn beard.

I had come to Asgard with a death wish. And though I had no doubt I would fall, I would do so as I'd lived. I would do so as the Myth Reaver.

"I dare it, Thunder Lord," I bellowed as loudly as I could. Even then, I couldn't be sure Thor would be able to hear me over the incessant noise of rain and thunder. "I am Finn Styrrsson, known as the Myth Reaver. I have killed countless warriors, monsters, beasts, and giants both in Midgard and Álfheimr. It is a wonder to me that you have not heard of me even here in the shining halls of Asgard. In the world of men, I am as feared in battle as you are. So I came to Asgard seeking undefeatable opponents. I crave a warrior's death that I might find welcome in the All Father's hall."

I nodded toward the corpses that lay so near us. Thor's glower twitched from me to the piles of meat that had once been his children.

I sneered at him. "My first adversaries were...less than able."

His mouth set itself firmer, his brows knit tighter, and the storm somehow managed to increase in intensity. Thor stepped from the back of his cart, taking several steps away from it. He considered me with smoldering black eyes while casually flipping Mjölner in one hand. He snapped his wrist when he tossed the hammer, spinning it so quickly I could barely make it out as anything but a blur. The rain spun from it in a pinwheel of droplets. He threw it up one last time, then snatched it from the air rather than let it land in his palm. He raised the hammer and pointed it at me.

"You know of the weapon I hold? You know the power of Mjölner?"

I nodded.

"Then you know that it cannot miss. It lands where and as hard as I wish before returning to my grasp. Knowing this, you must realize that my first throw missed you on purpose. I wished to warn you of your danger, yet leave you an opportunity to explain yourself. This you have not done."

"I'm sorry, Thunderer, that your sons' ineptness as warriors is not a defense you accept." I said, twisting my sword in my hand to bring the blade to bear.

No muscles twitched on Thor's massive frame. He held the hammer firmly pointed at me, even when forks of lightning struck it.

Luck and nothing else saw that I had readied myself for battle in time, raising my shield up to defend against the taller man. The lightning Thor wordlessly called down left the sky and bombarded me with sound and power, forcing me to my knees. I hunkered down behind Fathersbane, eyes shut tight, the wide circle of the shield covering me like a turtle's shell as bolt after bolt of the white hot onslaught fell on me.

I may have been there for a minute or a thousand years. I knew only the blinding dazzle of white and purple light filling my vision and the deafening boom of its aftermath. My body rattled with each strike as though weathering a physical blow, but though the stench of scorched air filled my nostrils,

I felt no burning pain. I wondered if this was what it felt like to die; overwhelmed but painless.

Then, as suddenly as it had begun, the barrage ended. My body and bones ached, I saw spots, and it felt as though cotton filled my ears. But I still lived.

"WHAT SORCERY IS THIS?" Thor howled loudly enough I heard it even through my muffled ears.

I unfolded myself, mostly unscathed, from behind my shield and looked at Fathersbane with wide, unbelieving eyes. The wrappings with my wolfshead mark had burned away, leaving not even ash. The boss in the center had blackened, leaving it melted and smoking. Yet the dragonscale beneath remained unharmed. With eyes still disbelieving, I looked around me. Where once I had stood amongst a copse of vigorous oak, only charred stumps as high as my knees remained. Once again, the sheer joy of surviving the moment caught me up, and I laughed.

"My dead brother tore this scale from the body of a sea wyrm, Loud One. But I think your forks are no match for a beast whose hide survived your wrath on the stormiest of seas."

Then I rushed him. I ran toward the Lord of Thunder, the hymn to him that I had sung with my men countless times on my lips. Again, my boldness wrong-footed one of the mighty Aesir. Thor froze, a look of shock plastered across his once-angry face. Far too late, he raised his hammer, but I had already closed in on him. I shoved the edge of my shield upward, into his face. I heard a moist crackle that echoed the smashing of my own nose earlier. A small cry of pained anger escaped Thor's lips as he backpedaled away from me.

But this gave me enough room to bring Moon Sliver to bear. I stabbed the long sword toward Thor's midsection. It sparked and slid from his strength-belt, the point burying itself deep in his thigh. His cry became a roar, and I jerked the blade free. I swung it around in a swift, short arc and its edge bit into his left arm, high and near the shoulder. I yanked the blade back again, seeing the pristine white of bone in the gash. I kicked my iron shod foot into the thunder lord's balls as hard as I could. The roar became a long, high squeal of anguish, and the humongous Aesir curled in on himself to protect his manly bits.

The strongest of all Aesir, the most powerful being in all the Nine Worlds save Odin All Father himself, crouched before me mewling like a kitten. Hot blood flowed freely from leg and arm, thicker than any man or beast's battle-dew I had ever spilled. Globs of it dripped and fell on the ground, hissing where it landed. Mad with bloodlust, my vision swimming with red rage of battle, I raised my sword high over my head, ready to deal the deathblow. A small part of my mind screamed at the impossibility, that I could not kill the mighty Thor. I hesitated. And, in that moment of delay, Thor struck.

He swung Mjölner, and the muscles of his uninjured arm rolled over one another like endless waves. The hammer blazed an arc as long as Thor's right arm. I threw myself to the side to escape it but only partially succeeded. The glancing blow of Mjölner hit harder than the pounding surf, and it threw me high up into the air. I crashed into branch after branch as I soared upward, the limbs pounding my body black and blue. But the branches slowed my ascent, else I may have simply flown high enough to fall from the branches of the World Tree and into an endless, starry abyss.

I came to rest finally high up in the boughs of an especially tall, strong oak. I had dropped my sword and shield somewhere in the flight and now hung weaponless. My breathing grew tight and sharp in my chest, probably because Mjölner or one of the branches had cracked some of my ribs. Some part of my mind questioned how I'd survived, but it was a small voice easily drowned out by the screaming call to kill my foe.

I looked down from the dizzying height and saw Thor, tiny at this distance, no larger than a child's doll. Even so, I could see his shoulders heave with anger, his upturned face crumpled and contorted into a grimace. He favored his wounded leg and blood still gushed from his arm. The hand that held Mjölner shook with fury and gripped the hammer until its gauntlet creaked.

I cupped my hands and called down to him, "If you concede the fight to me now, Thor, then I'll let you live. What say you?"

The Loud One roared in anger at my disrespect, re-earning that epitaph with each new crescendo of caterwauling. He brought his burly arm back as far as it would go, cocking the hammer. He paused, and the world went still. Then he let it loose, and the hammer screamed toward me like an eagle in flight. It scraped against the wind itself, glowing with the heat of it. My mortal eyes could scarcely track its movement, and the hammer hit me full in the chest while I still marveled at the weapon's golden glow.

The hammer struck my elven mail with a tone like a bell. My ribs lit up anew with furious pain; I curled around the hammer instinctively. For the second time in as many minutes, I found myself hurtling through the air. Thor had thrown the hammer so hard, and I flew so high I had time to wonder at the puzzle of my own survival.

Could even elven mail turn aside the blow of the Thunder Lord? Such thoughts seemed madness, and yet here I lay, broken but not killed despite two blows from the greatest killer of giants the Nine Worlds knew.

The hammer, with my body still curled around it painfully, slowed and reached the apex of its flight. It wobbled in the thin, cold air I tried vainly to suck into searing, bruised lungs. Then the weapon fell back toward the ground, and me with it. At this height, I surveyed the whole of Thor's realm and, as we fell, Mjölner and I, I saw my shield where I had dropped it. The dark-green, almost black, scale stood out against the pale ground. It reminded me of more than just a previous victory.

Understanding hit me like one of Thor's own lightning bolts.

Dragon's blood.

I had bathed in dragon's blood and who knew what other effluvia when I had escaped from the belly of a wyrm. Miraculously, I had come out of that ordeal with only minor wounds to show for the trip through its guts. I had been fully clothed and armored in otherworldly mail, so the bath could not have been complete. Perhaps I swallowed some of the beast's vein-water while in a berserker rage. Maybe I even chewed on its entrails as I passed through them. I had no memory of it, but something about the wyrm's life-juices had rendered me unkillable. I was not indestructible, I could be hurt and badly. But maybe, just maybe, I would not die.

I squinted into the rushing wind. The draft peeled my lips back from my teeth, but I would have smiled anyway. I'd come to Asgard looking for death only to find that I could not be killed. And I'd prove it, to myself and all the Nine Worlds, by killing Thor.

Thor grew large in my vision, and his eyes went wide with panic when he realized I flew straight for him. He turned to run, but Mjölner's magic aligned us to his new trajectory. We, Mjölner and I, barreled into Thor's back with bone-crunching force. He fell beneath me, and the three of us skidded across the ground, ploughing a deep furrow.

One of the oaks' knot of roots caught us as we dug deeper into the ground, and we both howled in pain as the thick roots jerked us to a sudden standstill. I lay there, panting, my bones all burning in my body like molten lead. Every inch of me had filled with searing pain, but I forced myself to my feet on leg bones that snapped like brittle sticks. They refused to support me, dumping me back to the ground. I lay in the mud, listening to horrible scraping, scratching, and cracking sounds. A flare of panic raced through my mind when I understood these to be the tortured noises of my broken, twisted body.

I realized that my vision had fallen half dark. I whipped my head around on a wobbling neck wondering why and felt the reason dangling on my cheek. One of my eyes had fallen from the socket and now hung only by gristle. I went to scream in terror and found my throat so mangled I could only hiss air through it.

Thor looked in barely better shape, yet he forced himself to stand, having better luck maintaining balance on limbs disfigured from injury. I looked in horror at his body, bending and twisting itself back into shape, then back to my own as it writhed to put itself aright. He reached out a mangled hand to Mjölner. The hammer twitched once then flew to his grip. His fingers closed on the haft, but the hammer immediately fell back into the mud at his feet with a filthy splash. Apparently his hands lingered in too much ruin for weapon handling. We looked at one another, murderous hate in our eyes but with bodies too broken to do anything about it. We had reached a stalemate, each too wrecked to finish the other.

I felt odd things happening to my body. Hurts that had been pure agony only moments before had lessened. I glanced down at my frame and heard wet snaps and pops as bits of my maimed members fixed themselves. Thor's fearful glare changed to a look of the same sort of confused interest I might have worn had I stumbled on a five-legged calf.

"No mortal can survive these traumas," Thor said, his voice thick with confusion. "Though such healing is the birthright of the Aesir, you are not one of us." He kept on with his odd, unblinking stare.

I noticed the forge-heat of my ruined body slowly tamping down to a mere hearth-warmth as things set themselves aright. I tried to stand again, and found myself able to stay upright on shaking legs. I felt a tug in my empty socket and a tickle on my cheek before the other half of my sight returned. At first it was murky but cleared quickly. For some reason, this brought the light of understanding to Thor's wide, stupid features.

"Sorcery," he said and spat. He reached across his body and wrenched a crooked arm straight with a freshly healed hand. Of course the wounds I'd given him with sword and shield had also closed. "I thought Odin the only warrior willing to learn such an unmanly art. No matter. I am Thor, Lord of Thunder, and no mortal, no matter what dark, womanish powers he calls upon, can best me. When I am able to move, I will crush each of your bones to dust. If they still reknit, I will pitch you into the fires of Múspellsheimr and watch you drift to ash."

I shook my head. "I know no sorcery. Though I am a master practitioner of another art many consider unmanly."

Thor's stolid gaze narrowed. "What art is that?"

"Cheating."

I grabbed a handful of sticky, wet mud and threw it into the thunder god's eyes, eliciting a surprised and annoyed noise in the back of his throat. Thor brought his hands up to rub the gritty slime from his face, but by the time he'd cleaned his eyes, I had already leapt up and charged. I dodged around the side of the hulking Aesir and leapt onto his back. I locked a forearm around his neck, grabbed its wrist with the other hand, and hauled backward.

Thor reacted instantly and violently. Mjölner leapt into his hand even as he spun to shake me loose. He swung the hammer awkwardly over his shoulder. Several blows landed but left me barely bruised. But one blow glanced solidly off my shoulder. The bone gave a sharp crack, and a blaze of pain shot through my arm. Thankfully the broken bone didn't weaken my grasp. I gritted my teeth through the jolt of pain and redoubled my efforts.

"You great, thick lackwit," I hissed in his ear over his grunts and gasps. "You've never seen anything like me; a *man* who can fight, kill, and mend like a god."

Thor wheeled backward, nearly sprinting in reverse, before flinging himself into an oak trunk wide as a small cottage. The tree shuddered, the trunk cracked under the impact, and something snapped in my back. My legs went numb, raising a spike of terror to rear in my mind like a frightened steed. But I took hold of my fear's reins, adding its power to the pressure I poured into Thor's adam's apple. The little lump of gristle trembled, then flattened beneath my choking arm. Pained noises grunted from Thor's ruined throat, and he thrashed all the harder.

His eyes bugged from their sockets. I kept whispering in his ear.

"I'm a new thing, unseen in all the Nine Worlds."

His swollen tongue lolled from his wheezing mouth. I sneered at him and made sure he could hear the disdain in my voice.

"And all *you* can think to do is end me?"

Thor's face grew purplish and blue. He fell to his knees, dropping Mjölner, and grasping my forearm with both thick hands. But lack of air had taken its toll, leaving the grips weak, barely able to break skin with tattered fingernails. I laughed a hoarse, ragged noise in his ear.

"I came to Asgard to die, 'tis true. But now my quest is become a crusade."

With one last spasm of strength, Thor heaved himself backward to land on top of me. My skull struck a stone, throwing stars across my eyes. But the move was desperate, weak. Still I clung to him, choking the last of his immortal life from his lungs.

"A crusade against the Aesir that starts with you, Thunderer."

The storm had stopped sometime during our struggle. Only the squelching of our bodies in the mud and the wispy, choking gasps of a dying god broke the quiet of the forest.

"Go to whatever fickle fate awaits foolish, cruel gods. Your father will meet you there soon."

Thor's empty chest heaved once...twice...a third time, then his body shook with a death rattle. I laid there, maintaining the pressure on his windpipe until my spine mended itself and feeling returned to my legs. I rolled the Thunder Lord's corpse from atop me and stood shakily to my feet.

I looked down on the blue, distended face that had been one of the most powerful beings in the Nine Worlds. His eyes jutted from their sockets. Foam and spittle flecked his lips and beard. In death, I found the Aesir looked just like every man or beast I'd ever killed. Ruined. Ended. Ugly. I found it...enlightening.

"Thank you, Thor, for showing me the way."

18. Omens and Portents

The aftermath of my battle with Thor was grisly, even for me. But my honorific had always been true. I reaved the myths I killed, plundering them for secrets, for trophies, or for weapons. Often for all three at once. The spoils of a battle with the thunder god would be the greatest spoils of a nearly lifelong campaign. I would have everything Thor's carcass had to give.

I stripped Thor's gauntlets and belt from the body quickly to avoid dealing with a stiff and bloated corpse later. Rumor said the iron gauntlets had been enchanted for handling Mjölner while the wide belt of dwarven make reportedly doubled Thor's considerable strength. Both items fairly hummed with power, but I set them aside near where Mjölner rested in the mud. I had other lost treasures in this forest. Perhaps they lacked the potency of this new trove, but they were mine and precious to me. I had to find my own lost weapons.

Working outward from the charred clearing created by Thor's initial onslaught of lightning, I circled an ever-widening area. After an hour, I began to despair. After another half hour, I found my helm. I picked it up and set it on my head, muck and all. It was no filthier than my hair.

I found Fathersbane after another couple hours of searching. When I had made the rest of that circuit, I found Moon Sliver nearly opposite where I'd found my shield. It lay half buried in the mud, its hilt barely visible. Replacing it in its weatherbeaten scabbard gave me a feeling of peace I hadn't realized I'd been missing.

This small satisfaction was my only comfort. Otherwise I felt hollow in both mind and belly. More to the point, I didn't know what I could do about either. Rest would not come soon nor easily with my horses and gear gone missing when Thor's idiot sons accosted me.

I returned to the battlefield. Much of the charred clearing still smoldered an angry orange, so I found it easily even in the gloom of coming night. Though useless for lighting the area, the constantly shifting dim light of so many stumps shined like a beacon.

Thor's two goats stood there, still hitched to their cart and knee deep in dirty sludge. They remained ill tempered in the way unsure animals always are. They eyed me angrily as though they knew I had done something horrible to their master. Could I handle the beasts or the cart? I didn't even feel like getting near enough to unhitch the animals from their harness. But I considered the alarm the beasts might raise if they returned without Thor, and I hesitated. My stomach growled loudly. I shrugged to myself, deciding that walking wouldn't kill me but starvation certainly would.

I slaughtered and skinned the goats, stoked one of the smoldering stumps to a full fire, and roasted them within it. While the meat cooked, I removed my soaking clothing and armor, setting them beside the bonfire to dry. Perhaps I should have been concerned who would see the fire and come investigating, but I was weary of limb and wet and hungry.

Once warmed by the fire, I devoured the meat of both goats. I filled my belly, and my eyes became heavy and drowsy. I quickly fell asleep on the ground, wrapped only in my wolfskin cloak and with a rock for a pillow.

I dreamt of Valhalla, as I had many times before. I was surrounded by glorious warriors, doughty and stalwart raven feeders all. The love and camaraderie of the valiant was, to me, like a blanket wrapped warm about a babe. Beautiful Valkyries served mead to everyone in the hall so that I didn't notice when a particularly young and beautiful shieldmaiden leaned next to me to refill my horn.

"This dream is no longer for you, Finn who is called the Myth Reaver," she whispered in my ear. Her warm breath and husky voice sent a shiver all through me. I closed my eyes. "This is a dream for mere men. But you are something new. Or had you already forgotten?"

She bit my earlobe hard, and my eyes flew open. No longer did I sit in the golden halls of the All Father. Instead, I stood in a shadowy glen, dappled by sunlight at play as though through a thick copse of leaves. A gentle breeze blew across me, but I heard no leaves rustle. I looked up and saw not thick boughs of ancient trees, but the massive foundation of *one* tree. I sat at the root of the very world, the root of Yggdrasill.

At the center of this glen, a well stood surrounded by blinding white clay. Near the well sat three women. The maiden I had thought a Valkyrie tended a loom, creating endless spindles of threads in all colors. Many of the hues I saw bore names I knew, but many more confounded me. A straight-backed matron pulled thread from the endless spools for weaving together into a vast tapestry. An old crone sat at a spinning whetstone, sharpening her silvery shears. When the matron came to the end of a thread's usefulness, although how she knew, I could not see, she held it out to the old woman. The hag would cackle through her toothless maw, remove the scissors from the stone, and snip off the thread.

My blood ran cold. These were the Three, the chiefs of the Norns who decided the fates of men. I knew in my terror that I had left my dreams. My sleeping mind glimpsed into the deepest reality.

"Or we have stolen you here," the crone said in her reedy voice.

It took me a moment to realize she'd answered my unspoken thoughts. I fell to trembling knees in horror.

"Worry not," the matron said. "You are a chosen and beloved instrument of ours, honed by the wyrd we created until you are sharp as the edge of our shears."

The maiden said nothing, though she did look at me and smile. Her smile spoke of intimate invitations. It put some steel back in me.

I cleared my throat. I asked, "An instrument for what? Am I, like your shears, merely meant to snip lives short?"

"Yes," the crone said, and her cackle rang out like a cock at morning.

"And no," the matron added.

At last the maiden spoke, and every word held a warm promise. "We honed you as a weapon, 'tis sooth. But a special weapon the likes of which the world has not known. You are a weapon to end the world."

I stewed in ultimate confusion, but I remained quiet. I hadn't even the wisdom to know what questions to ask.

The matron gave me a small, proud smile. "Good. It is good you know what it is you cannot know. You are a reaver and a bloody-handed man, but you are also more than these things. We *needed* you to be more than these things if you were to accomplish the wyrd we set out before you."

"What do you mean 'if' I accomplish it? Is my fate not known to you?"

The old woman chuckled. "A good question, a very good question. You chose well with this one, Urðr. Should he choose, he will be perfect for our intentions."

I looked to the maiden, Urðr, my eyes full of questions. Her cheeks colored, and she looked at me from behind her long hair so blond as to be nearly the white of fresh snow.

"Just as we chose you, so you must choose us, Finn. You are unique among mortals for we have laid out two wyrds for you."

My courage seeped back into me and I stood up. "What are they, then, that I might choose?"

"This we cannot say plainly," the matron said. "It is not for you to know more than the vague shape of things to come."

"You must either choose to end yourself, sweet Finn," Urðr breathed.

"Or to end *all things*!" the crone said, and cackled longer and louder than she had yet.

"If I choose only my own end, will I at least have glory?" I asked.

"You will not," the matron answered, her face creased with sadness. "That road does not end in glorious victory for the Myth Reaver."

"But I will have glory if I am the end of all things, then?"

"Yes," the matron said firmly.

"And no," Urðr said, a small frown creasing her forehead. "It *is* glory, the greatest kind of glory. But it is not the glory you sought all the years of your earthly life."

I glowered. "So you have brought me to a crossroads of your choosing, though neither path leads to my happiness."

The crone grew serious for the first time. She raised an admonishing finger. "Such is the way of wyrd. And so it has been in the Nine Worlds for all time. You are special among men, Finn Mythreaver, but not *that* special."

I contemplated this. The hag spoke truth, of course. Northmen never saw happiness as a true goal. We sought satisfaction: satisfaction in war, glory, or purpose. I now knew one question I had to ask.

"You three chose me and set me on the path that led to this tipping point. But did you manipulate all others in the Nine Worlds to bring me here?"

"Yes," the crone said, nodding.

"And no," Urðr said, shaking her head. "We spin the threads of life for every man, elf, giant, and god, and cut them as well. But Verðandi weaves them only where *they* will."

The matron, Verðandi, spoke. "I know your heart and what you seek though you know not the words. You wonder if, by weaving, we create the choices others make. I say to you, though we know you all better than you know yourselves, and therefore often know what you will do before you know it, we never force a hand." She looked me straight in the eye. "All choices in a life, all rules enforced or broken, are your own. This is true from the lowliest collared thrall all the way to Odin All Father himself. This is why we brought you here. To return to you the choice taken from you by those more powerful."

I understood everything then. This way could I have my revenge on the fickle, unjust All Father, even though it would burn the world down. I made my choice with ease.

"I will end all things, Sisters Three. I choose it for glory of whatever stripe. I choose it for satisfaction."

Though we four never moved, I found myself with the Norns in another place. I looked down to see my clothing splattered and dripping red with thick, hot blood. In one of my red hands, I held Mjölner. In the other, I held Moon Sliver. The sounds of battle intruded on my reverie, and I cast about to see Asgard under siege. Valhalla lay in ruins, razed and smoking. Fires licking across every golden roof of the Shining City tinted the sky a terrible crimson. Thick black smoke filled the air and choked the murders of ravens that crisscrossed the city pecking soft meat from the faces of dead gods. Somehow I would be responsible for all of this. Inwardly, I celebrated.

I smiled at the Norns, a smile of *satisfaction*. Verðandi and the hag smiled back at me, but sweet, lovely Urðr looked sad. She rose and crossed to me, then raised her hand to my face.

"Finn, you must know that you will be an agent of destruction. You will destroy all those you hate, all those who betrayed you, even your most detestable foe whom you've never met. All this will happen, but you must not despair when it fails to happen exactly as you wish it."

She leaned in to kiss me, but just as her soft lips brushed mine, I awoke with a start.

I lay there, blinking into the dawn sun rising over a land of gods. The dream had felt so true, but the harsh light of day chased it from my mind and left only wavering doubts. I shook myself. In the end, it mattered not. My crusade would be the same, had to be the same. Killing Thor had opened my eyes to new possibilities. Odin, despoiler of the afterlife, giver of capricious and cruel laws, ruled as a tyrant who needed knocking from his throne. The rest of the Aesir could help me or die beside him.

I was the Myth Reaver. But now I was also become Ragnarök, the twilight sun setting on the rule of Odin All Father.

Though I believed it, I could not make it happen with a foolhardy directness. I walked alone, only one man. An extraordinary man to be sure, the first of a new breed of superior being that would supplant the weak and stupid Aesir at the top of the Nine Worlds. But today, now, I fought alone. I could not lay siege to Asgard single-handed.

So I resolved to strike straight for the head. Cutting it off would lay the rest of the beast low. Grímarr had driven this lesson home to me. But first I'd have to slip past the beast's defenses unnoticed so as to strike once and cleanly.

I looked at the scattered bones and flaps of bleeding skin. The sight twisted my face into a grimace. I had been hungry...hungry and foolish. But unbidden, I recalled an old story, a tale of Thor and his servants. All was not lost if the stories held true. And if I now had access to Thor's power.

Again, I would have to cheat.

First I worked at the drudgery of filling the goat skins with bones. Thankfully I had been too tired to do much else than drop the bones where I sat. I'd even created two somewhat distinct piles corresponding to each goat. They were not entirely separate and sifting the greasy mess to make sure each pile had only one of each tiny bone left me disgusted. I vowed that, should this work, I would be more careful in the future.

I went to the small pile of gear I hadn't had the strength or will to deal with when I returned from my search the previous night. I glanced at the bloated carrion that had once been a thunder god, but it only confirmed what I already knew: the Aesir could die just like anything else. And I could kill them. I picked up the belt first, but with care. I'd never heard of anyone other than Thor wearing the belt. Would I even be able to? Would it strike me dead? There was only one way to know for sure.

I gingerly strapped the armored belt around my middle. The hum of power I'd noticed the previous night made my fingers vibrate lightly. I set the buckle in a notch and cinched the belt tightly around my middle. Instantly the hum of power moved from the belt into my very bone and sinew. I had always been strong, strong like no man before me. But this belt made me feel as though I could knock down mountains with the edge of my hand. I looked at my arms and fists, expecting to find them rippling with new muscle. I still appeared as I always had, though I felt more solid, more...real.

Anxious to test my strength and enjoy the greatest fruit of my labor, I grasped the haft of Mjölner with a bare hand. I lifted the heavy hammer with ease, but as soon as I held it aloft, lightning struck from a clear blue sky, landing directly on the hammer's head. The lighting surprised me, but worse, the now-red-hot hammer seared my palm. I dropped it in shock and pain. The weapon landed on the still moist ground, sinking deep into the loam with a hiss of steam.

My palm glowed an angry red all around a great cleft in my hand where the haft had directly touched me. If I flexed my fingers, I heard the crackle of burnt flesh and saw small white bones rolling over one another through the rent in my skin. Even as I watched, though, the restorative powers of the wyrm's blood took hold. The crimson flesh quickly turned back to white while the sinews and gristle of my palm worked to knit the wound's edges back together. In mere minutes, what would have been a crippling injury had healed to nothing more than a bright pink scar. Even that blemish lightened before my eyes.

Once my hand had healed, I lifted the iron gloves. They had been cumbersome due to weight the night before, even with my tremendous strength. Now, thanks to the belt of power, they felt light and supple as leather riding gloves. I tugged them on and once again grasped the haft of the hammer. Just as before, lightning struck the head when I raised the weapon. The hammer glowed from the instant heat, but my gauntleted hand remained impervious to scorching harm.

I turned to the goat skins stuffed with bones. I stood over them, literally crackling with power. I stared at them, wondering what to do. Had Thor a magic word? An incantation? Did he wave Mjölner over the hides in a ritualistic way?

I felt stupid, and that made me angry. As my ire grew, forks of lightning flitted out of the sky and struck around me. I gave my rage voice and screamed at the hides. "Baldur's hanging balls, you stupid goats! LIVE!"

A massive bolt of lightning struck each of the hides, leaving two large, mean-spirited goats in their place. The goats looked at me, blew steam from their nostrils, then came over and nuzzled me affectionately.

I petted their heads, then grabbed their horns in gauntleted fists and wrestled them around. "Did you forget I slaughtered and roasted you just last night? Or do you think I'm Thor? Either way you must be as stupid as your former master."

The renewed goats frisked and bleated at me, nibbling at my fingers. Thus did I discover another reason for Thor's mighty gauntlets. It felt nice, having someone to talk to again. Even if they were merely goats.

"So, how do I enact my plan? I have power like Thor's and most of Thor's clothing. Few of the Aesir would think to question me, I think, should I go traveling. In this guise, I should be able to get to the city of Asgard. Perhaps I might even gain all the way to Odin's side before he realizes I am not his son." I patted the goats' sides fondly. "But I am a stranger to these lands and know not how to reach Asgard."

Both goats licked me and bleated loudly. I stared down at their upturned heads, into eyes that met my own.

"Do you two know the way to Asgard?"

Both of them licked and nipped, then grunted excitedly.

"You are slightly smarter than your one time master. Well then, goats, I will hitch you to the cart and allow you to hie me to Asgard. It is past time for the All Father to meet the Myth Reaver...and his doom."

19. An Unexpected Ally

I wrestled the goats back into the cart's harnesses and bridles. This act seemed to bring back their cantankerous, ill tempers. They snapped at my hand so hard I had to clout their heads to settle them down. I bound Moon Sliver's scabbard onto the belt of power and lashed Fathersbane to the interior of the cart. My pale hair and beard did not match Thor's bright red, so I wore my helm in hopes it would hide my identity long enough to get into the city. Once readied, I stepped into the cart, took the reins, and slapped them against the goats' rangy hides.

"To Asgard," I roared. The goats took off like a bowshot.

The cart rolled along so quickly, the landscape blurred past me. Soon what seemed like neverending oak forests and steel gray sky gave way to rolling, green grasses and a sky such a startling, clear, crystalline blue as to take your breath away. The warm breeze, the subtle, pleasant scents, and over-all beauty of Asgard recalled to mind the Álfheimr, only without the sinister deepening of shadows beneath the lovely surface. In the distance, the mist-shrouded, rainbow-crowned city of Asgard grew ever larger. Even at such tremendous speeds, the wonderful countryside enraptured me. So swept up was I that when an old man stepped in front of the cart, I nearly ran him down.

I heaved back on the reins as hard as I could, yelling "WHOAH, WHOAH!" at the top of my lungs. The goats reared on hind legs and bleat-ed shrilly, but the cart rattled to a skidding stop with only inches between their muzzles and the old man.

"Lend an old man a hand," the cloaked figure croaked, extending a scarred stump from beneath his robes.

"Be ye gone, codger," I said in my most imperious voice. "You block the way of the mighty Thor."

"I most certainly do not. I block the way of Finn Styrrsson, also called the Myth Reaver," the man mocked. The teasing voice was eerily familiar. With his stump, he pushed back his cowl to display not the lined, craggy face of an old man, but instead the fair features of an Aesir. "I told you to make a better name for yourself, boy, and Myth Reaver was a good start."

Just as he had all those years ago in the forest where I'd killed the Fenrir pup, the indomitable Tyr addressed me. His crooked grin still mocked and his presence still commanded respect and fear. But the furtive glance he threw over his shoulder at the shining city still some way in the distance surprised me so. I might as well have expected a dragon to sneak on tiptoe. Turning back to me, he glared up into my face, and all was once again aright in the Nine Worlds.

"Now get out of that cart and send it on its way before you draw more attention to yourself than you can manage."

"Lord Tyr, I am honored by your presence. But how did you know I would come this way? And whom do you seek to confound with your disguise?"

I knew I frittered away time with foolish questions, but the shock of standing again face to face with the same Aesir I'd met so briefly and so long ago addled my wits.

"Later," he rasped. "When you are no longer screaming at the All Father how badly you want to die."

The import of his words finally sank home, and I snatched up my shield before leaping from the cart. I looked at the goats, then at Tyr, a question in my eyes.

Tyr gestured dismissively at the animals. "Just send them away. They know the way home, and the farther they are from us right now, the better."

I turned to the goats and patted their horned heads, a forlorn spirit upon me. Whether from enchantment or confusion, they had loved me. And it had been nice to have friends again. I frowned at them as they looked up at me with their wide, brown eyes.

Tyr looked backward to the city again. He put his hand on my shoulder. "We dare not dally further, Finn."

I nodded, never taking my eyes from the goats. "Return home with all speed. Go!"

The goats, with a final nuzzle, turned the cart and sped back the way we'd come.

Tyr nodded, his face serious. "Good, now let us hasten to cover. We have much to discuss."

He grabbed my arm and led me off the road into the sweet smelling forest of pine stretching for an infinite distance to both sides of the road. He guided me with sureness, though I could discern no path or markers. After several minutes we burst into a clearing where a small soldier's camp had been set up. A little fire crackled near the center, giving off meager puffs of smoke. A bubbling pot hung above the flame.

Tyr whipped off his cloak and tossed it near the tent. He shook out the mane of chestnut hair on his head and stood in the sun dressed in fine, glittering mail with a short, wide blade at his belt. He did not appear as physically imposing as Thor had, nor did he radiate the same kind of anger and power. But he gave off the same air of infinite, deadly competency he had all those years ago in another forest in another world. It seemed as though nothing could faze him or dent his courage. Thor had been a berserker, deadly in his madness. But Tyr exemplified the soldier born, dangerous in his precision.

He waved a hand toward the fire. "Sit, eat. We have much to discuss and little time in which to do it."

I had come to kill as many Aesir as I could, and yet something about Tyr's manner bespoke an offer of friendship. He looked on me with some affection, albeit the kind of affection a man might have for his favorite hunting dog, and I thought back to our first meeting. He'd promised he'd have an eye on me, though I wondered if that was for good or ill. I decided I'd never know unless I took the time to find out, so I dished some stew from the pot into a small tin bowl and sat.

"Surely you realized I'm not the boy you met before," I said to him.

He shrugged. "What of it?"

"I'm waiting for you to tell me why I shouldn't gut you like a fish right here, Tyr."

Seemingly unconcerned by my threat, Tyr sat down on the opposite side of the fire. He took a small tin bowl of the stew for himself. He balanced the bowl on his stump and scooped out a spoonful. He blew to cool it, then put the bite in his mouth. He chewed a moment, his eyes closed and a smile on his face.

"Mmmmm," he said after he'd swallowed. He opened his eyes to look into my own. "I miss food cooked over a fire in camp, shared with a comrade. There is something special in the good, solid fare of the soldier."

Now that he had eaten food from the same pot as my own share, I took a bite and chewed my food silently. He chuckled at me and took another bite. After swallowing, he said, "You don't trust me, eh?"

"I do not," I confirmed. "It seems everyone I meet since I left Midgard wishes me dead. Now that I come to kill Odin myself, I expect that trend to continue."

He laughed and slapped his leg. "Yes! That's what I've always loved about you, Finn, lo these many years I've watched. That willingness to see a job through. Your word is your deed and no sense in hedging."

Again, I wasn't sure what to make of this, so I used the excuse of chewing another bite of stew to keep my peace.

Tyr nodded at me with approval. "First, your questions at the road. I disguised myself that I might avoid bringing yet more attention upon a pretender to Thor's name traveling on the road to Asgard. I feared that Odin might see us from his high seat, so I stole a page from his book and went about as a berobed old man."

"It seems foolish to use a ploy invented by the one from whom you hide. Especially one as crafty as Odin," I said.

Tyr gave me an appraising look. "Odin is clever, but the problem with crafty people is that they often assume everyone else is very stupid. Loki taught me that, just before he tricked a blind man into killing everyone's favorite Aesir and got strung up in Hel for the trouble." He shook his head ruefully. "Truly, it's a fool who cannot heed his own advice."

"So that is how you came to be in disguise on the road waiting for a counterfeit Thunderer. But how came you to be there looking for *me*?"

Tyr threw his arms out wide. "'I'm the god of glory, Finn! The god of *heroes*. I take an interest in any living hero of whom men speak as though they are already legend. Does that sound like anyone at this fire?" He laughed again, the smile crinkling the skin around his clear, honey green eyes. "And I have taken a very special interest in you since you killed that whelp of Fenrir." He held up his stump. "That victory I could certainly celebrate with you, but I've cheered you on at the others as well."

I stared at him, searching him for duplicity. But what he said felt true; the words rang with sincerity. But he hadn't answered everything.

"But you seem to know of the red-handed deed I plan in Asgard. Why protect me from Odin?"

Tyr's clear, glad features turned dark before my eyes. He threw his bowl aside with his stump and squeezed the spoon in his good hand until I heard the metal creak. His voice held rage barely contained, a seething thing full of venom.

"Because you are a hero, the greatest in an age, and are mine to protect. Because I would not see your bright flame snuffed out rashly. And, foremost, because the considerable pride I take in you and your deeds is as nothing compared to the hatred I feel for that pompous, one-eyed bastard. Did I not warn you when first we crossed paths that you would grow to find him a cruel master?"

I nodded.

"Then I would deny him the satisfaction of killing a mere man so willing to defy him."

As genuine as had been his mirth, so now was his fury. Yet still I questioned.

"Why?"

Tyr closed his eyes, took several breaths, and when next he spoke, he did so only in reasoned tones. "Because he's not content to be god of wisdom, magic, poetry, the hunt, and a hundred other things including death. He also has to be god of war, battle, and victory. Because Odin stole my fame. Because he lets his loutish sons stomp around the place ruining everything, especially that glory hound, Thor. Because when Fenrir needed chaining, none other had the courage to do what had to be done, yet I had to prove my loyalty with the loss of a hand. Because he is Odin, father of hypocrisy and giver of capricious laws. Is that not enough? Is that not why you hate him?"

"Aye, Odin fans the same flame within us. But what can we do about it out here?"

Tyr snorted. "What did you plan on doing about it, pretending to be Thor and poorly?"

"I planned on pretending to be Thor until I reached Odin's hall. Then I will attack him and kill him."

Tyr looked at me dumbfounded. "Forget for a moment that everyone in Asgard knows Thor by sight and that you do not greatly resemble the brute.

What, pray, would you have done if the real Thor had appeared? Stealing his goats would slow him, but not stop him."

I shrugged. "The real Thor could not have given me away."

"And why is that?"

"Because he and his two fool sons lie in his lands feeding worms. Put there by my own hands."

Tyr's amused shock became full stupefaction. "You have killed the Thunderer? The belt and gloves you wear are not counterfeits made for your ridiculous disguise?"

"They are genuine, removed from his moldering corpse last night."

Tyr's gaze drifted away from me. "Ymir's massive skull." He didn't speak again for a minute then looked back to me suddenly. "You really believe you can do it, don't you?"

I nodded grimly. "I admit, I came to Asgard originally seeking one who would face me in battle and best me. None in Midgard would lift arms against me, and none in Álfheimr neared my battle prowess. Here in Asgard alone would I find someone to kill me with sword in hand that I might be taken into Valhalla. Or so I thought. Instead of the breezes I found in Man and Elf Home, I found only stiff winds. But they are winds I still mastered."

Tyr considered this, his stupor vanishing into calculation. Slowly he nodded at me. "I sought to save one who would be like a foolish child armed with a wooden sword for a fight with a bull. But now I believe fate is with you. You may yet have a chance to kill even the All Father. I would very much like to help you do it."

We looked into each other's eyes and into one another's minds, each taking the other's measure. I saw something unexpected in Tyr. I saw hope. And it would feel good to fight with someone by my side again, as I had with Dalk, Hallbjorn, and the others. Two would succeed where one might have failed.

"Then we are joined in this bloody deed? We two, stalwart Tyr and the Myth Reaver?" I asked.

"Aye, and you'll be thankful for my wisdom and strategy. There is a worm in the apple of your plans to slay the All Father."

I quirked an eyebrow. "Is there?"

Tyr considered me then spoke. "You would kill the most powerful being in the Nine Worlds in his capital city with...what? Without the tools to do the job properly, you have an orchard's worth of vermin in a single piece of fruit."

I chuckled but waved his protestations away. "It's true that despite hunting and destroying many beings and beasts more powerful than myself, you Aesir are a special problem. You're so hardy I find you nigh unkillable!"

Light dawned in Tyr's eyes and he said, "The constitution of an Aesir is truly a miraculous thing. But you said 'nigh unkillable.' I do not mean to belittle your efforts because Thor had tricks and power enough for a hundred thousand men. Even so, all-knowing Odin is another catch of fish altogether."

I nodded. "I need but one clean attack on the All Father. Should we receive such an opportunity, I will ensure it carries the proper potency."

Tyr slapped his thigh and smiled. "I know not of what you plan, Myth Reaver, but I trust you have something up your sleeve. Still, I'm never one to put all my eggs in a single basket."

He reached beneath his cloak and pulled forth a dagger. As the blade left its sheath, I watched a tiny drop of yellowish liquid drip from the point. The drop hit the ground and sizzled. In moments, a span of grass surrounding the drop's resting place turned yellow and died. Tyr sheathed the dagger and put it away.

"Poison rendered from the venom of the dread serpent that torments Loki in Hel e'en now. On the flesh of even an Aesir, it is unyielding in the pain it gives. In the veins..." Tyr shrugged. "We can only hope it's enough."

"Should my own strategies come to naught, we will have the chance to find out. You know the city, you know the All Father's habits, and you have a weapon designed for his demise. I ask no questions of your motives, god of heroes. Instead, I ask only one boon."

"Name it," Tyr said.

"When the light leaves the All Father's single eye, I wish to be close enough to see it gutter and die out."

Tyr's smile bared his teeth, like a death rictus. The warrior's smile. "Done."

We commenced to plan.

~

We walked the busy streets of shining Asgard. I nervously expected a guard to shout at us and demand an explanation as to why a mortal man wandered his city. Tyr put a calming hand upon my shoulder.

"Relax, Finn," he said to me quietly. "Most in Asgard are far too self-involved to notice you are mortal, let alone to care. Just keep your cloak pulled tight around you to hide Thor's...gifts, and we should be fine."

"But what of the All Father," I asked, just as quietly. "Does he not see all?"

Tyr chuckled. "One who trades an eye for wisdom is decidedly unable to see all. But worry not, for I ensured Odin's presence at his hall, Valaskjálf , before smuggling you into the city."

I looked at Tyr aghast. "Is that not the hall where he built Hlidskjalf, his High Seat from whence he can see all of the Nine Worlds? *This* is when you choose to smuggle in his assassin?"

Tyr's grip tightened on my shoulder and he maneuvered me into a short alley between two buildings. Once in the shadow, he grew serious.

"I would not speak such things out loud anymore, if I were you. I'm in this to the end, but I won't have some urchin passerby overhearing us plot the death of the Aesir's Battle Chief."

I nodded. "I'm sorry, Tyr. I realize surprise is paramount. Our job will be that much easier if Odin does not know we are coming. But that's why I question the wisdom of moving against him while he sits in his high seat."

"Think on this, Myth Reaver. If you sat in a place from which you could see all of the Nine Worlds, in what area would you be *least* interested?"

I thought a moment, then enlightenment dawned. "The area nearest me."

Tyr winked. "Precisely."

We exited the shadowy alley and rejoined the flow of traffic. At almost the selfsame moment I spotted two tall women in shining armor. They carried shields and spears and wore swords at their hips. Their helmets bore wings swept back from their temples. They looked dangerous, these Valkyries.

"And what of them," I said, inclining my head toward the shieldmaidens. "Will they not stand by the All Father's side?"

"Ah, another reason we should catch Odin at Valaskjálf. The bulk of his Valkyries will be at Valhalla, serving the legions of dead warriors there. Only his most trusted bodyguard will be with him today."

I grimaced. "His most trusted...and most skilled."

Tyr nodded, not looking at me as he navigated the streets. "Aye. But better the peerless handful than boundless peers."

Tyr spoke wisdom I found difficult to argue against.

We made our way through the vast city's center, taking hours to navigate its twisting streets. It was the largest settlement I'd ever seen. The longer we walked, the more I suspected every man, woman, and child I'd ever laid eyes on in Midgard could fit within Asgard's gleaming walls and still leave it sparsely populated.

Everywhere I looked, Aesir wore finery. It seemed they did not want for precious metals worked in fine craftsmanship or rich cloth in which to wrap their frames. And what frames they had, each citizen more beautiful or more handsome than the last. I remarked on this to Tyr. He chuckled.

"Did you know my parents are Jötunn?"

I stopped and stared at the back of Tyr's head. He didn't look back, so he didn't stop, and I fell a bit behind. I had to jog a few steps to catch up.

"I didn't realize. I thought Odin was your father."

Tyr glanced over his shoulder, his mouth turned as though he might spit. "He *honored* me with adoption into the All Father's family after this." He raised up his stump. "Because of my parentage, I felt I had to prove myself among the Aesir. So I volunteered to put my fist into the Fame Wolf's jaws. I did this knowing the Aesir would double-cross the beast and that it would be *me* who was punished for the betrayal." Tyr snorted. "It wasn't as though I had to fight my way to the front of the line. Only I stood brave enough. Or stupid enough. And so Odin 'rewarded' me with sonship."

"You don't look like any giant I've ever seen."

He stopped and turned to face me, an eyebrow cocked. "You mean because I'm not two miles tall with two heads and fangs?" He shook his head. "Do you know the true difference between Aesir and Jötunn, Finn? Jötunn can look beautiful or like monsters, and either visage may hide a noble heart. Aesir can only appear beautiful. And are only ever monsters inside."

Tyr turned and continued on his way. I followed him for a while longer, when I noticed a change in the crowd. Most of Asgard had been jovial and pleasant, as though the entire city celebrated a fair or market day. But the tenor of the crowd changed. I overheard whispers between men with serious faces, and gasps of shock between women. The lighthearted, festive atmosphere took a decidedly sinister turn.

"Tyr…" I started, but he held up a hand, cutting me off.

"Yes, I see it as well," he said, standing next to me and surveying the crowd. A frown creased his forehead as he watched the subtle shift in the throng. "Wait here, I'll see what I can find out."

I lost Tyr in the crush, but I stayed where he'd left me. Foreboding ran up and down my spine and sweat beaded my forehead. I frantically scanned the crowd with flitting eyes for any sign of Tyr's return. I almost felt shame at the relief that flooded me when he reappeared.

"Come along," he said, grabbing my arm. "We need to move faster."

"What's happening?"

"It appears your handiwork has been found in Thor's lands. The lady Sif, concerned for her missing husband and sons, went out looking for them and found only their rotting corpses. Did you not hide them?"

"It didn't occur to me," I murmured.

"No sense in crying over spilled blood," Tyr said, concern written across his face. "Everyone is treating it like a rumor right now. But rumors like the murder of Thor cause turmoil, even if the populace can't bring themselves to believe it yet."

He picked up his pace again, now almost running as he dodged us through the crowd. The darkening mood of the throng now mirrored our own until, finally, Tyr pulled me up short.

"We're here."

I looked up at Valaskjálf. The colossal hall sat on a sheer cliff face that jutted upward from the city's center. The hall's high, proud walls reached toward the sky, scorning the meager architecture of men. Some white gem made up the walls and they glittered in the sun with a dazzling array of colors. The innumerable silver shingles that covered its vast rooftop from edge to edge gleamed like a gargantuan mirror. Rising from the center of the silvery roof, a tower soared to lofty heights. It rose so high that I felt I might topple over backward trying to look toward its summit. Cloudbanks thankfully obscured its highest reaches and saved me from the shame.

Tyr slapped the back of my head lightly. "No time for gawking. Let's go."

We ascended the thousands of stairs cut directly into the stone of the cliff, winding back and forth until we reached the tall, golden doors. Two Valkyries stood stoic watch at the portal, but Tyr simply acted as though he would walk right past them. One of the Valkyries dropped her spear in front of us. She stood tall and straight, armed to the teeth, and wore shining armor that made her hard to look at for long. What you could see around the helm held fine features, though she had flinty eyes. When she spoke, her voice rang as cold and clear as glacier ice.

"No one summoned you, Tyr. What business have you with the All Father?"

Tyr gave her his most winning smile. "Well met, Hrund. I'm merely on a visit to sate my curiosity. There are ill tidings on the wind and I'd like to hear how they started. I figured Odin knows nearly everything anyway, so I may as well ask him."

Hrund's eyes narrowed. "Ill tidings like the death of Thor?" She snorted. "Ridiculous, of course. It is far too balmy a day for Fimbulwinter, so worrying about Ragnarök seems a bit foolish."

Tyr chuckled. "Aye. That's why I came not to ask the truth of the rumor, but only to see how such a rumor could get its start. Is the All Father too busy to see me?"

Hrund shrugged. "I have no particular instructions that he should be left in seclusion. You may proceed." She nodded toward me. "Who's your friend?"

Tyr kept smiling and slapped me on the back. "This? Just a hero I've had an eye on. Seemed the time for him to visit Asgard."

Hrund considered this, then shook her head. "The All Father will not be seeing your pet man, Tyr. 'Twould be unseemly."

Tyr's smile turned brittle. "I'm very sorry to hear you say that, Hrund."

Faster than the eye could follow, Tyr snapped his stump up and across the battlemaiden's face. She gave a small grunt, but made no other noise as the light went out of her eyes. Tyr caught her as she slumped.

I turned to see the other Valkyrie's eyes go wide, though the surprise didn't stop her from bringing her spear to bear. I caught it as it came down, though, and yanked it from her hands. I curled my free hand into a fist and smashed it into her face. The crunch of bone and meat followed, and the Valkyrie's body snapped backward into the wall head first. I stood there a moment, amazed at the power of my own blow, before shaking myself alert. Thor's belt of power...

I turned to Tyr, who had thrown Hrund over one shoulder and was muscling a hall door open with the other

"Don't just stand there," he snapped. "They can sense when one of their own has fallen. We'll be swarmed in minutes if we don't get inside."

I helped him swing the door open far enough for us to slip through, then I pushed it back as he dropped Hrund into a room. The doors met with a thud, and I bolted them shut.

Tyr let out a ragged sigh. "I'd hoped to avoid that. Now we'll have a platoon of Valkyries to fight. *If* we survive the battle with Odin."

"I'm sorry," I said. "I didn't know. And Thor's belt, I...I forgot my own strength."

But Tyr ignored me. He busied himself by casting about the hall.

"Bar the doors," he ordered. "Use whatever you can lift."

I looked around for the best materials to build a barricade. The interior of the hall was even more spectacular than the outside. Precious metals worked into exquisite filigree or gems carved into intricate designs covered every surface. Passageways spread out from the main hall like a spider's web leading toward uncounted rooms. The staircase that led to Odin's High Seat, the throne from which he could survey the universe, dominated the center of the hall. Arrayed around the staircase in every direction were chairs, benches, and tables nearly filling the main hall.

I ran to the far end of the room, picked up the largest table I could find, held it in front of me like a massive shield, and pushed toward the front doors. With my strength doubled by Thor's belt of power, it was a mean feat to shift several hundred pounds of furnishings in front of the main doors. In minutes, every stick of furniture in the hall had been fashioned into a makeshift barricade.

Tyr watched this with amused shock.

"What?" I asked, suddenly self conscious. "Will that do?"

He barked a laugh. "Oh, it'll do." He held up a hand and cocked his head to the side.

I listened with him and heard several sets of hoofbeats pounding somewhere within the hall. Several somewheres, actually, but converging on us.

"The rest of Odin's Valkyrie bodyguard," Tyr said. He pointed at the massive staircase. "Quickly, we need to be on the move."

We raced to the spiraling staircase and climbed it frantically. Our own stomping steps echoed back to us from pounding hoofbeats drawing nearer and nearer. Our breath came in heaving gasps and my whole world focused on moving each foot in turn, one step higher. Despite this grand effort, the colossal, vaulted ceiling still loomed overhead. The round aperture where hall ended and tower began still lay ahead of us.

"Faster," Tyr panted. "We must reach the safety of the tower."

But it was too late. From different branching halls, Valkyries in full battle tackle burst into the main hall. They rode their steeds low for speed but leveled their spears in front of them for a charging attack. Their tall, muscular stallions' hooves struck the ornate stone floor of the hall, throwing off sparks. Each of them, upon entering the hall, pulled back on the reins, causing the horses to rear and whinny. The Valkyries' swiveling heads hunted for signs of the danger. Finally one of them looked up.

She pointed toward us with her spear tip and shouted, "There!"

As one the shieldmaidens spurred their war horses and burst back into a gallop. I chanced a glance downward as they came near the lowest stair. Rather than gallop up the stairs, the horses raised their front hooves and ran on thin air! The sound of hoofbeats still filled the room, sparks still flew when the hooves *should* have struck something, but they rose, galloping on nothing!

I grabbed Tyr's cloak and pulled him to a stop. "It's too late," I gasped. "We'll have to fight them off."

Tyr looked down at the horsemaidens riding ever-rising circles around the staircase, supported by naught. A frown marred his smooth features. He drew the short sword at his waist, and it rang like crystal.

The angle of the staircase covered us from any attacks from below, but it also kept us from striking downward. Tyr stood, bouncing his sword lightly in his hand. I unhitched Fathersbane from my arm and laid it securely on the stairs. Tyr looked at me in consternation.

"Defense will not win this," I said, but before I could explain further, the first of the Valkyries rode level with us. She'd already drawn her spear back, readied for throwing. I saw the light of recognition gleam in her eyes and, her arm a blur, she let the spear fly.

"LOOK OUT!" I yelled to Tyr. He dropped flat on the stairs without hesitation or backward glance. The spear flashed through where he'd been standing, tearing strands of still fluttering hair from his head, so close did its deadly point come to a killing blow.

The spear flashed toward my heart. I sidestepped, lashing out with my hand, and caught the haft. I spun with the weapon's momentum, cocking the spear backward as I did, and let it fly on exactly the path it had followed to me.

The Valkyrie's eyes went wide behind her helm's face shield, but my throw was too hard, too fast. It hit her full in the chest, sinking halfway up the shaft before the augmented force dragged her from the saddle. She sailed backward across the expanse of the hall until the spearhead protruding from her back embedded itself in a far, stone wall. The vibrating spear extending from the dead warrior woman's chest hummed and smoked.

Tyr rose to his knees, looking over his shoulder at the warrior woman pinned to the distant wall. He looked back at me, and the look sent chills of horror through me. Tyr, a master of immortal wars, looked upon me with the same awestruck gaze I received from mere men. The god of heroes from the sagas looked upon me as though I were a warrior out of legend. It was...unnerving. And yet a part of me recognized it as entirely appropriate that the lords of Asgard should fear me.

The other Valkyries screamed their defiance and swung around to charge us.

"Go," he croaked from a dry throat. He swallowed. "Take a steed and ride for Odin's High Seat while I finish them off."

I nodded once, snatched up my shield, and ran for the edge. I leapt and my amplified leg thews carried me across the vast empty space in an eye blink. I landed solidly behind one of the Valkyries, her stallion lacking even the time to flinch. Before she realized what had happened, I grasped both sides of her helmeted head and twisted it sharply sideways. Her silent, lifeless form slid from the back of the still galloping stallion. I snatched her spear from a now limp hand as she fell. Mastering the reins and digging my heels into the horse's side, I directed the stallion up the stairs.

My steed shot up toward the hole leading from hall to tower, and I entered the towering cylinder at a speed unmatched by even Thor's cart. Over the sound of hoofbeats, I heard the distant noise of battle as Tyr made his stand against the Valkyries. I cast back a wish for luck, though he wouldn't need it. They were Valkyries, but he was *Tyr*. He would be along. I focused my mind on the coming battle.

Soon I would face the All Father.

20. Clash at the Top of the Worlds

The stallion sped up the tower, flashing hooves never touching the stairs. I know not how long I rode through that lofty tower at the top of the Nine Worlds, because the blurring, featureless walls gave no indication of height. I could have ridden for an hour, a day, or a hundred years. At last, in the distance, I saw a pinprick of pure white light. The tiny light grew larger and larger in my vision until it spread into a wide, gaping mouth. We shot through it, and the close, stale air of the tower vanished so howling, frigid winds could slap me in the face.

The horse and I shot up into the air, but I yanked the reins and wheeled my steed around to trot onto the roof of Hlidskjalf, the hall from which Odin could look out over the entire universe. Once his hooves were planted again on solid ground, I dismounted quickly and slapped his flank to spur the beast. As the stallion sped away, I spun to face Odin All Father.

Snow blew and drifted across the broad plateau at the tower's peak. Ancient and dying stars cast a wan light that sparkled on the ice crystals and only dimly illuminated the area. The hole leading down the tower and, eventually, back into the hall lay at one end of the flat space, while at the other squatted a massive throne. Carved of hard, sharp-edged obsidian, the throne had been festooned with gold and jewels enough to make it sparkle. The shape of the throne was difficult to discern at first, but then there came a great grinding noise of stone on stone. The massive chair rotated. Looking full upon the chair's face, I cringed.

The high back of the chair, which towered over the seated figure, was carved into the form of two distinct horses. Though joined to the other like a freak of birth, one of the horses appeared sleek and muscular, powerful and graceful, a perfect example of its kind. The other looked a horrific thing with snakes for a mane, sharp teeth for rending and tearing, and a hundred other monstrous features besides. If one resembled the perfect dream of all things equine, the other illustrated the perfect nightmare. The conjoined trunk of the horror-horse left the statue with eight legs that formed the base of the throne. When the chair turned, the eight legs shifted sinuously in a way that turned my stomach sour.

Upon the throne sat a figure neither imposing nor terrible at first glance. An aging man still stout of frame and powerfully built despite the appearance of advanced years, Odin slouched with unconcerned nudity while the biting winds tugged at him. For his only clothing, he wore a long cloak the blue of deep twilight draped loosely around his torso. Though simple and unadorned, the cloak was obviously well made and of fine cloth. His bare feet had the toughened and scarred soles of a constant traveler. His large hands ended in thin, clever fingers slackly grasping Gungnir, the long, dark spear. Gungnir's haft leaned against the armrest of the throne.

No neglected heirloom hung upon the wall to admire, the spear shaft showed shiny with wear. The head of the spear stretched an ell long and glittered silver in the wan light. The point and edges looked wickedly sharp, cutting the winds that blew across them in a way that recalled Moon Sliver's own deadly edge. The golden runes etched deeply into the silvery metal writhed beneath my gaze.

Two tall, hulking ravens perched upon Odin's shoulders, twitching their heads back and forth to consider me with their glittering, perceptive eyes. Their stare was both intelligent and malevolent. The birds of prey were blacker than the space between stars. The deep red of old blood stained their beaks. They cawed and cooed into their master's ears, their voices a vicious, cruel sound.

Finally I looked to the All Father's careworn and craggy face. His hair and beard were white and shimmered as snow in the sickly light. He wore a high crown upon his head consisting of a thin gold circlet and two steel raven's wings sweeping upward and back from his temples. His mouth turned downward in a frown that could have been anything from disapproving to pitiless. Soft, wrinkled flesh covered one eye socket while the other held an eye that stared so sharply it seemed it could draw blood. The eye looked into me, knew me, and understood me in a way no one else, be they staunch friend or intimate lover, ever could. It was a cold, dispassionate knowledge, as though all my life's moments of transcendent joy or abject misery could be reduced to alchemical formulae. I felt lessened by his stare, rendered less than human.

I returned that baleful glare as much as any mortal is able. I pointed at the reclining figure.

"Fire-Eyed All Father of the Aesir, founder and exemplar of that accursed and degenerate race. Know that you face Finn Styrrsson, the Myth Reaver. I come to rain down on you the storm of battle until your blood is spilled upon this frozen ground. Here, at the top of the Worlds, I bid all who live and all who have died, all who yet suffer and those who suffer no more beneath your cruel and reckless dictates, to bear witness. By the authority of the Three Norns, the Myth Reaver calls you to account for your crimes. Your Ragnarök is upon you, and I am its strong right arm."

At first, Odin remained utterly impassive. His broad form did not twitch, nor did his face flicker in reaction. He merely considered me as I stood, that single eye sifting my past, my present, my future, and my soul. Then he did something utterly unexpected.

He laughed.

It was not the belly laugh of the ruffian seeking to bait me. It was not the hearty laugh for a true and worthy jest. It was not the fake laugh of the fool who fails to apprehend the clever quip.

No, it was worse than any of these. Odin laughed the demeaning laugh of the overindulgent parent. He dismissed me as a misguided moppet.

He sat up straighter in his seat and leaned forward, the twinkle of humor in his single eye. When he spoke, his voice sounded deep and resonant, the voice of a skald, of an orator, of a warrior-poet. Though not loud, it yet carried across the expanse and not even the freezing tempest could whip it away as it traveled from his lips to my ears.

"Tell me more, child. Tell Odin, who traded an eye and then died to learn the wisdom of what sorrows and troubles would befall both men and gods. Tell Odin, who drank of the well for the knowledge of *why* these must befall the men whom I made. Tell me, child, of my cruel laws and shortsighted mandates." He leaned back, stroking his beard and chuckling.

His dismissive words infuriated me. He could have struck me down where I stood. He could have welcomed me into the family. He might have threatened me or become angry. But I could not abide Odin's dismissal. The battle rage rolled over me like the waves at sea.

"Since my own words fail to make you understand, Wanderer," I said through clenched teeth, "I will use a language I know you speak."

I drew back the spear I'd taken from the Valkyrie below and launched it with all my strength high and far into the air. It sailed up and over Odin and his High Seat. As it soared, the All Father stood to watch my declaration of war vanish into the starry darkness. I bared my teeth in a wolfish grin. As usual, these prideful Aesir, so sure of their own superior might, never expected a mere mortal to dare an attack. Taking his eyes from me would be Odin's final mistake.

Whipping Moon Sliver from its sheath, I leapt toward the Hanged One and slashed the stout blade across Odin's midsection. The taut flesh ripped like thin paper against the elven sword's razor edge. Guts and entrails, gray and ropy, fell from the Aesir Lord's belly and pooled at his feet. Fecal stench filled my nose as god's blood sprayed across my clothing. The sudden movement startled his ravens, which screamed and flapped away from his shoulders to rest on the back of his looming throne. I howled my triumph and drew the sword back, then stabbed its tip through Odin's still-beating heart.

I leapt backward, leaving the sword lodged in his blood-bellows, and eagerly waited for the All Father to fall. He slowly turned to face me, still wearing the indulgent smile of a grandparent for his favorite child. He grasped Moon Sliver's hilt and drew it slowly from his chest. The tip left his torso with a quiet slurping noise. Never taking his eye from me, he spoke a word.

The word sounded unlike any I'd ever heard before. If put to the torch, I could never repeat it. It wasn't meant for any tongue in the Nine Worlds, and its utterance burned me as though a red hot worm had nestled in my ear. I watched as the sucking wound in Odin's chest knitted itself back together and the gut strands fed themselves back into his belly. When the belly-snake had rewound itself, the tear sewed itself shut.

The All Father tossed my sword back to me. I caught it easily and fell into an aggressive stance, ready to attack again. Before I could charge, my back exploded in pain, and my left shoulder blazed suddenly afire with agony. The heat swiftly spread down the arm like a brand and I found myself too weak to support Fathersbane. The shield clattered to the ground.

I tried to turn to see my attacker, but my knees buckled, and I fell into an awkward crouch. Stepping around me and into my sight, Tyr solved the mystery. He clutched his envenomed blade in his hand, my blood dripping from its tip along with the toxin. He beamed triumphantly first at me, then at Odin. Confusion flared across my brain. What game did Tyr play? Would he sacrifice me to stand near enough to Odin to sink the blade into *his* back?

"All Father," Tyr said and knelt. "I heard of a battle with your Valkyrie bodyguard and rushed to your aid. I arrived in time to save you from this marauder."

Even through my feverish, befuddled thoughts I understood. Tyr had no elaborate scheme. He offered mere betrayal.

"Liar," I croaked. "Villain. Traitor. You *aided* this marauder, god of heroes." I tried to spit at Tyr, but my parched mouth failed me. "Did your heart quail when the day was not won by the first onslaught? Did your betrayer's blade yearn to bite into whatever flesh was at hand?" I coughed harshly. "You know nothing of even simple courage. Coward."

Tyr stood, his eyes bulging with terror. He looked from me to Odin and back, his jaw working soundlessly. I gathered my strength and lunged at Tyr with Moon Sliver, determined to take him to death with me.

Odin's lip curled in a sneer, and he kicked me in the jaw, sending me reeling backward. He barked another terrible word, and Moon Sliver erupted into a million sparkling fragments. To add insult to my injury, he hissed another sorcerous syllable at Fathersbane, and the shield melted into stinking rot.

Fury gripped me. My chance to annihilate Odin vanished like smoke in the breeze, but Tyr deserved a back-stabber's doom. My rage burned hotter than the poison in my veins and I lunged at him again. This time I moved too fast for Odin. I grappled Tyr, who let out a woman's terrified cry. I lifted him over my head, and threw him so far and so high that he flew out over the edge of Odin's High Seat. His long, shrill scream grew fainter as he fell the impossible distance back to the ground.

I spun, ready to use whatever strength still lay within my waning limbs to make Odin remember me after my death and defeat. But the All Father had expected this and buried Gungnir's tip in my belly. His runed blade cut through my elven mail as though I wore armor of paper. It stabbed deep into my guts, and the stench of a dying man once again rode the wind. The fire in my bowel joined the blaze speeding through my veins. But as it had so many times before, the fire of wounds bolstered me.

I gripped the haft of the spear, and, pulling on it, took a halting step toward Odin. The spear burrowed deeper into me.

"What's this?" Odin asked, his one eye widening in surprise.

I took another step and felt the tip scrape my spine and tear through thick muscle before exiting my back. I clenched my jaw so hard the bones creaked and I feared my teeth would shatter in my mouth. But I took step after step until I had ridden Odin's spear high enough that we stood eye to eye.

The pain burned so great and my muscles were so weakened, that I feared I'd crumple to a heap if he let loose his spear. But Odin's astonishment had shifted to proud approval. He nodded to me, a small smile tugging at the corners of his mouth.

"Truly, Myth Reaver, I have never seen your like. You spit defiance until the very last. For that I applaud you. But you must realize the battle is over. There's nothing you can do now save stain my cloak with your blood."

"A gift..." I wheezed and grasped my chest through my ruined tunic. "A gift from Thor."

The hand at my chest tore my tunic free and brought forth Mjölner. Mjölner that never missed. Mjölner that struck as hard as its master wished. Mjölner that could shrink down to fit into its master's pocket, remaining ever at hand. Mjölner, whose whereabouts these prideful, stupid gods had never thought to ask of the mere mortal.

The hammer instantly grew to its full size. Lightning flashed from the night-black sky, slamming into its head and flaring it red hot. With the last of my strength, I swung the hammer wide and hard. The broad head smashed into Odin's cheek with the noise and force of a thunderclap. His face distorted under the tremendous impact. His head snapped to the side, shattered teeth and bloody drool splattering across his High Seat, desecrating it.

Odin turned loose of his spear, his hands coming to his face in fear and shock. The weight of the weapon pulled me to the ground, and Mjölner fell next to me, my grip far too weak to hold it. I lay there, my toxic lifeblood leaking from a hole in my middle. The stars wheeled and whirled around my head. I laughed loud and hard until I coughed. Flecks of blood sprayed from both convulsions, but I didn't care.

I heard Odin utter another eldritch word, though it was pained and garbled by his ruined mouth. I hadn't the strength left to twist and watch him, but I heard every bit of his discomfort. It brought on another fit of laughter.

Odin stepped back into my view, once again hail and whole. His renewed face darkened with true anger now. I celebrated the victory of enraging the All Father just as a defiant whelp appreciates the annoyance of an indolent parent. I chuckled, bringing more blood up from my raw throat.

"Rebellious child," Odin sneered at me. "What, pray, finds you so mirthful as you lay there dying?"

"I'll have died," I rasped, still giggling and coughing by turns, "in battle. I'll have the death of a warrior and a hero. My eyes will close here, atop your High Seat. But they will open in your shining hall of Valhalla." I smiled warmly. "I receive *almost* every gift for which I came to Asgard."

Now Odin laughed, a cruel and terrible noise. His ravens landed on his shoulders in a crash of feathers and coupled their own mocking calls with his mirth. Every bit of it made what little blood I had left run cold.

"You think yourself a valiant warrior because you killed my sons? So you are. You think yourself a hero because you defied me, wounded me? So you are. But you are no true danger to me and mine. I will resurrect Thor and his sons with a word. Tyr, as well, should I desire. They still have parts to play before our Twilight. You, Myth Reaver, are no Ragnarök, no doom to me and mine, no matter how much you wish it."

He leaned down over me so he could look straight into my face. He spoke quietly.

"And you are not welcome in my hall."

I shook my head in desperate denial. "No. No, I followed your rules. I came here to die in glorious battle. What fault is it of mine that I had to defy you to find my match? They are *your* rules, and you must abide by them!"

"Oh, Finn, you poor fool. They *are* my rules, my absolute law. But because of that, they are mine to uphold—and to break—at my whim."

Odin stood and walked back to his High Seat. He sat in it, and spoke to me a final time.

"I, Odin Doomgiver, do consign you to Hel, Finn Myth Reaver. There will be no Valhalla for you, no place in Freyja's fields." He shook his head, his face the picture of affected sympathy. "Your worthiness, sadly, far outstrips my generosity."

My limbs lay immobile and cold. Every weakening beat of my slowly stilling heart pumped less and less of my lifesblood onto the floor. I felt numb in body, mind, and spirit. I thought it could get no worse. I believed there could be no further indignity. Even in this, I underestimated the All Father.

"I tire of him staring at me," Odin said, his eye still meeting mine, though he no longer spoke to me. "Hugin. Muninn. See to it."

The great, black birds screamed and spread wide their ebon wings. They floated as one down to me and landed on my chest. They cocked their heads, their glinting, wicked eyes considering me. Then their blood-red beaks flashed in concert. Twin searing sensations burned through ruined orbs.

I beheld only darkness.

Epilogue - All Across Midgard...

In the North there is a mead hall. It is not so different from a thousand other mead halls. Indeed, on this night, it is very like *all* other mead halls, for its denizens are about to hear a tale. Nay, a *legend*. It is the same legend told all across the frozen North in these dark days.

The hall is filled with boisterous, celebrating warriors. At the head of these warriors is a king. To the left of this king, there is a skald. The skald steps from beside his king and makes his way to stand by the fire. The fire crackles at the center of the warriors at the center of this hall which, on this night, is so like every other hall in the North.

The warriors fall silent as the skald, who is like all other skalds in all other halls this night, clears his throat dramatically. When he speaks, the skald's voice is clear and strong and proud. It is sonorous and sweet. It is precise and true. Every warrior, every servant, every slave, even the king falls silent and leans toward the skald. So it is all across the North this night.

"Let me tell you a tale, O Northmen, of the mightiest warrior. A warrior so powerful, so stalwart, so true that he stood in judgment of Odin All Father. Even unto death."

"Let me tell you a saga...of the Myth Reaver."

Don't miss out!

Visit the website below and you can sign up to receive emails whenever Joshua Unruh publishes a new book. There's no charge and no obligation.

https://books2read.com/r/B-A-HB-MB

Did you love *Saga of the Myth Reaver*? Then you should read *Hell Bent for Leather* by Joshua Unruh!

Chet Leather can see things others can't. Ghosts. Demons. Lies and truth. This sight beyond sight has made the supernatural a part of his life.

But things get even stranger when the Devil takes his friend's soul in a deal gone bad.

To save his friend, this haunted cowboy must ride into the herd from Hell and rescue the lost soul from the Devil himself.

The whole damned world is Hell bent for Chet Leather.

It's going to be a hell of a ride.

Hell Bent for Leather is the first story in Six-Gun Supernatural, a series with tales of a West much weirder than what's in the history books. It stars Chet Leather, the haunted cowboy.

Approximately 63,000 words.

Read more at www.JoshuaUnruh.com.

Also by Joshua Unruh

Arcanoir
Hob Lesatz for Hire

Gripping Tales of the Impossible
Werewolves of Mass Destruction

Six-Gun Supernatural
Hell Bent for Leather

Standalone
Saga of the Myth Reaver

Watch for more at www.JoshuaUnruh.com.

About the Author

Joshua Unruh writes all the things. He has developed webseries and television pilots that have never been produced, comic books that have never been drawn, and roleplaying games that have never been played. But he always publishes the stories!

Through his imprint, Pulp Diction Press, Joshua specializes in modern retro fiction. Action scientists, haunted cowboys, girl super spies, diverse superheroes, and marauding vikings are just some of what he offers through PDP.

Joshua strives to make everything he writes clever, interesting, or funny. Like Meatloaf said, two out of three ain't bad.

He makes his home in Oklahoma City with a wife, a son, a dog, and no room in the storm shelter when the inevitable tornado hits.

Read more at www.JoshuaUnruh.com.

About the Publisher

Pulp Diction Press specializes in modern retro fiction like action scientists, haunted cowboys, and diverse superheroes.

We shoot high caliber fiction straight from our imaginations through your eye holes.

Stay in the loop on new releases and any other hot news at www.pulpdiction.biz